LAND OF THE LAWLESS

The land around Mexican Hat was lynch-crazy. A white man had been murdered and all the evidence pointed to an old Indian as the killer.

But Lee Banner knew the real killer was still free. And he also knew that there were three possible witnesses to the crime . . . and one of them was an Indian named Adakhai who would as soon kill a white man as talk to one.

LAND OF THE LAWLESS

Les Savage, Jr.

First published by Barker

This hardback edition 1999
by Chivers Press
by arrangement with
Golden West Literary Agency

ISBN 0 7540 8047 1

British Library Cataloguing in Publication Data available

Printed and bound in Great Britain by
Redwood Books, Trowbridge, Wiltshire

TO BUTCH, MY SON

**And I could search the world
and never find a better one**

1

In the cell, in the heat, in the stripes of blinding sunlight that slanted through the barred windows, the droning of the fly was the only sound. It circled above the Indian. It settled on his swarthy cheek. He made no move to brush it off. He sat on the rusty cot, staring fixedly at the adobe wall. His eyes were as blank as glazed beads.

"Jahzini," Lee Banner said. *"Sixoyan bica dahndinza?"*

The Indian's slack lips worked soddenly at the words. *"Do ya ah-shon dah . . ."*

"No good?" Banner's voice sounded exasperated. "Of course it's no good if you won't tell us anything." He turned helplessly to Cristina. "My Navajo's not up to something like this. Explain to him that we can't help him unless we know everything that happened."

The girl began speaking to her father, intensely, swiftly. Banner could only catch a word here or there and gave up trying to follow. He leaned tiredly against the barred door, tall, blond, broad-shouldered, in a blue serge filmed at the cuffs and coattails with Arizona dust. He had a high forehead, sharply squared off at the temples. His deeply recessed eyes gave his lean face a brooding quality that made it appear older than his twenty-five years.

Cristina broke off finally, waiting for her father to speak. Sunlight made a shimmering circle on her black hair as she turned to Banner.

"He will not even answer me."

Banner shook his head defeatedly. "I guess there's nothing more we can do, then."

Her eyes widened, dark with plea. She had spent six years at Carlisle, and spoke English with the peculiar precision of one who had learned a foreign language well. But here and there

1

were the guttural inflections, the swallowed word-ends of her Navajo origins.

"Lee, in your heart do you believe my father killed Wallace Wright?"

Banner stared into her delicate face, knowing it would haunt him now. This was really the first time he had seen Cristina since her return from Indian school a few weeks before. She had left a child; she had come back a woman. Yet there would always be a childlike quality to her, no matter how she matured. The fruitlike curve of her cheek, glowing like sun-tinted copper. The reedlike slimness of her body, in the boarding-school dress of flowered calico. The hair parted in the center like a little girl's, so black it drank in all the light and left only the faintest sheen over the top of her head.

He reached out to grasp her arm. "You know I can't believe Jahzini did it. The man I remember couldn't kill anyone. I may be in the prosecutor's office, Cristina, but I'll do everything in my power to help your father." He watched that draw a shining hope into her eyes, and then turned to call: "We're through now, Charlie."

There was the raucous squeak of a swivel chair. Charlie Drake appeared at the end of the cell block, rattling the keys on his ring. Sweat made dark half moons under the armpits of his shirt. He unlocked the door and pulled it open with a wheezing breath.

"I don't see what you hoped to gain out'n that Indian. They got 'nough to hang him a dozen times over."

Banner walked through with stooped shoulders. "What would you do for a friend, Charlie?"

The sheriff wheezed again, pulling the door shut after them with a clang. "Don't get sucked into anything, Lee."

Banner's boots beat a hollow tattoo against the cement floor. The outer door creaked dismally on unoiled hinges. He allowed the girl to go out and followed her into the furnace of Mexican Hat in June. The jail fronted on Reservation Street at the northwest corner of Courthouse Square. Banner's eye automatically registered the picture—the buildings across from the courthouse, the curlicued façade of Blackstrap Kelly's saloon jammed up against the row of enigmatic adobes, the false fronts of Sam Price's Mercantile, and the harness shop, with their white paint scabrous and peeling from sun and wind and sand. For six blocks it ran, the old and the new, fronted by the inevitable sagging hitch racks, the rusty ring posts. Then it met the desert. Wherever a man stood on any street in the county seat, he could always see the desert at its end—the heat waves dancing along its ridges, the mirages forming in its flats, the never-ending alteration of its colors.

He felt Cristina's hand on his arm, and realized they had reached Jahzini's old Studebaker wagon, its split front axle bound with rawhide. He halted awkwardly here, not knowing what to say. Cristina's lower lip trembled with her attempt to smile. He saw how ripe it was for such a delicate face.

"Judge Prentice has a pretty full docket," he said. "They haven't set any date for the trial yet, but I imagine it won't be till late summer. Maybe something will turn up by then."

She seemed about to answer. She didn't. The shadow of a man came into Banner's vision. It touched the wagon. It stopped.

"Checking up on the case, Lee?"

"Doing what I can, Arles."

Arles took a deep drag on his cigarette, smiling loosely. He was tall, dour, slack as a piece of old hemp. Beneath the battered brim of a ten-gallon hat his face was burned almost black by the sun. The movement of his eyes from Cristina to Banner made a shuttling gleam in the shadow of the brim.

"I thought Henry Dodge had already questioned Jahzini."

"He has, Arles."

"Doing some leg work maybe."

"Not exactly."

"Oh. Not exactly." Arles took a last drag on his smoke. Then he pinched it out between his thumb and forefinger. He saw their eyes on it. He smiled his slack smile, looking at the thumb, the finger. "Most folks won't believe them rope calluses are that thick. I can pinch a match out the same way. Don't feel a thing."

"Don't you?"

Arles flicked the cigarette butt away. His narrow head turned to Cristina. "Rainbow Girl," he said. It brought a flush to her face. "Maybe you asked Banner to defend your father," he said.

"You know it's as good as an insult to use their Indian names," Banner told him. "Why do you keep on doing it?"

Arles looked at Banner. "You going to defend Jahzini?"

"Why don't you let it go, Arles? It's been hard enough on Cristina."

"Dodge wouldn't like you defending Jahzini. Not when he's prosecuting the case. Be like his own son turning against him. Dodge always said you was like his own son."

Banner's voice was thin. "How about Hackett?"

"Hackett wouldn't like it either. Nobody would. There's a lot of feelings against the Indians about this. You know how much trouble they've caused us over that railroad land. The case is open and shut. You'd only lose and make a lot of people hate you."

"That sounds like something Hackett told you to memorize."

Arles's eyes made a gleaming flicker in the hat shadow. The loose grin formed slowly, with palpable effort. "Don't make me mad, Lee."

"This isn't any of your business, Arles. Why do you bother with it?"

"I just wanted to put you right, Lee. You've got too big a future in that prosecutor's office. You don't want to ruin it over some old drunk Indian that never did any good for——"

"He's not an old drunk!" Banner was surprised at how loud his voice was. "He's my friend and he was my father's friend before me——"

"Take it easy, Lee. You'll bust a gut."

"Then leave us alone, Arles. Cristina's in no shape for this kind of thing."

Arles chuckled softly. His eyes passed over the girl slyly. "I hadn't thought of that," he said. "See you so much with Julia Wright, I hadn't thought of that at all. Maybe you're not doing it for old Jahzini, after all. You'd be a fool to mess your whole career up over some little desert slut——"

Banner's violent lunge cut Arles off, driving him back so hard he crashed into the wagon. As he went, Arles slapped at his gun. But Banner grabbed the wrist in his left hand, pinning it against Arles's side. With his other hand he bunched the man's shirt up across his chest and threw the whole weight of his body into holding Arles against the wagon. Only then, with their two bodies straining against each other, with their breathing filling the air in husky gusts, did Banner feel the full effect of the exploding anger that had driven him into the man. The blood throbbed like a drum through his temples. His voice shook when he spoke.

"I told you to leave her alone, Arles. Now get out of here. Get out, and don't ever let me hear you talk that way about her again."

He held Arles a moment longer. The man's frame was rigid against Banner, and though he made no move to tear free, there was a vicious rage stamped into his face. Banner stepped back, releasing him.

Arles's whole body came forward involuntarily, his hand gripping the gun. But he could see Banner was unarmed.

"They'd lynch you for that," Banner said. "Not even Hackett could save you."

Arles hung there a moment longer, on the point of drawing. But at last he brought his rage under control. His voice had a rusty sound.

"Mighty safe without your cutter, ain't you?"

"You can have it any way you want it. All you have to do is unbuckle your belt, if you aren't through."

The man's narrow head lowered a little, till the brim of his tall hat almost hid his gleaming eyes. He did not speak. He did not move. The breath passing through him had a husky, animal sound. Finally his boots scraped softly against the sun-baked earth.

"You're a damn fool, Lee," he said.

He glared at Banner a moment longer. Then he wheeled around. His shadow slid off the wagon. The shaggy Indian pony stamped fretfully in its traces. Banner felt Cristina's hand on his arm.

"It is always like an explosion when you get mad."

He tried to relax, tried to smile, couldn't. "He built me up to it."

"He has always hated me," she said. "Ever since he tried to make love with me at the trading post that time and I scratched his face."

Banner was frowning now, still watching Arles cross the street. "Why should he have done that—any of that?"

"He was probably speaking for Hackett. Why wouldn't Hackett want you to defend my father?"

"I'd like to know," Banner said.

After Cristina said good-by, after she got into the wagon and turned it down Reservation Street, Banner remained in front of the jail, watching her go. She would be returning to her mother, out there in the lonely hogan beyond Yellow Gap. Banner had spent a year in that hogan, after his father's death. He had been twelve years old, and Jahzini had been his father's only friend in this barren country. The old Indian had taken the boy in, had treated him as his own son, till Banner's uncle had come West to care for him.

All the memories of that year welled up in him now, stronger, more nostalgic than they had ever been. He could see Jahzini, sitting cross-legged in the hogan, kindness and warmth in every seam of his nut-brown face, holding Banner and Cristina round-eyed and spellbound as he recounted the ancient myths of his people. He could see Jahzini half drunk on *toghlepai,* a chuckling little gnome lying on his back and thumping his belly like a drum and singing the Clown Song till the children and even his sober wife were doubled over with laughter. He could see Jahzini forcing his portion of mutton on a hungry boy when a bitter winter had left them without enough to go around.

In this mood he crossed the street toward Henry Dodge's law offices. Before he reached the bank, the outside stairway coming down from above began to tremble, and finally Banner's uncle stepped out onto the plank sidewalk. Fifty, white-haired, ruddy-faced, Dodge was inclined to paunch and seat. His gnarled thumbs were perpetually hooked in flowered galluses that held up rumpled serge trousers. He saw Banner and halted on the walk, grinning at him.

"Looking for you, son. The sheriff got permission from Fort Defiance to impound all of Wright's official papers till the trial. Might be some evidence among them that would help the people. I'd like you to pick the stuff up."

"Isn't that Sheriff Drake's job?"

"He and I both thought it would be easier on Julia if you did it," Dodge said. "You've been so close to her, she's gone through enough already, what with her father being killed. You'd better take the wagon. Might be a load."

Banner's mind was hardly on what Dodge was saying. "Henry, I can't believe Jahzini did this. There's something funny about it. He's so changed, so dazed. All he does is sit there and tell us it's no good——"

"—and claim he didn't do it," Dodge finished. "Of course he's dazed. I'd be dazed, too, with the evidence piling up against me like that." Dodge put a fatherly hand on Banner's shoulder. "I know how far back your attachment for Jahzini goes, Lee. But he was drunk when they found him. A man ain't in his right mind when he's drunk. And you know the trouble Jahzini had with Wright. The Indian was on one of those alternate sections the government gave to the railroad. Wright got the order to move him to land just as good. Jahzini wouldn't go. He was drunk that time, too, and he threatened to kill Wright if the man came again. And now we got a statement from Jess Burgess saying that he had arranged to buy wool from Jahzini in town on the day of the murder. That'd mean Jahzini was coming through Yellow Gap about the time Wright was killed there. Cristina herself said Jahzini started out with the wool. He never reached town. To top it all, they found Wright's burned saddlebags in Jahzini's hogan."

"That's it," Banner said. "Why would he want the saddlebags?"

"Those Indians are natural-born thieves——"

"Now you're talking like Hackett."

"What's Hackett got to do with it?"

"That's what I'd like to know. Why should Hackett be afraid I might defend Jahzini?"

Dodge's twinkling eyes went blank. "You defend Jahzini?"

Banner's voice lowered till it was barely audible. "Hadn't you considered the possibility, Henry?"

A little muscle twitched in Dodge's cheek. His voice came from deep in his throat. "Son, you might as well stand out here on the street with everybody watching and slap me in the face."

Banner grasped his arm, suddenly contrite. "It won't come to that, Henry. You've always said a prosecutor owes as big a duty to the accused as he does to the people. I know you'd do everything you could to get Jahzini free if you thought he was innocent. Now tell me about Hackett. Why is he so interested?"

"How would I know, Lee?"

"He's one of your principal constituents, isn't he? Without his support you wouldn't be district attorney today. And now he's pushing you toward that superior bench——"

"Now you're goin' off halfcocked like you always do, jumpin' in with both feet before you even know what's there——"

"Or maybe you don't want to know what's in Hackett's mind," Banner said. "Maybe you're afraid to dig any deeper than this."

A ruddy flush began to creep up Dodge's neck. "Son, stop it. We never talked like this before."

"Maybe it's time we did."

Dodge's voice sounded guttural with restraint. "Don't make me mad, Lee."

Banner frowned at him. "It's funny," he said. "That's the same thing Arles told me."

2

It was one o'clock when Banner came back to Reservation Street with the cut-under spring wagon. He was still depressed and confused from his talk with his uncle. Was Dodge right? Had his usual impulsiveness led him to jump to the wrong conclusions? He tried to tell himself Dodge would not compromise on this case. His faith in the man's integrity went back too far.

Moodily he pulled up before Blackstrap Kelly's. Under the curlicued façade, in the deep shade of the slanting overhang, the saloonkeeper sat on an upended barrel, lovingly blowing the head off a beer.

"I swear," Banner said, "you get more kick blowing that foam off than you do drinking the stuff."

Kelly thumped the barrel with his wooden leg. "Head's the best part. Look at this now. Frothy. Lacy. Like something a woman would wear."

"Tilfego inside?"

"As usual. Out back, proposing to my cook." Kelly sent him an oblique look from beneath his shaggy brows. "You going in?"

Banner had started to turn, but checked himself, frowning down at the man. "What's the matter?"

Kelly brushed a bulbous thumb across his nose. "You ain't really takin' that Injun killer's case, are you, Lee?"

Banner's voice grew low. "You, too, Blackstrap?"

The man tapped his wooden leg uncomfortably against the barrel. "Don't say it like that. I'm sick of this Injun trouble as anybody. Some of my best friends got holdings north of the railroad. Only last week some Injuns run off a hundred of Elder's cattle."

"Which they claimed he originally cheated them out of."

9

"That ain't true. He bought 'em from Hackett. He's got a legal bill of sale."

"Then maybe it was Hackett that cheated them."

"They're always claiming something like that. You know they're weaned on lies. What are they makin' such a fuss over losin' a few acres for anyway? They've still got half of Arizona. They signed a dozen peace treaties——"

"All of which we broke."

"Damn it, Lee"—the man twisted angrily on his barrel, looking up at Banner with a flushed face—"that's exactly what I mean. You keep on talkin' this way and you'll lose every friend you have in this town. These Navajos have pushed us too far. Burn us out, run off our cattle, shoot up our riders. This murder is the last straw. There wasn't a better man in the world than Wright. He didn't have an enemy in this town. If he couldn't settle this trouble with the Indians, nobody could. He never raised a hand to 'em, he did more for 'em than their own people would. And what do they do? Kill him. Shoot him from ambush like the dirty coyotes they are."

"Is that the feeling in town?" Banner asked quietly.

Blackstrap looked morosely at the plank walk. "I've heard talk of lynchin'."

"So you wouldn't want me to come into your saloon any more if I was going to defend Jahzini."

With one aggravated blast the man blew the rest of the foam off his beer. "Damn it, Lee, I didn't say that——"

"I'll tell Jigger to bring you out another beer," Banner said.

Somberness left Banner's eyes half lidded, made his face older, as he went into the saloon. He hadn't fully realized until now what the feeling of the town was about this killing. Absently he caught Jigger's attention, jerking his thumb toward the front door, and the bartender began pouring another beer for Blackstrap. Banner went on through the reek of stale whisky, stagnant cigar smoke, dank sawdust, passed the trio of townsmen at the bar, the bored faro dealer smoking over an empty layout. He pushed open the kitchen door. At the big table on the left-hand side of the room sat Tilfego, broad, squat, sloppy. He had the cook on his lap, poking at her amplitude with a hairy finger.

"So much ripeness I have never see. If someone they do not come along and pluck you, Celestina, you will fall off the bough."

"Will you really marry me, Tilfego?" she asked.

"You and six hundred others," Banner said.

They both turned in surprise. Then Tilfego grinned. It tilted his eyes till he looked like a Chinaman.

"You are just in time the best man to be, Lee. Celestina, this is my very good friend, my best friend, my only friend. He and I we grow up together, both of us."

"You have tell me a hundred times," she said.

"How about a little hunting?" Banner asked.

Tilfego's eyes glowed eagerly. "Hunting?"

"You'd better," Banner said. "A married man doesn't get out much."

"If you will allow me to rise, my dove, my pigeon, my little *chilipiquine*," Tilfego said, "married we can get upon my return."

"I don't think you mean to marry me at all," she said.

"On the honor of my grandfather."

"The horse thief?" Banner asked.

Banner finally got him out into the wagon. As they were rattling down Reservation Street toward the desert, Tilfego slid off his ancient sombrero and ran thick fingers through hair that sprouted from his Neanderthal brow like the roached mane of a horse.

"*Qué barbaridad*," he sighed. "What a barbarity. I never see so much heat. Hunting you do not want to go in this furnace."

"Not really. I just didn't want to talk in front of Celestina. You been tracking for the Army lately?"

"No. And something I got to make soon. My money he is all spend."

"How about reading some sign at Yellow Gap? I'll buy you a beer afterward."

Tilfego slapped him on the back. "Who cares for beer? I

have not see you enough lately. And now is this business of Jahzini. And you do not think he kill Wright."

Banner glanced at him, grinning ruefully. "I hope you find sign that easy at Yellow Gap."

"Is not hard for to see how you feel, Lee. Perhaps the land she will tell us what we want to know."

They had left the town. They were in the land of illusion. They were in the Painted Desert, where the colors were constantly changing with the caprice of heat and light and desert dust, where vast distances staggered the eye. They crossed a meadow of sacaton grass that rose to meet them like the restless swell of a tawny sea. They dipped into a gorge cut by aeons of wind and water. Its eroded walls were twisted and tortured, streaked with the vivid reds, the browns, the glittering blues of exposed rock strata. They finally reached its eastern end and rolled into an endless greasewood plain, studded with castellated mesas that were flung across the earth like the gargantuan playing blocks of some giant child.

The cutoff to Yellow Gap was ten miles east of Mexican Hat, the gap itself three miles north along the cutoff. It was fissured and shelved by erosion, its walls sculptured into weird mosques and minarets that scrawled twisted fingers of shadow across the glaring yellow earth of the bottom. The road followed the rim for half a mile, then shelved down the west wall. It was a sandy, slippery descent, with the brake shoes shrieking most of the way. The horses hit the bottom, blowing with relief at escaping the treacherous trail. Far ahead they saw the towering column of rock near which the Indian agent's body had been found. Tilfego made Banner stop the wagon a hundred yards from the spot, and they went the rest of the way on foot. Finally Tilfego halted, staring at the yellow earth beneath the rock column.

"*Qué barbaridad!*" he said. "What a barbarity! Look at the mess they make."

"I guess that's why nobody else could read much sign," Banner said. "The bunch that came down to get Wright's body wiped it all out. But I've seen you pick sign out of worse messes than this."

All Banner could see were the imprints of shod hoofs and boots and the wheel tracks of wagons crisscrossing the sand. But Tilfego finally began picking his way carefully through the marks until he reached a spot a few yards distant. He squatted down there and traced the outline of a man's figure with his hairy forefinger. It was like dawning light. Banner could see clearly the depression the body had left, with all the other prints superimposed upon it.

Squatting there, the seat of Tilfego's greasy buckskin *chivarras* shone wetly across his broad rump. The Mexican was studying the surrounding terrain now, his brown eyes squinted almost shut with concentration. In his restless habit, Banner slid his flat-topped hat from his head, running long fingers through his sweat-dampened hair. Finally Tilfego pointed at a patch of creosote twenty feet away.

"Somebody he stand there. Twig he is break."

"Could it be the bunch that got the body?"

"Many men they would have break more brush." Tilfego rose and moved over to the creosote, studying the earth for a long time. The heat drew the purpled pattern of whisky veins to the surface of his coarse jowls. "He come down here from the east rim, then he go back up," the Mexican said at last. "While he stand here, something she make him jump. You can see where his boots they have change the position. If it was behind him he would have turn. But he did not turn." Tilfego raised his primitive head slowly, till he was looking across the canyon. "I think she was something up on that west rim."

They got into the wagon again, drove back up the road to the rim. They left the wagon in some greasewood and worked their way northward along the rim. It was a long, maddening search. It took the Mexican over an hour to find it. At last, in a thick growth of prickly pear, he squatted down.

"One man. On a shod horse. Coming from the north. About three days past."

Excitement lent Banner's face a boyish eagerness. "The day of the murder."

Tilfego rose, following the tracks toward the rim of the gap, halting again in a stand of wind-twisted junipers that overlooked the canyon. He studied the surrounding trees for a long time, finally fingered a wisp of something from the rough bark.

"Horse he is a bay. Scrape his hair off here."

"It couldn't have been the killer?"

"No. This man he did not even go down into the gap. He wait here awhile, then he turn and go back north."

"Then that's what startled the killer, down in the canyon. He saw this man up here."

"Maybe not the man. Trees hide him. Maybe just his movement."

"What's the difference? There's every possibility that this man saw the murder. Do you realize what an eyewitness could mean, Tilfego? If Jahzini didn't do it, this would save his life."

"Not so quick, not so quick," chuckled Tilfego, holding up his coffee-colored palm. "Henry Dodge he is right. Always you are jump before you look. Let us read some more."

He spent a long time studying the sign, recounting a myriad little details about the horse and rider that would have amazed anyone who had not known Tilfego's uncanny ability to read the signs left on the earth. But added up, they did not give Banner much more to go on.

They returned to the bottom of the gap at last, and Tilfego began to work again. Going to where the unknown man had stood in the creosote, near the body, the Mexican began backtracking along the man's trail, up to the east rim. He was silhouetted at the top among the ocotillo, their spiked rods swaying in the breeze like scarlet-tipped wands. Then he disappeared back of the drop-off.

Banner paced restlessly around the wagon, making sure not to spoil any sign. It must have been half an hour before Tilfego reappeared. He came down from the rim and stopped in the creosote ten feet from Banner.

"This man he hitch his horse way back in the piñon where the rim she starts to drop off."

"Not the bay again?"

"No. This is different man. The horse I know. She got three nail is missing in the left hind hoof."

"Whose horse?"

"In them rocks a long time he hide. A lot of cigarette he smoke. Then he shoot Wright."

"Why did he come down here?"

"To see if Wright was dead for sure, I guess. And while he stand here, the movement of that man on the bay catch his eyes."

"What have you got in your hand?"

"I tell you he smoke cigarette. He try to grind all the butts out with his heel. But one get shoved under a rock."

He brought it over to Banner. The butt was about half an inch long. One edge of the paper had been folded over neatly an eighth of an inch.

"An ordinary man, he crush it out against the ground," Tilfego said. "This one is pinched out, like between the fingers."

Banner raised his eyes to Tilfego's sweating face. His voice had a hollow sound.

"Arles?" he said.

3

After that they went to the agency. It took them an hour, through the castellated mesas and the tortured gorges and the mesquite-choked washes. Then the horizon flattened out and the buildings appeared as if rising from the ground. Timber was precious in this land, and the buildings were all of adobe, beaten by the wind, the sun, the rain, till they had taken on the hues of the earth itself. Calico Adams's trading post was first, a tawny cube of a building. The viga poles forming its rafters thrust their ends out at ceiling height and dropped a striped shadow pattern over the sallow adobe. The other buildings were behind the trading post, the schoolhouse, the agency living quarters, the shaggy ocotillo corrals. There were a pair

of Navajo ponies racked before the post, heads bowed, tails
frayed by the wind.

"You won't mention what we found," Banner said.

"My mouth she is sealed," Tilfego said. But his eyes were
on those ponies. His whisky-veined nostrils began to flutter.
"Chilipiquines!"

"Chili peppers," Banner snorted disgustedly. "How can you
tell there are any women around? Just a couple of ponies.
More likely men."

Tilfego's grin tilted his eyes into their Chinaman slant. "I
don't know. When there are *chilipiquines* around something
inside me just start for to buzz like the bee. I look around, I
sniff the air, I turn the corner. *Hola!* Chili peppers."

Banner pulled up by the door of the trading post. "Get off,
then. Be careful of those Navajo girls. You know what they
think of Mexicans."

Tilfego climbed off the seat, chuckling. "Before I am Mexican"—he thumped his chest—"I am man."

At any other time it would have drawn a grin to Banner's
face. But his mind was too filled with that cigarette butt and
its implications. He shook the reins out and drove the wagon
around the trading post toward the agency quarters. He saw
that there was a sweat-caked roan standing ground-hitched
before the long building, and a man at the doorway.

He turned sharply as Banner approached, and Banner recognized him as Victor Kitteridge. He made a tall and narrow
shape in the doorway, his faded denim shirt and jeans so worn
they were paper-thin at the elbows and knees. The suspicious
calculation in his eyes seemed to have sucked all the warmth
from his face, leaving his mouth sour and pursed, rendering his
face hollow and sunken beneath the sharp angles of his cheekbones.

Julia Wright stood behind him, just within the doorway,
and Banner tipped his hat to her before speaking to the man.
"Didn't realize you knew the Wrights, Kitteridge."

The fine weather graining looked like tiny scars at the edges
of the man's lips. "Man should stop to pay his respects," he
said laconically. *"Ipso facto,* Counselor."

Banner's grin was wry. "No law against it. How's the round-up coming? They tell me your increase has been so good you had to hire a Mexican hand."

"Did they?"

Banner's grin faded. "Get any more beef and you'll have to lease some of that railroad land like the rest of the outfits."

"Will I?"

The hammerheaded roan stirred restively. Kitteridge slapped his hat against his leg, bringing a puff of dust from it, then pulled it on his narrow head. The roan grunted tiredly as the man stepped over and pulled the latigo tight. He took up the reins, toed a stirrup, and swung aboard. Glancing obliquely at Julia, touching the brim of his battered hat, he turned the horse down the road. Banner watched him go, frowning.

"Lived out here three years and I don't think he's been to town a dozen times. Do you really think he's on the dodge?"

Something passed through Julia's face. She turned sharply toward him. "I don't know. Dad did him a favor once. He stopped to express his regrets."

Banner swung from the wagon, wrapping the lines around the whipstock. She waited for him silently, her eyes fixed to his face. The strain, the grief of the last days had left her face pale and drawn. She was a tall woman, almost as tall as Banner. The swell of her breasts was deep and round against the bodice of her watered silk dress, the nearest thing to mourning she could approach in this outpost.

He had heard her called a handsome woman. It was a good word. Something more than prettiness, something even beyond beauty. Something that struck a man with distinct impact, and held him. Her brows were heavy saffron sickles above eyes so blue they were almost black. There was a honeyed abundance to her high-piled mass of golden hair. As he turned to her, something close to a plea lifted her chin, widened her eyes. He stepped to the door and caught her hand. He saw the tension die a little at the corners of her lips.

"I'm so glad you came," she said. Her voice was low, husky

with strain. "You helped so much the other day. I guess I needed it again."

He pressed her hand. "I'm sorry I couldn't make it sooner. I'm on an unfortunate errand. Dodge got permission from Fort Defiance to impound all your father's official papers till the new subagent came out. It was really Sheriff Drake's job, but both he and Dodge thought you'd been through enough already."

Her hand slid from his, some of the strain crept back into her face. She gave a little shake of her head. "It does make it easier, having you do it. But why impound anything? Isn't that a little irregular?"

"Dodge thinks there might be something among the papers that would help the prosecution."

She nodded, turned to lead him across the room. It was cool in here, the coolness of thick adobe walls and heavy earthen roof. The furniture was simple, massive, hand-carved. Navajo blankets sufficed for rugs. Their barbaric designs leaped up at Banner out of the gloom. Julia led him into her father's office. It still smelled faintly of his pipe tobacco.

She threw open a small trunk. "Most of his official stuff's in here. The more recent letters are in the desk. He had one ready to mail to the commissioner when he—left." She sat down at the old roll-top desk with a rustle of watered silk, began pulling documents from the pigeonholes. Then she spoke again, in a strained voice, without looking up at him.

"Did Cristina ask you to defend her father?"

He knew a vague surprise. "Were you in town today?"

"Hackett was by. Arles had told him about it." Tension dug a little crease in the soft flesh beneath her chin. "How could Cristina ask such a thing? She must have known what a position she put you in. Dodge is like your own father. To take the case against him——"

"She didn't ask me to do that," Banner said. "You can't blame her. After all, Jahzini was one of my oldest friends in this country——"

He broke off as she flung up her head. Her eyes were filled

with a more naked anger than he had ever seen in her before. He stepped forward, involuntarily, grasping her shoulder.

"Julia, I know how you feel, but——"

"Do you?" she said. It was as if the words brought her to her feet. She stood so close her breasts came against him with a silken pressure every time she breathed. "That you could even talk to that woman." Her voice was vitriolic. "Or with Jahzini——"

"Julia, I had to——"

"Why? What could you possibly gain?"

"I didn't mean to discuss it with you today, Julia. I wanted to spare you. But if you insist, I doubt very much whether Jahzini murdered your father."

The blood drained from her face till it was the color of putty. He saw a little vein surface in her temple, beating frantically.

"How can you say that? Every shred of evidence points to Jahzini. I saw him fight twice with Dad over moving from that land. They found Dad's saddlebags right in Jahzini's hogan! All she had to do was come up and ask you. The way she swings her hips——"

"Julia!"

"You're defending them now. That filthy dirty swine murdered my father, and you're——"

"Julia!"

He almost shouted it, catching her by the arms and shaking her with the intensity of his desire to stop her. When he realized what he was doing, when he saw the pain his grip brought to her face, he stopped. She stared up at him, eyes flashing, and he thought she was going to lash out again. Then, abruptly, all the sand went out of her. Her head dipped against his chest; all the weight of her body sagged against him, and she was crying. The sobs were deep and hopeless and lost, causing her whole frame to shudder. He held her tight against him, speaking in a husky voice.

"That's better. You should have done it the first time I came out. You can't keep it all inside."

She didn't answer. She continued to cry, the sobs racking

her body. When at last it was over, she leaned against him, wet cheek pressed to his lapel.

"I'm sorry, Lee——"

"I guess you had to let it off somehow." He took a handkerchief from his pocket, wiped at her eyes. "Why don't you come back into town with me? The sooner you get away from here the better."

She shook her head. "I've thought it over. I don't have anywhere to go. No relatives in the East. This has been my life the last five years. I'd miss teaching those Indian kids. I'd have to get another job somewhere anyway. Mrs. Adams said she'd put me up at the post when the new agent came."

"Maybe you're right. I don't think they'd ever get anybody as wonderful with kids as you."

She put a hand on his wrist, and he could see the effort it caused her to bring the words out. "Now, what was it you said about doubting whether Jahzini—Jahzini——"

"I don't want to upset you again."

"Tell me," she said. "I can't be like that again. I won't."

He frowned. "Julia, what about that trouble your dad had last year with Hackett over Broken Bit cattle grazing on Indian land?"

"They settled that."

"To the Indian Bureau's satisfaction, maybe. But was your dad satisfied?"

"You know he wasn't," she said. "That's one of the few things I thought he was wrong about. Hackett acted in good faith."

"Did he?"

"Lee, what are you driving at?"

He glanced at the papers in the trunk. "If your dad had been working on anything out of the ordinary, concerning the Indians, it might be in those papers."

Her chin lifted. "Would we have the right to go through them, Lee?"

"If it meant a man's life——"

"How do you know it means a man's life? What are you going on, anyway?"

There was a rising edge to her voice, and he saw how this was angering her once more. He had the impulse to tell her what they'd found at Yellow Gap. Yet he knew it was not completely conclusive, and would only upset her again.

"Maybe I'm wrong, Julia," he said. "I shouldn't have imposed this on you in the first place. Forget it."

"I will," she said. She touched his arm with sudden contrition. "If you'll forget what I said about Jahzini and—the girl."

"Of course I will," he said.

And knew, somehow, that he wouldn't.

With all the letters, the documents, the forms in the small trunk, he left Julia and drove back up to the trading post. He halted the cut-under wagon beside the ratty Navajo ponies, swung down, went inside.

There was a richness to the cool gloom of the room. A richness of barbaric colors blazing from hand-woven blankets, of dully gleaming silver heavy to the hand, of *yei* masks topped with the exotic splendor of guacamayo plumes from Yucatán. The counter ran down one side of the dim room, with the shelves behind it, carrying the beads, the coffee, the tinned fruit, the bolts of gay cloth, the rack of Winchesters. Calico Adams stood there, trying to trade with a pair of Navajos. They were hardly listening. Their attention, sullen, watchful, was on Tilfego.

The Mexican sat on the *bayeta* blankets piled against one of the peeled cedar posts that supported the roof. The girl on his knee was buxom for an Indian. When Tilfego saw Banner, he grinned and pinched her cheek.

"Like the peach, no, *amigo?* Did you ever see one so ripe? She is going to marry me."

"Do tah," the girl said. She giggled and pushed his hand away. *"Do tah."*

Calico's snowy head glowed like a nimbus in the gloom of the room. "Can't you get that Mex'can out of here?" he asked Banner. "He's ruining my business."

"I've got the papers," Banner told Tilfego.

"How you like the tickle, *chilipiquine*," Tilfego said, probing at her with a sly finger. "I never saw a chili pepper giggle like you."

"Tilfego," Banner said.

"Let us stay a little longer, Lee. The best man you can be."

"You'll have to walk back."

"What a barbarity," Tilfego said. He gave an immense grunt, getting up. The girl almost fell off his lap. She stumbled backward, sputtering angrily. Tilfego shrugged helplessly. "Tomorrow, *chilipiquine*. Tilfego will come back an marry you then."

Outside, in the wagon, in the heat, rattling down the road, Banner said, "I don't see how you do it. The ugliest man in the world."

Tilfego grinned blandly. "Have you ever see a bird charm by a snake?"

"You should be more careful with those Navajo girls."

"She was not belong to the men. Her Mexican name is Rosita. She always is hang around Calico's place."

"You still ought to be more careful. Those Indians were mad enough to do a scalp dance."

Tilfego shook his head sadly. "Always you preach. Like the voice of my conscious."

"Conscience."

"*Sí*, conscious." Tilfego raised his head, splayed nostrils fluttering. "Somebody coming."

Banner could see nothing at first. But he had long since come to have implicit trust in Tilfego's primitive faculties. Four riders finally appeared on the horizon.

"One is Arles," Tilfego said before Banner could differentiate between horse and man. "Clay Hackett. Big Red." The Mexican squinted. "The fourth a stranger is."

The quartet were coming down the road at a ground-eating canter, and Banner could make out Clay Hackett now. One of the biggest ranchers in the county, his six-foot body had a slouched ease in the saddle, broad-shouldered, lean-shanked. His face was narrow to the point of gauntness, its prominent cheekbones, its hard jaw molding it into a wind-scoured handsomeness. His grin was broad and confident, but his black eyes could take a bite out of a man. He pulled his horse down, black as sin, without as much as one white stocking on it, and let the animal stir up the yellow dust with its nervous little dance.

"Glad to find you, Lee," he said. "Henry told us you'd come out to impound those papers. We can take them off your hands now. This is the new agent. Claude Miller."

"Claude R. Miller," Arles said.

Banner nodded at the agent. He was slim, dark, in well-cut blue serge. He had a little mustache and a string tie and in a country where the sun made even the white men dark, his face looked pasty. Big Red sat a roan just behind him. Red was three inches taller than Hackett and weighed two hundred and fifty pounds, no fat. His face would never burn; it had a ruddy glow, like a bull's-eye lantern on a dark night.

"You got a court order for the papers?" Banner asked.

The heavy muscles rippled through the chest of Hackett's black as it fiddled in the road. "Dodge said we didn't need that. The sheriff would have to be along to make this official."

"I'm acting for the sheriff," Banner said. "They're officially impounded as of the time I got them."

"Miller just wants to go through them and see if there's anything that might be necessary for his administration," Hackett said.

"He'll have to see Dodge about that," Banner said.

Tilfego grinned blandly at Arles. "You better get the new left hind shoe for that horse. Three nail she is already gone."

Arles was rolling a cigarette. "I'm thinking of running her barefoot," he said. He carefully folded one end of the cigarette paper over an eighth of an inch.

Hackett gave a vicious jerk on the reins that stopped his black from fiddling. "What the hell," he said. "Henry told us to pick the papers up."

"That's the gospel," Arles said. He licked his folded cigarette paper, sealed it, looking at Banner all the time.

"I'll be getting along," Banner said.

Hackett leaned forward in his saddle, fixing Banner with his eyes. "Not till you give us the papers."

"I can't give them to you."

"I think I should have stay back there with my *chilipiquine*," Tilfego said.

"Get them, Red," Hackett said.

Big Red reined his short-coupled roan around the slim dark agent, around Arles, around Hackett. He checked it beside the wagon.

Banner's eyes took on a chipped-glass glitter. "Don't do it, Red," he said.

"Arles," Hackett said.

Arles took a long drag on his cigarette, sidled his horse around to help the redhead. Big Red's saddle creaked as he put all his weight onto his left stirrup, swinging off into the bed of the wagon. He bent over to lift the trunk onto the rump of his roan. Arles reined his horse against the outside of the roan to hold the trunk once it was on the horse. Banner jerked the whip from its holder and lashed it across his nigh animal.

The horse screamed in fright, rearing.

Banner hit the other horse. They both bolted. He heard Big Red shout behind him, pitched off his feet. The whole wagon shuddered as the man's great body struck its bed. Hackett had to dance his black aside to keep from being struck by the rig as it shot by him.

Dust spewed from beneath spinning wheels, iron rims clanged against the rocks of the road. Banner heard a running horse off to his left and saw Arles spurring his mount to catch the wagon. His animal had a lot of quarter blood, quick on the jumpoff. It caught up with the rear wheel, drew toward the front. Banner snapped the whip over the team again, trying to get more speed. He heard Big Red scrambling to hands and knees in the bed behind.

Then Arles drew abreast of the front wheel and jumped off his horse at Banner. His body smashed into Banner, knocking him over against Tilfego. Sprawled on top of the lawyer,

Arles braced one leg against the dasher, straightened up, hit Banner in the face.

It knocked Banner into Tilfego again. Blinded by the pain, he felt the reins torn from his hands. He lunged back up into Arles. It almost knocked the man off the wagon. The only thing that kept him from pitching out was his hold on the reins. It pulled the team hard to the left. Banner felt the wagon slew beneath him as the animals turned sharply.

"Jump," Tilfego shouted. "She is going——"

The horses plunged into the ditch siding the road and went down. The wagon overturned.

Tilfego's form flashed by Banner, like a jumping cat. He pushed off after it. He had a dim sense of Big Red pitched from the bed as the wagon went on over. And of Arles, jumping too late, caught by the edge of the seat as it came down on him.

Then Banner hit, balled up, and rolled, and came to a flopping halt in a spiny patch of creosote. He turned over and saw that the horses were down, kicking in their traces. Arles was pinned beneath the overturned wagon, apparently unconscious. Big Red was on his hands and knees in the road, shaking his head like a wet dog. Then Hackett came up on a running horse and pulled it to a vicious halt above the trunk, where it had been thrown from the wagon into the road. He leaned out of the saddle, scooping at the handle. Banner got to his feet and scrambled out of the ditch and ran for the man.

Hackett straightened, the small trunk in his arms, and tried to wheel away. Banner caught up with him, grabbed his arm. Hackett fought. Banner pulled him out of the saddle.

When he realized he was going, Hackett let go of the trunk and tried to come down on Banner. The lawyer jumped away.

Hackett hit on hands and knees and came up like a rubber ball. Banner blocked one of his flailing arms and hit him in the face. But Hackett's rush carried him on into the lawyer and he kept driving, and it knocked Banner off balance and finally spilled him.

Banner rolled over to see Hackett still coming in, jumping to spike him with high heels. He flopped out from under and came to hands and knees before Hackett had wheeled back. The man tried to reach him while he was still down, but Banner got to his feet as Hackett rushed. One of Hackett's bony fists rocked his head and he felt himself stagger backward. He caught himself, blocking the next blow, coming inside it. He hit the man in the belly twice. They were short, vicious blows. They stopped Hackett.

Banner shifted his feet and struck again. Hackett tried to block. Those first two blows had slowed his responses too much. Banner hit him in the belly again. He put all the weight of his body behind it. Then he hit him in the face.

It straightened Hackett to his full height and spun him around on his heels and pitched him full length to the ground. He lay on his belly, making sobbing sounds into the dirt. Banner stood above him, panting, waiting. Then he heard something behind him and turned to see Big Red coming toward him, still shaking his head.

"No," Tilfego said. "You better not."

Big Red stopped. Tilfego sat in the ditch, grinning blandly. He had his gun out.

Hackett had a lot of trouble getting to his hands and knees. He crouched there, swaying. Blood dripped off his face into the dirt.

"You still want that trunk?" Banner asked.

The breath sounded squeezed out of the man. "I'll get it." He spat a tooth. "Damn you. I'll get it."

He tried to get up and almost fell. When he finally gained his feet he spread them wide, swaying dizzily, wiping blood from one edge of his mouth. The new agent sat his fiddling horse a dozen feet back of the overturned rig, face filled with a foolish expression.

"Look here," he said. "Look here."

"Those horses don't look like they've broken any bones," Banner said. "You can help us get this wagon turned back over. If you want to look at the papers, they'll still be in Dodge's office."

Tilfego chuckled. "What a barbarity."

4

Henry Dodge was in his office when Banner got back. The door was open, he was sitting tilted back in his chair with his white-stockinged feet propped up on a pulled-out drawer. The awesome reek of his cigar filled the room, and ashes littered the calf-bound copy of *Coke's Commentaries* in his lap. As Banner walked in, carrying the small trunk, the old man's leonine head lifted. Then he put the book hurriedly on the desk, swinging his feet off the drawer at the same time.

"You got it. Good!" The chair shrieked as he leaned forward, rummaging through the litter of papers on the floor. "Just lemme get my shoes on now and we'll go through it. They were here somewhere."

He stopped, holding to the tongue of a shoe he had uncovered. He looked up again, as if the bruise mottling Banner's cheek, the jagged tear in his coat sleeve had just made their impression on him.

"What in the johnny-hell happened to you?"

Banner heaved the little leather-bound trunk onto the desk, breathing heavily with the effort of carrying it up the stairs. "Hackett tried to take it away from me."

Dodge sat the shoe on the pulled-out drawer, frowning at Banner. "Didn't he tell you? I said it was all right, son, if he met you on the way back. I didn't expect that new agent so soon. He'll probably need some of the stuff himself. He told me he'd hold it all for whenever I wanted it."

"His name is Claude Miller," Banner said. "Isn't that Hackett's cousin? The man who's been clerking for three years at Fort Defiance, waiting for Hackett to pull some strings and get him an agency?"

"I suppose so. He looks like he'll do all right on the job. I don't see why you wouldn't hand the papers over. They're his by right now."

"And since he's Hackett's cousin, I don't doubt Hackett will get a look at anything he wants. Why should Hackett be so eager for those papers? It made me suspicious right there. So suspicious I went through the trunk on the way in here."

Dodge's eyes widened. "You? A lawyer——"

"Don't cite the book at me now, Henry. I'd break a hundred laws if it would save an innocent man's life." From his pocket, Banner got the envelope he had opened, pulled the letter from it. "Wright had written this to the commissioner the very day he went out to be killed. Want to read it?"

Dodge snorted. "I won't compound a felony."

"I'll tell you what's in it then," Banner said. "Wright told the commissioner that for the last six months he had been gathering proof against Clay Hackett. Wright claimed that now he could prove in court, beyond a doubt, that Hackett was mixed up in one of the dirtiest swindles that had ever been perpetrated against the Indians——"

"You're talking about that grazing trouble again. It was all settled last January."

"In this letter Wright said that the January arbitration was just a farce. Hackett hasn't observed a single article of his agreement. Wright claims he has statements from two sub-agents that Hackett used his influence with the Indian Bureau to have at least six different families forced off their rightful lands, some of the best graze in the Corn River bottoms. He has depositions from two white ranchers that Hackett used force in a dozen instances to drive other Indians off their graze. He has a hundred statements from Indians and traders of beatings and burnings and mass slaughter of their sheep."

Dodge leaned back in his chair, a deep frown ridging his forehead. "I can't believe it. I just can't believe it." He looked up. "Those depositions, statements——"

"I couldn't find them. They weren't in the trunk. We even ripped out the lining. I think Wright must have been carry-

ing all that proof with him. Remember the burned saddlebags they found in Jahzini's?"

Dodge spread his hands. "But without them——"

"We've still got a case." Banner pulled the stub of the
cigarette from his pocket, put it on the desk. "We found this
at Yellow Gap. Not ground out against a rock or a wall, not
stepped on, the way an ordinary man would put it out.
Pinched out. Who else around here but Arles puts his cigarette out that way?"

Dodge stared at it, tucking horny thumbs inside his galluses. "Arles might have stopped for a smoke on that rim
any time during a week before or after the killing."

"There was other sign. Tilfego recognized the tracks of
Arles's horse, the back left shoe with the nails missing. Arles's
own tracks led down from the rim to a spot near where
Wright's body was found."

"Would you swear they were Arles's tracks?"

Banner hesitated, frowning at him. "I——"

"You know you're not that good. And how much would
Tilfego's word mean to a jury? He's already been in jail on a
perjury charge."

"That stupid case about the horse. He was proved innocent——"

"Stupid or not, he lied under oath. A prosecutor would
bring that out. You know what it would do to the jury——"

"You're quibbling," Banner said. It stopped the older man.
Banner stared at him a long time, feeling the bleak expression
narrow his face. "You're overlooking the whole point entirely.
I know just about how significant this proof would be in
court. I've seen you tear a lot stronger evidence than this to
shreds. But we're not just talking about the legal technicalities of evidence. We're talking about a man's life."

"Lee——"

"What's happened to you, Henry? I've seen you actually
hand items like this over to the defense. You always bent over
backward to see that a man you were prosecuting got a fair
trial." Banner drew a soft little breath. "But those cases didn't
involve Hackett, did they?"

The old man's eyes flashed up to his in an instant of anger. Then they dropped to the cigarette butt again; he settled into his chair; the lines seemed to deepen in his face.

"You shouldn't have said that, Lee."

Banner wheeled to the window, unable to bear the hurt he had caused in this man who had been a father to him. He took his hat off, whipping it against his leg a couple of times. He ran his hand irritably through his blond hair. Then he grew quiet, staring out at the twilit town through slitted eyes. Tilfego was still sitting where Banner had left him, in the cut-under wagon at the hitch rack before the office stairs.

Dodge's chair creaked softly with his turning motion. "Lee, I know what kind of a man Hackett is. I watched him grow up in this town. You know how no-good his folks were. It didn't leave Hackett much. All he's gotten in this world he's gotten the hard way. It's left him a hard man, I guess. But not the kind of a man who would murder."

Banner saw Tilfego's head raise. The man seemed to be sniffing the air. In the twilight his sudden grin was only a dim flash of white teeth in the swarthy pumpkin of his face. He climbed out of the wagon and disappeared around the corner.

"I disagree," Banner said. "Everybody knows Hackett's land south of the railroad is drying up. If he doesn't keep what he's grabbed north of the railroad, he's through. If Wright's proof was ever brought to light, the Indian Bureau would push Hackett back to his old pastures if it took the United States Army to do it. Everything that he's fought for ten years to build here would be wiped out. He's up against the wall, Henry. I think he's quite capable of murder, under those circumstances."

Dodge did not answer. Banner could hear his breathing in the room, labored, stertorous, the breathing of an old man.

Tilfego reappeared on the street below, hanging onto the arm of a girl. He pulled her halfway across the street before she stopped, trying to tug free. He whispered something in her ear. She giggled. She went on across the street with him. They disappeared into Blackstrap Kelly's.

"Did you ever wonder why I wanted to be a lawyer so badly?" Banner asked.

It took Dodge a long time to answer. Finally he sighed heavily. "Natural, I suppose. Growing up in the house of one."

"Not just any lawyer's house, Henry. That wouldn't have burned it into me the way you did. You used to wonder why I played hooky from school so often? It was to watch you try a case. I used to sneak out of school to watch you when the other kids were sneaking out to go fishing. For years, Henry, before I even started studying for the bar, I wanted to be a lawyer like the other boys wanted to be Billy the Kid or an engineer on the A. and P. It's something to watch you in court, Henry. A man couldn't see you in action without wanting to be a lawyer."

"Lee——"

"I guess that's the same way you've wanted to sit on the superior bench, isn't it? I guess I didn't really know how much it meant to you till just now. You've been talking about it ever since I can remember. I didn't really take it in, how much it meant to you. That's why I'm trying to understand this now. If you want that judgeship as bad as I wanted to be a lawyer, I guess I should understand——"

"Lee, don't——"

"And you won't get the bench without Hackett's support, will you?"

"Damn it, Lee, here you are goin' off half cocked again——"

Dodge's husky shout lifted him up out of the chair. He stood in his stocking feet, face ruddy with anger, hands opening and closing at his sides. Through the window Banner heard a shrill feminine squeal from Blackstrap Kelly's. Then a sharp slapping sound. The batwing doors flapped open as the girl pushed through them and ran down the street. Tilfego came running out behind her. He stopped on the sidewalk, staring after her figure. His hand was up to his face. His mouth was open foolishly.

"Qué barbaridad," he said.

Banner put his hat back on, taking a deep breath. "You'll turn Wright's letter and that cigarette butt over to the court as items for the defense?"

The ruddiness had faded in Dodge's face. He spoke in a low voice. "Of course."

"And that's all."

Dodge held out his hand. "Son, we can't swear out a warrant on this evidence. What else can I do?"

That somber look settled vague shadows beneath Banner's prominent cheekbones, drew his eyes half shut. He shook his head tiredly.

"Nothing you don't have the courage to do, Henry," he said.

5

Dusk was a stain on the town when Banner reached the street. Tilfego was not in sight, and Banner supposed he had gone home. The young lawyer climbed into the wagon and lifted the reins and turned down Aztec to the house he and Dodge shared. He felt steeped in a sort of gray fog, unwilling to bring clarity to his thoughts, to face the implications of what had just happened. Vaguely he tried to find an excuse for Dodge. Had he been too harsh in his judgment? It was true that the evidence he had brought was not conclusive enough for any formal indictment of Hackett. Yet Dodge's reluctance to commit himself went beyond the evidence.

This was seething through him as he passed the jail on Aztec Street. He found himself staring at the barred windows. It took his mind off Dodge. It brought him the picture of Jahzini again. Not as he had been this morning, dazed, incoherent, shrunken. Not even as most white men would always see the Indian, stoic and uncommunicative, and enigmatic. He was seeing a man so much more human than anyone in Mexican Hat would ever realize, a man whose intense affinity with the earth and the sky had molded into him a strange mixture of childish naïveté and aged wisdom, making him one moment a clown, the next a mystic.

Banner could remember a pot-bellied little gnome whose black eyes twinkled with mischief, teaching a blond boy to play *nanzosh* and running with him after the hoop and shouting as gleefully as another child. Or he could remember sitting out on a lonely mesa with the dawn-tinted statue of a man, so steeped in his closeness with the earth that they could unspeakingly know things together which no white man with all his words and all his sophistries would ever know. . . .

These memories still filled Banner's mind as he reached Dodge's house. It was a long adobe, shoulder to shoulder with a row of other long adobes that fronted right on the street. Banner passed through the wide gate in the patio wall and drove across the flagstoned garden to the stables. Unharnessing the team, watering them, putting two quarts of grain in the trough, he went inside and washed up. Dodge's bustling Mexican cook fixed him something to eat, but he had no appetite. Finally he took a pot of coffee to the study, tried to settle down to work. He had some conveyancing to do, a codicil to add to a will. Though Dodge had been d.a. for six years, lawyers were so scarce out here that he was still forced to maintain his private practice. But Banner found himself unable to fill out the codicil; the proper phrasing would not come. His mind was still too filled with memories of Jahzini and with what had happened this evening. And with a bay horse.

Finally that was his uppermost thought. A man on a bay horse who had seen a murder.

He put the deed away, staring blankly at the wall. It seemed hopeless at first. There were thousands of Indians north of the tracks. A dozen white ranchers and squatters. Hackett himself ran a crew of thirty men. Or it might have been a stranger, wandering in from nowhere, disappearing again into the vastness of the country.

But Banner's mind clung stubbornly to it. Actually, would it be any of Hackett's men? Tilfego had not recognized the bay's prints. That practically obviated the possibility of it being a Hackett rider. It wasn't even logical that Hackett would allow another of his men to wander down that way, knowing Arles would be waiting to kill Wright.

And how about the stranger? The tracks had come out of the north. If it was a stranger, that meant he would have passed through a lot of Indian land. He couldn't do that without being seen, or at least without his tracks being seen. It would be almost impossible for an outsider to pass through that country, unknown to the Indians, as vast and desolate as it was.

And if it had been one of the Indians themselves. This was shearing time, when they all stayed close to their hogans, joining in the work. That cut it down considerably. Banner had seen only a few in town these past weeks. The route through Yellow Gap led only to Calico Adams's trading post or to town. It would not be hard to find out what Indians had been at those two places the week of the murder.

As it began narrowing down, he realized what had been at the back of his mind all day now. It would take work, an immense amount of riding. But he was still remembering Jahzini. . . .

He went to his bedroom, making a blanket roll. He buckled on his gun. He put enough grub for a couple of days into his saddlebags. He left a note for Dodge saying he had gone hunting. Then he saddled up and rode off.

The alchemy of darkness had changed the vivid hues of the desert. The amethyst ridges were yellowed by a full moon; the crimson strata of sandstone were silvered by reflected light; the chocolate earth of canyon bottoms was turned to black velvet by the shadows. He rode till the moon began to fade and then stopped to sleep in the shelter of a ridge. He awoke with false dawn flushing the sky, and started again without breakfast, for he knew that would be waiting ahead. He was deep in the reservation now. He came upon the hogan at dawn.

It was what the Navajos called a logs-stacked-up house, made of piñon logs, boughs, cedar bark. It looked indescribably lonely, huddling there beneath a lone cottonwood on the edge of a wind-swept wash, with the desert stretching out as far as a man could see on every side. Banner drank in the bittersweet taint of wood smoke on the air and hailed the house.

In a moment the door of woven yucca stalks was pushed aside and Cristina stooped through, straightening to stare at him. He heard the catch in her voice as she recognized him and came swiftly forward.

"Lee, what are you doing this far north?"

His center-fire rig creaked softly as he stepped off the horse. "I have reason to believe your father isn't guilty of the murder, Cristina. I'm traveling north to try and find out. My Navajo isn't as good as it used to be. I could use your help."

He saw her lips part. In the milky dawn light the piquant oval of her face held a waxen hue. Her figure was a slim stain against the growing day, the rondure of her breasts vaguely shadowed in her velvet tunic. When she finally spoke, her voice trembled with suppressed emotion.

"There is great hurry?"

"Time to tell you about it."

"Come in then. You surely have not eaten breakfast."

She turned, with an intimate rustling of voluminous skirts, and led him into the low doorway. Banner stooped through, straightened within the mingled smells so characteristic of these dwellings. The greasy reek of mutton seemed to pervade everything, and with it the penetrating odor of the sumac and piñon gum with which they made their black dyes. It brought the past back so vividly that he almost expected to see Jahzini sitting over by the fire, eyes twinkling roguishly with some new, secret mischief that had always lain between them. But it was only the bent old woman, shawled in her worn bayeta blanket, Jahzini's wife, who had been mother to Banner during that year. She came to him with her hands held out.

"*Ahalani, shiyaazh* [Greetings, my son]."

"*Ahalani, shima* [Greetings, my mother]."

She stood a long time gripping his fingers in her sinewy brown hands and staring at him with eyes almost blind from

a lifetime of bending over smoky cookfires. Then she waved
at the pallets along the wall. He turned right, as was the custom of Navajo men upon entering, and seated himself upon
one of the rolled sheepskins. Cristina ladled mutton stew
from the copper kettle into a pottery plate traded from the
Pueblos. The firelight played smokily over her figure, deepening the shadows beneath the breasts till they looked full
and heavy. And as she bent to put ash cakes beside the stew,
it drew her heavy skirt tight across one hip, revealing surprising fullness. For the first time he began to realize how deceptive her apparent slimness might be.

As she took up his meal, he told them about Wright's
letter, recounting as much as he could in Navajo so the old
woman would understand. Then he told them what he and
Tilfego had found at Yellow Gap.

Cristina had just poured a cup of coffee, and she turned
toward him, still holding it. "Arles," she said. There was a
thin bitterness to her voice. She was looking right through
Banner.

"I think he's our killer," Banner said. "He must have done
it for Hackett. At first we thought he came down to the body
to make sure Wright was dead. Now I think he did it to get
those saddlebags. All the proof Wright had been collecting
against Hackett must have been in them. Arles burned it, but
the bags weren't completely destroyed, so he planted them
here in your hogan while you were out with the sheep to make
it even worse for your father."

She handed him the food, her eyes focusing on his face.
"There is a chance, then? If we find this man who saw the
murder, this eyewitness on the bay horse?"

"Haat iish baa yanilti?" the old woman asked.

Banner realized that he and Cristina had reverted to English, and the old woman had asked what they were talking
about. Cristina turned and explained the last part of it. The
squaw's face remained expressionless, the lines of weather and
age and sorrow engraving it deeply. But when Cristina finished,
the old woman turned to Banner, and her smoke-squinted eyes
were luminous with grateful tears.

"Ah-sheh heh, shiyaazh."

Banner turned to Cristina, frowning. "I don't remember the first word."

"Perhaps you never heard it," she said, smiling softly. "It is a word we hardly ever say, even to each other. She said, thank you, my son."

They went outside after breakfast and walked to the corral, and Banner helped Cristina rope out a shaggy little pinto, lifting the saddle for her. She worked in silence, tugging the latigo tight. Her profile was like a glowing copper cameo; the thin morning light made a dull shimmering in her thick black hair. There was a sense of innate wildness to her movements, to the very scent of her, like a doe captured but never quite tamed. She must have felt his attention on her; she looked up self-consciously, cheeks flushed. "We will start with the Indians first?"

"They'll be the biggest job," he said. "But we'll do two things at once. They'll know if any strangers passed through the reservation going toward Yellow Gap. We can find out at the same time what Indians went south last week."

The old woman was standing by the door when they left the wash, frail and lonely in her ancient bayeta. They rode out a narrow arroyo where paloverde spread up the eroded bank like a fountain of gold. They topped a ridge and looked out over a desert turned to a green ocean by the early morning light.

"This is the trail north," Cristina told him. "It will take us by horseback at a walk by many hogans."

Banner found himself taking his usual pleasure in the exotic turn of her speech. A Navajo never simply went somewhere. In his own language, the means by which he went and even the speed at which he went were implicit in the verb stem chosen. It was one of the thought patterns that insisted on transferring itself, no matter how fluently a Navajo learned to speak English. It gave Cristina's speech a childlike quality that never failed to enchant Banner.

They dropped down off the ridge into the vastness of the

desert. Barrel cactus crouched on every side like furrowed
dwarfs all leaning toward the southwest. The sun rose and
bleached the sky till it shone like naked steel and the world
became a furnace. Before noon they reached the encampment
of Cristina's cousins at Red Forks. Three logs-stacked-up
houses and a big corral, the flock of sheep held in a brush
corral by the boys, the sacks of unwashed wool piled against
the houses. The sweating faces and the shy smiles and the
greetings. And the questions.

"Any strangers?"

No strangers.

"How was Mexican Hat?"

"I have not been to Mexican Hat since the Mountain
Chant."

*Wasn't that one of this clan down by Yellow Gap last
week?* None of us have been down that way in a long time.
Perhaps a cousin. Yes, a cousin, from up by Chin Lee. *When
did he go?* In the month-of-the-big-crust. *That's January.*

That's January.

They rode again. Banner lost count of the hogans they
had stopped at, the grinning faces, the disappointments. But
at none of them had they heard word of a stranger. There
had been a new trader up by Ganado. But he had come in
by wagon, and had gone on to the north. Nobody had even
seen the tracks of a stranger heading south.

In the afternoon they began to run into big bunches of
Hackett's Broken Bit cattle fanned out through the black
and white grama grass. Banner saw the angry flush it brought
to Cristina's face. This was far north of the checkerboard
sections the railroad leased to Hackett. This was deep into
the Indians' land.

They finally reached a country of gorges and canyons and
were soon lost in the aimless meanderings of a chasm cut a
hundred feet down into the surrounding tablelands. When
the horses first started to spook and shy, Banner thought it
was the heat and their weariness. Then he felt the trembling
of the earth. The girl pulled her pinto in, turning to stare at
him.

"What is it?" Her voice sounded small.

Before he could answer, the first whitefaces plunged around the turn ahead, spilling from the narrow notch into the broad canyon floor on which they stood. Banner spurred his chestnut up beside Cristina and then neck-reined left, forcing her dancing pinto over to the canyon wall. There was a narrow cleft with a studding of scrub oak abutting its upper lip. The cattle were turned away from the wall here in a little eddy, and they flooded on by, bawling plaintively. For a moment the canyon was filled with a sea of plunging backs and tossing horns, and then they were past, and the dust was whispering back into the earth. A quartet of riders appeared in the notch behind the cattle. Banner saw Hackett's black horse. As he passed the cleft, Hackett caught sight of Banner and the girl. He waved two of his riders on after the cattle, and turned his black toward the wall, pulling it down to a walk. Arles wheeled to follow, a cigarette in one corner of his mouth.

"Looks like we almost wiped you off the walls," Hackett said. He wasn't smiling.

"Couldn't have done better if you'd tried," Banner said.

"We could have done lots better," Arles said, "if we'd tried."

Hackett touched his hatbrim. "Afternoon, Cristina."

She dipped her head soberly.

Arles shifted in the saddle. "My back's still sore."

"I was hoping maybe that wagon broke it," Banner said.

Hackett ran a finger inside his lip. "I'll have to get me a new tooth. Dentist said it'd cost twenty dollars."

"An expensive fight," Banner said.

Hackett chuckled suddenly. It was a bold, rough sound. It shook his whole body.

"Just like when we was kids, Lee. Remember how we used to fight all the time?"

"It wasn't serious then."

The humor was wiped off Hackett's face. "No," he said. "It wasn't serious." He leaned forward in his saddle. "What's on your mind, Lee?"

Banner's eyes grew veiled. "A lot of things, Clay."

"Nosing around?"

"I guess so."

"Finding out a lot of things?"

"Enough things."

Hackett slapped a hand across his saddle horn. "That's what you get for talking to a lawyer, Arles. Go around in a circle. Come right out where you started. Damn it, Lee, why in hell did you want that trunk so bad yesterday?"

"Why did you want it?"

"You raised my back hairs. It was Miller's by rights. You know you didn't have any official hold on it."

"The sheriff has it now, if you want it."

"Charlie Drake?" A crooked smile crossed Hackett's face again, suddenly, surprisingly. "Well," he said, "maybe so." He wiped sweat-caked dust from his angular brow with the tip of a dirty neckerchief. "Got to be getting on after my beef."

"Isn't it a little north of your leases?"

"Few strays get over the line. You know."

"More than a few."

"Don't take too big a bite, Lee. A man can only chew so much." He sent Cristina a sharp glance. Then he put one hand on his saddle horn and leaned against it. "Did it ever occur to you, Lee, that you might be getting sucked into something?"

"It's pretty evident what I'm getting into, Clay."

"Is it now?" Hackett looked at Arles. Then he gathered his reins, emitting a rueful little snort. "You're a damn fool, Lee."

"Am I?"

Staring at Banner, Arles took a last drag on his smoke. Then he pinched it out between his thumb and forefinger and dropped it. "Yes," he said, "you are."

Hackett laughed. Arles glanced at him. Hackett spat. They lifted their reins and necked their horses around and spurred them into a gallop. The dust rose in a choking cloud and Banner turned his face aside, squinting against it, till it began to settle again. He and the girl sat silently till the men were out of sight.

"Did you see how Arles was watching you?" she asked. "He never took his eyes off you."

"I saw."

"Do you think he knows, Lee?"

"That I know he killed Wright?" Banner asked. "Maybe."

"That's bad, Lee."

"I know, Cristina."

And, looking at her, he realized that from this moment on it would always be with him.

6

They rode on down the canyon after that. The horses kicked dust up to a buttery haze and the sunlight waned from the narrow strip of sky above and the shadows darkened and Banner found himself looking over his shoulder more and more often. And finally he pulled up, angry with himself, yet knowing that this was the way it would have to be from now on. Cristina checked her horse and sat wordlessly ahead of him while he searched the canyon walls until he saw a bench. He rode toward it and scrambled his horse up the ledge that led to the top and Cristina followed him. They sat their blowing animals behind a screen of junipers for a while, watching the canyon below.

"Is there any other way he could follow us?" Banner asked.

"No. If he is following us he will have to come by horseback down this canyon."

They waited. The horses fiddled beneath them. A brightly banded gecko lizard slithered from under a rock and stalked a fly like a tiny tiger. That was all.

"Let's go. If he was coming he'd have showed up by now."

In the canyon bottom now there was no highlight, no shadow, only a gray blackness lying over everything, robbing it of life. They rode steadily northward, with the rocky walls rising against the sky above them, tousled with grama grass and the ghostly silhouettes of scrub oak. Finally Banner pulled up again.

"Am I just jumpy?"

"We could climb a mesa. We could see some distance from there."

"We'd better."

He started to wheel his horse. The shot made a deafening smash. His horse reared and he pitched off the rump.

Hitting hard, with the breath knocked from him, rolling over, he heard Cristina's animal grunt, heard the sudden clatter of its hoofs as it broke into a wild run down the canyon. He kept rolling over, dazed, knowing only that he had to gain some sort of cover. There was another shot. Sand kicked up three feet to his right. He kept rolling till a scrubby juniper stopped him. He flattened against the ledge of rock on its other side, beneath its thick branches.

He could hear the sound of the horse down the canyon. It faded, died. He was no longer dazed. The pain was coming. His head was beginning to ache, his whole back throbbed. He got his six-shooter out. The oiled oaken grips were reassuring in his palm. He was thinking of Yellow Gap, and the cigarette stub they had found on the rim, and of the impression the body had left in the saffron sand.

He shifted over to one side, trying to see the rim. But dusk was thickening, rapidly becoming night. He couldn't lie here long. His greatest impulse was to go after Cristina. But if her horse had run away with her, it might go several miles before she could stop it. And if the gunman was still on the rim, Banner would only expose himself by going down the canyon.

He hunted for a way up to the top that would not leave him open. He found it, finally, a fissure, choked with brush. He began to crawl toward it, along the ledge of gray limestone. He thought he saw motion above, and stopped. He was sweating. His mouth was dry and cottony.

When nothing happened he moved on.

He reached the fissure and began to climb. It seemed to grow lighter as he rose. He reached the top to find that twilight still turned the sky pearly up there, while the canyon bottoms were black as ink.

The mesa spread out to the east, yellow with flowering greasewood. Erosion had turned it to a labyrinth of shallow gullies. He began to work his way down one of these, the mesquite crackling softly to his passage. Then he heard the horse snort.

It registered a definite shock against his nerves, stopping him sharply. It had seemed to come from his right. He took a chance, worked his way to the top of the gully. The greasewood was knee-high here, so thick he could not see through it. He bellied down and began a snakelike passage across the sandy flat. The horse snorted again, closer, but still to his right. He started to veer that way when the other sound came. It was a soft click. It sounded like a cocked gun.

He stopped, trying to cover his breathing. The click had come from his left, and ahead. Was he taking a direction that would put him between the man and the horse?

Carefully he eared back the hammer on his own gun. Then he began to crawl again, more slowly, more painstakingly. It was growing darker. He could barely distinguish the feathery edges of greasewood against the sky above him. Finally he reached the edge of another shallow gully, which ran out to the wall of the main chasm.

At the mouth of the gully, behind the rocks, looking down into the canyon, crouched the man. His figure made a vague silhouette. The silver bow guard on his wrist, the silver conchas on his belt gave off a dull glitter in the last of the twilight. But the weapon in his hand was no bow. It was a Winchester, with its lever pulled out to half cock. Banner finally made out the edges of his hair against the coppery sheen of his flesh. It was long hair, uncut, and Banner knew he could not use English.

"*Taadoo nahi nani,*" he said. "Stand still."

The Indian stiffened. Then, slowly, he turned his head till he could see Banner, holding the gun on him. After a long moment he let his Winchester slide to the ground.

Cautiously Banner made his way down into the gully,

moved toward the Indian. He could see that the man was young, maybe twenty. He was naked to the waist, wearing only buckskin leggings, a pair of Apache war moccasins curling up at the toes. He turned to Banner. The impression of his face was vague, narrow, like his body, the whites of his eyes gleaming like marble in the growing night. Banner tried some Navajo on him. The Indian would not answer. Then Banner heard the rustling in the lower canyon, and knew what the man had been watching. He moved forward, keeping his gun on the Indian, till he could make out the shadowy movement below. Two horses, only one ridden.

"Cristina?"

"Lee? My horse ran away. Are you all right?"

"I've got our bushwhacker. Stay down there."

He jerked his gun back into the gully. The Navajo started walking. Banner followed, till they reached the horses. There were three of them, one with a pack slung over its back. Banner got their lead ropes, then went back to the edge of the gully with the Indian. It became a fissure, crawling down the canyon wall, slanting enough to take the horses. Banner slapped them on the rumps and they began scrambling down, squealing angrily. Then he picked up the Winchester, followed the Indian down after them. Cristina rounded the animals up as they hit the bottom. She dismounted when they were quieted, coming forward to meet Banner as he slid into the sandy flats after the Indian.

"*Ahalani, tineh* [Greetings, young man]."

The Indian did not answer. Cristina tried again, asking his name. "*Haash yinilege?*"

For a while Banner thought he would not answer this either. Then, sullenly, "*Nishtli Adakhai.*"

"He says he is Adakhai," she told Banner. "It means The Gambler. I know him now. He comes from Chin Lee. He is the most famous gambler on the reservation. He is also known for his hatred of whites."

"No wonder he won't talk to me. Ask him why he shot at us."

She spoke to the Indian again. He answered, a long speech,

with angry gestures. Finally she said, "He says he did not shoot at us. He has been south, hunting, and was riding home. He heard the shots and came over here to find out what they meant."

"Do you believe him?"

"I don't know. You can see his hair is not cut. He is one of the wild ones, who will not adopt the ways of the white man. Most of them at Chin Lee are that kind."

"Would they know about a stranger?"

"No stranger could pass through this country without their knowledge."

"Then let's go on up there with him."

"It might be dangerous, Lee. If they all feel against the white men as this one does——"

"And yet they might be the very ones who could help save your father. We've got to go, Cristina."

She stared into his face, eyes luminous. Then she spoke in a low voice. "Very well. We will go."

Banner was reluctant to give Adakhai his rifle back, but Cristina asked him if he would use it if they returned it, and he said no. He did not want to take them to his clan, but Cristina told him they would go anyway, that she knew where it was. Sullenly the Indian mounted one of his animals, picked up the lead rope, started down the canyon. They left it in a short while, breaking onto a desert bounded on the south by a great rock-ribbed escarpment that seemed to run endlessly to the east. They followed the base of this wall, riding behind Adakhai. Dust hung acridly in the air and set Banner's chestnut to snorting. The footing was treacherous and there was the constant ring of iron shoes against sliding rocks, the husky grunts of the animals lunging to stay upright. Cristina dropped back.

"Did you notice his horses?"

"Hard to see anything in this light."

"One of them is a bay."

Banner looked at her sharply. Then he heeled his horse into a trot, trying to catch up with Adakhai's spares, trying to see if they were shod. But it was too dark. He heard the ring of shoes against rocks, didn't know which horse had made it.

Then the darkness was spattered with light.

It came from ahead, winking, dying, at a half-dozen points. It finally became the wavering plumes of cookfires. The Indian shouted something. The fires were blotted out by the fluttering passage of running figures, swiftly gathering around Adakhai and Cristina and Banner. There were a few women in velvet tunics, voluminous skirts. The men were all thin and stringy, the copper of their bodies grayed with caked dust. Few of them wore shirts; their pants were buckskin, and some wore only G-strings. They wore their hair long, tied in two squashlike knots at the back of their heads.

"It is doubtful if you will get any English," Cristina said "See their hair?"

"I've seen," Banner said.

With a soft rustle of moccasins in the sand, a slight tinkle of heavy hand-hammered silver, they were gathering. None of them spoke. None of them were smiling. Cristina sat straight in her saddle, face blank, eyes moving slowly through their ranks. She seemed to be waiting for something.

Adakhai had slid off his pony and was unlashing what Banner had thought was a pack. He saw now that it was the carcass of a deer. A pair of boys helped him, and he spoke to them in short, thumping gutturals. They were the only ones paying any attention to him.

An old man was shouldering through the other people now. He was short and squat and bow-legged, with stringy gray hair and a scarred face. He moved with a limping, froglike dignity that would have been ludicrous in anyone else. But the utter savagery of his figure robbed him of any comedy. He halted before Cristina, speaking in a guttural voice.

"Ahalani, cikeh."

"Xozo naxasi, natani. Sa ah hayai bikehozoni."

She called him chief. Called him *natani*, and wished him long life and happiness. Half a century of winds and suns must have scoured his face, leaving it rough textured, deeply furrowed. But the eyes glittered with undimmed light, staring intently at Banner. He waved at the cookpots, inviting them to eat.

Cristina stepped off her horse, and Banner put his weight into the left stirrup, hesitating just a moment, and then swung down. They stepped back for him, a stirring of moccasins, a tinkling of silver. It was like stepping into a den of wild beasts. The smell of wildness was so strong, so rancid, he almost gagged on it. Staring at their gleaming coppery faces, their glittering eyes, smelling their stench, he had the sense of being transported in time, in space, cut off from all he had ever known. A man could have come here a thousand years ago and found these same people, speaking this same language.

He looked at Cristina, and she nodded at the saddles. He stripped the sweat-sodden gear from both animals, carried it to the fire. Then he led the two jaded beasts to the picket lines behind the hogans.

These were not the logs-stacked-up houses he was so used to. They were the more primitive type of dwellings. They were the forked-together houses whose form and structure had been handed down by the Talking God.

The Indians were shifting restlessly around the fires. None of them seated themselves until Banner returned and lowered himself cross-legged on a sheepskin by Cristina. She was handed a dish of Pueblo pottery. He was handed a dish. From a communal pot stew was ladled out. One by one the men began to seat themselves. The youth named Adakhai sat across the fire from Banner. Watching with those smoldering eyes. They were all watching. They ate silently, watching. It was only the sound of the spitting fires. And all those eyes, watching.

"I told you it would be bad," Cristina said in a low voice. "This is a wild clan. This last year has made it worse. They cannot understand why the government gave some of their land to the railroad that way. I see many of the Talk in Blanket clan. I heard they came north by wagon after being forced off their land in the Corn River bottoms."

"That wasn't the government's fault," he said. "Hackett brought pressure to bear in the bureau."

"Hackett?" she said. She stared at him a moment, anger moving over her face like a cloud. Then she, too, looked at her food. Her voice had a muffled sound. "It does not matter. All these people can see is that their treaty has been violated."

She began eating once more. Sitting cross-legged beside him, the firelight catching up vagrant little glitters in her eyes, eating the stew with her hands, licking the grease off her fingers, she was robbed of the civilized veneer he had known; she seemed to take on the primitive savagery of these people. When she was finally finished, she put the plate down. She looked at the chief, around the circle of gleaming bronze faces. Then she made a ceremonial gesture with one arm.

"*Di banaxosinini. Toaxei Mexican Hat. Hosteen Jahzini la yah abi do-lte* . . . [Of this you have been told. At the place called Mexican Hat, Old Man Black Ears has been put in jail]."

Banner followed it that far, but she was speaking so swiftly, with the glottalizations, the swallowed-word ends, the subtle mutation of verb stems which so mystified the white man, that he soon began to lose it. After she finished, the chief spoke to her, and then turned and spoke to some of the others. It went along too fast for Banner to get more than a vague idea of what they were talking about. Some of the others began answering, sullenly, warily. Then Cristina asked the chief something. He answered. Cristina looked quickly at Adakhai and asked something. It stopped there.

The silence fell like a blow. They all sat like graven statues, staring at the girl, at Banner. The fire snapped. A horse stamped far out.

"What was it?" Banner asked.

"They have seen no strangers," Cristina said. "I asked if any of them had been as far south as Yellow Gap. The chief said Adakhai had hunted down that way."

"And Adakhai wouldn't answer?"

"I asked him if he had been through Yellow Gap. He was silent."

"That alone sounds suspicious. Did you explain we were looking for an eyewitness to Wright's killing? That it would save your father's life."

"I explained that. They are not convinced that you have truth in the heart. They say how can I trust you when you work for Henry Dodge, who will prosecute the case? These are the wild ones, Lee. They do not understand. I think we can find no more this way. I will be sleeping with the women in the hogans tonight. Perhaps I can learn more from them."

The crowd began to disperse. The women washed the dishes, the kettle, the few utensils in sand. Half a dozen of the men began playing conquian with Mexican cards. A few rolled out their sheepskin pallets by the fires and lay down. Cristina was taken to a hogan by a pair of old women. Banner felt vaguely suffocated, to be left alone, with the pressure of their hostility a palpable thing on every side, with Adakhai sitting across the fire staring at him from those smoldering eyes.

He built a cigarette, offered it to the Indian. Adakhai rose and walked away. Banner lit the cigarette and smoked it himself. Then, despite his tension, the weariness of the long ride began to creep over him. More men were sprawling on their pallets now; the fires were dying. He unrolled his army blankets, put one under, one on top. He turned on his side and met the unwinking eyes of a Navajo lying on a sheepskin five feet from him. He turned the other way. The Navajo on that side was sitting up, watching. He turned on his back, staring at the sky. Even the stars seemed to be watching.

He smoked the cigarette down, put it out. He thought he would go to sleep then, he was so tired. But he didn't. The breathing around him gathered volume, grew stertorous. The card game broke up and the men rolled in. Still he could not sleep. Finally he knew why. Adakhai's bay horse was on his mind again.

The Indian had been south hunting. Had just returned. That could mean he had been there during the week of the murder. When they asked him about Yellow Gap he had refused to answer. It all fitted in. But the bay horse on the rim of Yellow Gap had been shod. If Adakhai's horse was shod . . .

The impulse ran through Banner so strongly that he almost rolled over. He held himself still with great effort, listening to the snoring, the breathing, the soft sleep sounds all about him. He knew the chance he would be taking. If they caught him, and misinterpreted it, there was no telling what they would do. Yet he had to take it. Adakhai was already suspicious. If he was really the one, and did not want it known, he might get rid of the horse during the night. Banner knew he had to find out now.

He slipped his boots off. Then he listened again. He rolled to one side and stared around the circle of men, dark mounds in the moonlight. All of them seemed asleep.

He slid from his blankets, rolled to hands and knees. A man flopped over. Banner froze. The man settled back, snoring.

Banner crawled away from the blanketed bodies into the night, behind the forked-together houses. The horses were picketed here. They shied nervously, began shifting around, snorting as he came to his feet among them. In the moonlight he saw his chestnut. It whinnied softly. He moved among the animals, seeking the bay. At last, near the end of the lines, he found it.

The horse tried to sidle away from him but he followed it to the end of its rope and caught it there, murmuring to it, soothing it, till he had the animal quiet. The moonlight pooled shadows beneath its body and he could not yet see if it was shod. He put his weight against the horse, shifting it off balance, and then bent to lift its right front leg.

There was no shoe. The hoof looked strange. Its heel was pinched, the frog squeezed in. But there was no shoe.

He dropped the hoof and straightened with the sense of fluttering motion from the hogans. The horses began snorting and running on their picket ropes. Then he wheeled, with the shocking surprise of the shape hurtling out of darkness upon him, and the guttural shout.

"*Tchindi!*"

The body came into him so heavily that he stumbled backward, falling. He had the instantaneous impression of moonlight making a glittering sliver of something above his head, and all he could do was throw his arm up to block it as it came down.

He landed on his back, a stunning blow, with the man spraddled above him. Breath knocked out of him, he felt the shift of the body, heard the grunt as the man struck again. He jerked aside. The knife ripped his collar, dug hilt-deep into the earth by his ear.

The man's face was a foot above Banner's. It was Adakhai. Banner hit him with an upflung elbow. Adakhai's head jerked back. Banner caught his wrist in both hands and used it as a lever to heave the Indian over.

He rolled on top, still holding the knife wrist in both hands. He twisted it, heard the Indian shout in pain. But before he could get enough leverage to make Adakhai drop the knife, the man lunged up beneath him.

The tigerish fury in the narrow body shocked him. He tried to block it and keep his grip on the wrist too. It was what defeated him. He couldn't retain his wristlock and stay on top. Too late he let go. He was already pitching over.

Adakhai came on top of him. Smashed him full in the face with his free fist. The stunning pain of it incapacitated Banner. Dimly he felt the knife wrist torn free of his pawing hands. Saw Adakhai raise the knife to drive it down. Tried to jerk over. Couldn't.

Then the Indian gave a great shout. His weight was torn from Banner. A shrill voice was screaming something. Banner rolled over, dazedly, onto his hands and knees. The horses were squealing and rearing and running on their picket ropes all about him. And off to one side he saw a slim figure writhing with Adakhai on the ground, shouting.

"I-chai . . . tchindi . . . juthla hago ni . . ."

Cristina.

Adakhai rolled her over, tore free, tried to come to his feet and lunge at Banner again. The girl caught at him. Banner saw her hand flash before Adakhai's face. Saw the four parallel stripes leap into Adakhai's face, from brow to jaw.

The Indian shouted in pain, eyes squinted shut, and reeled back. By then Banner had gained his feet, shaking his head to clear it. Running figures were pouring in between the hogans now. A pair of them blocked Adakhai off as he tried to lunge at Banner again.

The chief ran between Adakhai and Banner, a squat, frog-like shape in the moonlight. The others gathered around until the wild smell of them gave the air a rancid weight. Adakhai stopped fighting, held by the two men. He was trembling with rage. The girl's nail scratches on his face were dripping blood onto his naked chest.

"What was it?" Cristina panted. "What were you doing?"

"The bay," Banner told her. "I had to see its feet."

"Lee!" Her eyes were wide and dark with anger. He had never seen her reveal so much emotion. "Why could you not wait? Why must you always do things without thinking?"

"I couldn't wait," he said. "Adakhai was suspicious. If he's the one, he might have gotten the horse away tonight."

She shook her head, mouth twisted. "But this was the worst way you could have done it. He was probably watching you. He must think you were trying to steal the horse. I thought you understood us better than that. I thought you were one of the few white men who knew how our minds worked."

Defeat left a sick taste in his mouth. "Try to make him understand, Cristina. I was only doing it to help your father."

She shook her head, eyes squinted almost shut. "It will not help. I doubt if you will ever learn anything from them now. You have violated——"

The chief cut her off with an angry gesture, turning to speak to Banner. *"Doya deinnzin, do bilhojolni itaeda, tlish bizedeigi, bik-ee dinishniih, doo ylldin da——"*

"He says he is very angry with you," Cristina told Banner. "You are warlike, you cannot keep a confidence, they all hate you. He says you must go."

Banner's shoulders sagged. "What about you?"

"They will not let me go off with you at night, a white man. They will take me back to my home tomorrow."

"You'll be all right?"

"These are my people, Lee."

He stared around the circle of their hostile, Mongoloid

faces. He had seen the same wooden expression in Cristina's
face when she met Hackett, or Arles. The special blankness
reserved by the Indians for the despised *belinkana*. It gave
him a painfully clear sense of the impenetrable wall between
his mind and the minds of these people. As he turned to go,
he saw Adakhai's eyes. They glittered like a naked blade in
the moonlight.

7

Banner did not go far that night. He was too played out. He
found a *tchindi* hogan about four miles from the Indian camp
and slept there, knowing he would be safe, for no Navajo
would approach a building in which someone had died. The
body was always removed through a hole knocked in the
north wall and the wind howled through this all night long
like the plaint of the lost souls supposed to inhabit these devil
hogans.

It took him all of the next day to get back to Mexican Hat.
He reached the house sodden with fatigue and turned his
horse into one of the stalls in back, forking out hay and dropping his saddle beneath the ramada where all the rigging was
kept.

There was a light in the parlor and he heard Dodge's soft
laugh. Going down the hall, he felt a rush of warmth. How
many times had he come in like that to hear the old repro-
bate chuckling over some ironic twist of a case in Chitty or
Coke?

"Henry?"

There was the creak of a hide-seated chair, the sound of
boots on hard-packed adobe. "Lee. Where in the devil have
you been?"

"Up to Chin Lee, Henry. Trying to turn up the eyewitness
to the killing——"

"The eyewitness!"

"We found his tracks out at Yellow Gap that time. You

didn't give me a chance to tell you about it in your office. A man on a bay horse who saw the murder."

"Now, son, this isn't the time to talk about——"

"It can't wait," Banner said. "I think I've found the witness. An Indian boy named Adakhai, up by Chin Lee. He was down there hunting during the week of the murder. He has a bay horse. When——"

He broke off as the other figure was silhouetted in the doorway. Dodge made an apologetic gesture.

"I told you it wasn't the time to talk about it, Lee."

"Go ahead," Julia Wright said. The light made a golden corona of her high-piled hair, silhouetted the flare of mature hips in their tight-fitting silk. Her voice had a strained sound. "Did this Adakhai say he'd seen Jahzini murder my father?"

"You know I'm not trying to convict Jahzini," Banner said. "I think he's innocent, and I'll prove it."

"By stealing my father's trunk and going through his papers?" Her voice was bitter.

"Julia, I had to do that. I'm sorry, but I had to. Did Henry tell you about the letter I found?"

"That's exactly what I came here for tonight. You got those papers under false pretenses. Claude Miller says the only one with authority to impound them is the sheriff. This whole thing is so stupid. The case against that old Indian is open and shut, and here a man right in the prosecutor's office is trying to mess the whole thing up. Lee—I——"

She broke off with a sound of utter exasperation. Most of her face was in shadowy silhouette, but he could see the hard line anger gave her cheek. Then she turned, tight-lipped, and walked across the living room, snatching her cloak from a chair. She had opened the front door and stepped outside before Banner caught up with her. He grasped her arm, pulling her back around.

"Julia, this isn't like you at all. Would it help your father now to kill an innocent man for his murder?"

"But he isn't innocent. All the evidence against him——"

"—is as circumstantial as the evidence I've found defending him," he said.

She started to fight, then the tension went out of her suddenly and she sagged against him, face turned aside so that her hair brushed his cheek.

"Oh, don't go over it again, Lee. I'm so tired, so confused. You're the only one who could really give me any help, and here you are fighting me . . ."

She broke off, leaning heavily against him, and turned her face up. It was soft now, like satin in the moonlight. He felt all the anger drain from him. He dipped his head to hers and kissed her. He held her against him and kissed her because it was something he should have done long before this, when it had all first happened, when she had first needed him so badly. He was filled with an impulsive sense of betrayal at having failed her.

For a moment she met it with the old passion; her ripe body straining against his. Then he sensed the subtle change. Her lips altered their shape, grew stiff and unyielding, slid off his mouth. It brought her cheek against his chest, with her face hidden from him.

"You're not still angry with me, Julia?"

"No."

"If it was that, I could understand."

"What do you mean, Lee?"

"I've felt it before. What is it, between us, Julia?"

"Nothing, Lee. Nothing!"

"There is something." He caught her chin in a cupped hand, forcing her eyes up to his. "I always thought it was something in your past. You came from Denver three years ago. Every man in Mexican Hat started buzzing around. You wouldn't have anything to do with them for months. Then, suddenly, the barriers came down. For a while I didn't know whether it would be Hackett or Elder or me."

She fingered his lapel, pouting. "You knew there was never any question, Lee."

"But even then you wouldn't talk about Denver," he said. "It always chilled things to bring it up. With both you and your father. What was it, Julia? Was it a man, back in Denver?"

She tried to pull away. "Lee, please——"

"It's got to be something like that, Julia. I keep feeling it, between us. Not all the time. For a while I think I've broken it down. I think you've forgotten it. Then, kissing like this, sometimes just talking to you——"

"Lee, will you stop it! Will you *stop* it!" Unable to break loose, she hid her face against his chest. "I can't talk about anything like that now. There's nothing. It's all in your mind. Please don't. Please——"

He held her tight, eyes turned bleakly to the darkness beyond. "I'm sorry. Maybe I'm wrong."

Her breathing seemed to abate; she was quiescent in his arms a moment, her full body softly molded to him. She spoke so low he could hardly hear.

"You'll come to see me tomorrow evening, then? I get so lonely."

"If I can. We'll probably be in court during the day. That Morgan litigation."

"And you won't go riding all over the country like that?" She waited for his answer. She tilted her head up when he did not speak. "There must be a hundred men with a bay horse around here, Lee. A dozen of them could have passed through Yellow Gap during that time."

The expression on his face stopped her. He stared down at her with the realization of what an illusion the past few moments had been. She grasped his hands tightly.

"Lee, you won't——"

"How can I promise that?" he said stiffly.

A dull red flush crept up her neck into her face. She stepped back, out of his arms. Her voice was barely audible when she spoke.

"Maybe you hadn't better come to see me tomorrow night."

Dodge was sitting in his big leather chair by the fireplace when Banner came back in. He had pulled off a shoe and was bent over, rubbing his white-stockinged foot.

"Much better," he said, with a relieved sigh. "That's the trouble with women. A man can't really relax." He leaned back in the chair, propping his other foot on a knee to unlace the shoe. "Clear things up?"

"No," Banner said emptily. He shook his head. "Her hatred of Jahzini seems so blind, Henry."

Dodge finished untying the shoe and grunted heavily, pulling it off. "She's had a shock, Lee. Always been a self-contained girl. But I know what's happening inside her. Give her time to get over it."

Banner lowered himself into a chair, staring moodily at the floor. "I suppose you're right."

"Yes." The shoe dropped with a heavy thump. "Well." Dodge put his hands on the arms of the chair, tapping absently with his fingers and frowning around the room. Then he heaved himself up and went to the ivory-topped table, padding across the floor in his white-stockinged feet like a grumpy old lion. He pulled open the drawer and shoved aside the ancient Dragoon Colt he kept in there, to get at his box of cigars. He bit off the end of a long black smoke and padded over to the fireplace to spit it out. He lit up, rolling it between thumb and forefinger till it was drawing well. Then he cleared his throat.

"Just how much did you get out of this Indian—this Adakhai?"

"I told you the important part."

The awesome reek of the cigar was beginning to fill the room. "Don't you see what flimsy evidence the whole thing would be, son?"

Banner stood up. "We went through that before, Henry. I walked out on you before too. I didn't want to carry it any farther. I guess I was afraid to. But we've got to do it sooner or later. Why do you keep insisting on the technicalities of the case? I've turned up more than enough to cast doubt on Jahzini's guilt."

"All right. I'll admit what you've turned up changes the aspect of the case. But that's as far as I can go, Lee. Even if I accept the cigarette butt and the tracks you found as valid evidence, they aren't conclusive proof to me that Hackett had

Wright killed. Whether Hackett was one of my principal constituents or not, I couldn't accept it. He just doesn't operate
that way."

Banner stared at him a long time. "You've changed in the
last years, Henry. I guess I've been working too close to you.
I wasn't aware of it. You look older. Suddenly you look
older."

"We all get older, Lee."

"And as we get older, Henry, do we get more afraid? Does
our job, our position, get to mean so much to us that we can't
face anything which might endanger them?"

"Son——" Dodge said it sharply, rocking his weight forward. Then he stopped, staring wide-eyed at Banner, the
blood darkening his face. At last he settled back, the choleric
anger mingling with a look of helplessness.

Banner forced himself to go on. "Jahzini doesn't have
money for a lawyer. I understand the court's assigned Farris,
from Flagstaff."

Dodge seemed to dredge it up with great effort. "Yes."

"I know how Farris feels about Indians. I certainly wouldn't
feel safe having it in his hands." Banner frowned intensely at
the floor, knowing he had to say it now, that he could avoid
it no longer. "Farris wouldn't be needed if Jahzini already had
a lawyer, would he?"

Dodge held out his hand. "Lee—son——"

"It's got to be that way," Banner said in a strained voice.
"I've got to take the case, Henry. I've even got to leave this
house——"

Dodge grasped his arm. "You'll ruin your whole career
this way. You don't have enough evidence to win the case,
son. Lose it and you'll never get a private practice in this
town. The feeling's too intense——"

"That's why I've got to move out of your house, Henry.
The Indians know you're prosecuting the case. I'll never get
anything out of them as long as they think I'm still with you."

A stricken look filled Dodge's eyes. Then he turned jerkily
to face the fireplace. He put the end of his cigar against the

mantel and slowly ground it out. When he finally spoke, his voice was rusty and trembling with suppressed rage.

"I guess you're right. You'd better go."

8

Aztec Street ran six blocks southward from Courthouse Square, then dipped into Gayoso Wash, becoming no more than a wagon road, and ran three blocks more to the railroad. In these three blocks was the Mexican section of town. The cross streets were narrow alleys that meandered haphazardly through squalid adobes and tarpaper shacks. At the street called Calle de los Leperos, Banner turned off Aztec, riding between sagging spindle fences that surrounded dark dooryards.

Banner's portmanteau was on the rump of his horse and he was still sick from leaving Dodge under these circumstances. He realized his own anger had led him to hurt the old man, to express suspicions he wouldn't have put into words if he had stopped to think.

He drew his horse up sharply as a screaming voice burst from one of the adobes farther down the alley. A woman's voice, shrill, vitriolic, cursing in Spanish.

"Tu bribón, se las tendra que haber con ella papá, lo agarro con su manos en la masa——"

There was the crash of crockery, a man's voice shouting wildly, *"Madre Dios,* what are you make——"

Light blossomed from a door flung open. The man's figure was silhouetted in the yellow rectangle, squat, bowlegged, primitive. A dish hit him and broke all over his skull. He howled and ducked low, wrapping his arms around his head. A clay jug spun over him and struck the street and shattered.

"Vayase con la música á otra parte!" screamed the woman.

The man was running toward Banner; the woman was silhouetted in the door, heaving another plate. It spun by and smashed against a wall. Other doors were opening, people were shouting ribald advice, laughing. The man wheeled into a cross alley. Banner reined the horse in after him, impulsively cringing as a plate flew by and smashed into a spindle fence. At the other end of the alley, the man came to a halt, puffing from his run.

"So she caught you red-handed," Banner said.

The man brushed pottery from his hair, muttering angrily. "I was just show Carmilla how they do it in Durango. She tell me her mother won't be home till midnight. What a little liar."

"So you'll have her father to answer to."

"Is that what the old witch she was shouting? What an old *brujà——*" The man broke off, turning, staring at Banner. "*Amigo!* I thought was the voice of my conscious."

"Conscience."

"*Sí.* Conscious."

"How about bunking with you?"

"Is pleasure." Tilfego rubbed at the back of his neck, staring up at Banner. "So you're going to defend Jahzini. And Henry Dodge he has kick you out."

"Is it that clear?"

"Your bag you got. I see it coming a long time. You cannot have the blame for Henry. Even I can see that you do not have enough evidence for the court."

Banner shook his head dispiritedly, without answering. He had been over it so many times in his mind he was beginning to wonder if he was right about any of it.

The Mexican's two-room adobe was farther up the Street of the Beggars. They turned Banner's horse into the spindle corral out back and went into the house. While Tilfego lit a candle Banner slumped wearily on the bed, head in his hands, and told Tilfego about Chin Lee, about finding the pinched heel and squeezed frog on Adakhai's bay. Tilfego agreed that it might mean the horse had been recently shod, for that condition usually developed from poor shoeing. The Mexican had seen no sign of the bad frog in the tracks at Yellow Gap. However, it was possible that the condition had developed after the Indian had been to Yellow Gap, and he had subsequently removed the shoes to let the hoof get better. It gave Banner a little hope.

He slept like a dead man that night, not waking till ten the next morning. Tilfego was out back, currying Banner's chestnut. Banner helped him rub the horse down and then they went into town for breakfast. There was not much movement on Reservation at this hour. A pair of dusty riders passed by, the desultory talk of idlers came softly from a corner. Banner was about to cross the street with Tilfego when he saw the wagon coming in from the east.

It was like the shock of a blow at the pit of his stomach. Jeremiah Mills was driving the wagon, a creaking Owensboro that had seen its best days. And one of the horses in his team was a bay.

Tilfego put a hand on Banner's arm. "You jump too quick again, Lee. I thought that was too easy, ride out over the week end and find everything."

"But it all pointed to that Indian——"

"You did not really think you would be that lucky."

Banner's shoulders sagged. "I guess not. I guess I realized this was bound to happen sooner or later. Mills is north of the tracks, isn't he?"

"Way north."

"And he'd have to come through Yellow Gap to get to town. Is that a cinch sore on the bay?"

"Looks like it. She has been under saddle, and not too long ago."

Mills pulled into the rack before Price's Mercantile, climbing slowly out of the wagon. He was tall, gaunt, with the chronic stoop of the dryland farmer in his heavy shoulders. He shambled into the store, rubbing the gristly creases of sun-reddened flesh at the back of his neck.

Banner and Tilfego walked the half block to the Mercantile, and Tilfego squatted down to study the hoofs of the horse, lifting one at a time.

"Same size as that one at Yellow Gap."

Excitement robbed Banner's face of its brooding quality, making it young, eager. "Could this be the one?"

"Hard to say. The one at Yellow Gap have little dent on rear hind shoe. This one she is smooth."

"Riding over a lot of talus could have ground it down."

"Maybe." Tilfego rose, shaking his head. "Remember that was cold trail out at the gap. I could not swear to it, Lee. Not like I could swear to Arles's horse."

"But there's enough anyway. A bay, the same size———"

He broke off as Mills came through the door with a fifty-pound sack of flour on one shoulder. The man glanced dourly at Banner and lowered the sack into the bed of the wagon.

"That's a pretty bay," Banner said.

Mills leaned against the wagon. His heavy-boned face had been baked by the sun and whipped by the wind till the wrinkles lay like pleats in the leathery flesh. "She ain't good for nothin'," he said. "So lame I can't ride her."

"You ain't had her long?" Tilfego asked.

"Not long. Victor Kitteridge owed me some money for alfalfa. He couldn't pay it. I needed a wagon horse so I took the bay instead."

Banner stepped close to him. "You know Wallace Wright was murdered in Yellow Gap last Thursday, Mills. That same day a man on a bay horse rode through the gap. We have every reason to believe he saw the killing."

The first shock left Mills's face blank. Then his eyes narrowed till they were almost shut, receding deeply into their network of wrinkles. "I didn't have this horse then."

"If you're saying Kitteridge gave it to you after the murder, I can check with him easily enough."

"Go ahead, damn you." The man turned to climb into the wagon.

"Are you *that* afraid of Clay Hackett?"

It stopped Mills, with his hand on the wagon. He turned to look at Banner again, surprise in his eyes. Then something else filled them, almost a look of pain. They swung away, and he lifted his foot to climb in. Banner stepped up beside him and put a hand on the side of the wagon. It blocked Mills from stepping up. The man stared down at Banner's arm for a mo-

ment, cholericly. When he finally spoke his voice was thick
with the phlegm of anger.

"Take it away, Lee. I'll bust you open like a sack."

"Will you, Mills?" Banner asked softly.

The man continued to look at the arm for a long time.
Banner could see the pulse throbbing in the cup of his
weathered neck, the dull red flush filling his face. But there
was something else working insidiously at the man, counter-
acting his anger. His chin sunk down till it was pressed
against his chest and the furrows beneath his jaw were deep
and leathery. Without looking up, he spoke, his voice strained
and husky.

"What do you want?"

"I always thought hard work put that stoop in your shoulders, Mills," Banner said. "But that isn't it. You're afraid.
You've been afraid so long you've forgotten what it's like to
give a man a good punch in the nose. Five years ago it was
another big man you were afraid of, back in Missouri or
Arkansas or wherever it was. Now it's Clay Hackett."

It was that strange expression of pain in the man's face
again, till the cheeks looked sunken, the eyes filmed and dead.
It drained all the anger out of him. He settled slowly, heavily,
against the wagon, letting a husky breath flow out of him,
staring at Banner's arm without seeing it. For a long time
Banner thought the man would not speak. But finally Mills
drew in a shallow breath and the words began to creep out,
not directed at Banner, or anybody in particular, just words.

"We were a long time getting this place. I owned two farms
back in Missouri. I was flooded out. Owned one in Ohio.
Crop failure lost me the mortgage. Homesteaded in Wyoming.
The Johnson County War finished that. I guess I've squatted
in a dozen places between here and there. Sometimes the cattlemen squeezed me out, sometimes the land failed me. It
digs into a man to lose that many times, Banner. It digs into
a man."

"And if it wasn't for Hackett, now, you couldn't even stay
where you are."

Mills's head lowered. "He could kick me out if he wanted

to. I had squatter's rights on that land. Even the government recognized them till the railroad come through and they gave it alternate sections along the right of way. My land fell in one of those sections. The railroad leased it to Hackett. I know cattlemen, Banner. Ninety-nine out of a hundred would have kicked me off. He's let me stay."

"Has it ever occurred to you why? Your land runs right across the northern end of the railroad section, doesn't it? Ever had trouble with the Indians?"

"A dozen times. You know that."

"Don't you see what a buffer you make for Hackett, Mills? He's using graze he'd have to fight the Indians for if you weren't there. They don't understand this business of the government giving land to the railroad that was theirs by treaty. Whenever they get heated up about whites on their land they see you there. It's you they strike out at. That plays right into Hackett's hands, after the brush he had with the Indian Bureau last year. All the reports that come in have you in trouble with the Indians in that section, not Hackett."

Mills stared intently at him, mouth working faintly. Then he shook his head. "Don't try to twist this around, Banner."

Banner felt a frown pull his brows in. "I hadn't realized before how many people in this town were under Hackett's thumb. How can you live on your knees all the time, Mills? I'd vomit."

Blood crept darkly into the man's face, his concave chest started to swell. Then he settled back, staring at Banner with helpless, empty eyes.

"You never had a family, did you, Banner?"

Banner looked into those eyes. It was like looking at a hundred years of bitterness, pain, defeat. He let his arm drop off.

"All right, Mills," he said.

The man stared at him a moment longer, then started to wheel and climb into the wagon. He checked himself, looking beyond Banner. His mouth opened a little. His face took on a color of old putty.

"You aren't going to believe everything the counselor says, are you, Mills?" Hackett asked.

Banner wheeled to see the man standing on the sidewalk, behind the hitch rack. He had his thumbs hooked in his gunbelt and his feet planted wide in that swaggering way. There was a crooked smile on his face.

Mills licked his lips. "I mind my own business, Hackett. You know that."

"Sure you do," Hackett said. "The counselor's just out rustling up a few votes or something. I hear he's stepped out of the district attorney's office. Going to run against Henry in the next election or something."

"I was just leaving," Mills said.

"Sure you were," Hackett said.

The Owensboro creaked as Mills stepped up, settled himself on the seat, shoulders deeply stooped. The little bay snorted, tossed its head, wheeled with the other horse as Mills reined them around. Hackett shifted restlessly on the plank sidewalk. It made his great cartwheel spurs clank. They always seemed to be clanking.

"This Adakhai," he said. "Do you really think he saw the murder?"

Banner was unable to keep the surprise from his face. His voice was bitter. "Does Henry run to you with everything?"

"Haven't seen your uncle in several days," Hackett said. "I dropped in on Julia last night, though. Must have been after she'd seen you. She was right upset, had to let it out on somebody. She told me the news you'd brought back. Do you really think that Indian will testify against a man of his own race?"

"If he testifies, it won't be against Jahzini."

"Won't it now?" Hackett lowered his head till his sardonic black eyes were barely visible, staring dourly at Banner from beneath his hatbrim. Then his smile came again, crooked, humorless. "Well," he said absently, "maybe not." He glanced beyond Banner, at something down the street. "Maybe not." He turned and walked toward Blackstrap Kelly's, his spurs setting up a jingling clatter in the quiet street.

"He sure like to drag them cartwheels," Tilfego observed.

Banner did not answer. He turned to see what Hackett had looked at. Arles was sitting his horse near the corner of Aztec and Reservation. He met Banner's gaze for a moment, his face almost black in the shadow of his hat. Then he reined the horse around and rode toward the desert.

They ate breakfast at one of the Mexican cantinas, and then Banner went back to Tilfego's house to get some paper and pencils from his bag. He had known he would have to start the process of elimination sooner or later. Mills's appearance with the bay this morning, upsetting all Banner's calculations about Adakhai, convinced him that he might as well begin now. He went to the extreme west end of town first, meaning to work eastward. The station was the last building on Reservation. From his cubbyhole of a ticket booth, Si Warner saw Banner coming, and turned back into the larger waiting room. Banner and Tilfego followed him in. The man had his back turned and was assiduously sweeping out beneath the seats.

"When I was a kid," Banner said, "you used to tell me stories about the time you were an engineer for the A. and P."

The man stopped sweeping, thin shoulders hunched over the broom. "Don't make it hard on me, Lee. Blackstrap Kelly's my friend too. I got to eat my meals there every day. I got to drink his liquor if I want to see my other friends."

"I knew the feeling was bad in town, Si. I didn't know it extended to you."

"Damn it, Lee." The man shook his head exasperatedly. "Everybody in town knows you're goin' to defend Jahzini. Dodge's cook heard you pull out from the old man last night, and you know what a gossip she is. Feeling's high on Reservation Street and you're goin' to run smack into it. Like this rumor that some Injuns are goin' to try and bust Jahzini out of jail. A lot of men are sayin' we should hang Jahzini before they can try anything. Caleb Elder said anybody that defended Jahzini ought to be hung too."

"Let me hear him say it," Tilfego growled. "I'll string him up by his thumbs."

"Elder's got a right," Si said. "Some Injuns burned out his Cherry Creek line camp last night, hurt one of his boys pretty bad."

"Without provocation, of course," Banner said sarcastically.

"That don't matter. It's the feelin' in town that counts. A man's either on one side or the other now."

"I've still got to ask you some questions, Si. Did you see Jeremiah Mills in town on June the twelfth?"

"Can't recall."

"If I have to bring you into court, Si, and you lie, they can jail you for perjury."

Slowly, the parchment-faced old man turned around, his eyes glittering with birdlike anger in their hollow sockets. Finally he shook his head.

"Damn it, Lee, I still didn't see him."

"Victor Kitteridge, then."

The man's eyes went blank with his effort to remember. "Seems so," he said reluctantly.

"Riding a bay?"

Again the hesitation. "Seems it was that hammerhead roan of his."

"What time, Si?"

"How the hell can I remember all that? Morning, I think. I don't know . . ."

After Si, it was Sam Price. And then Blackstrap Kelly. And all along the way he met the same resentment, the same withdrawal, the same anger. It left a sick feeling, to see so many of his friends turn from him. But he persisted, and by the end of the day he had gotten down to Fifth Street. He had filled five sheets of paper on both sides. He had the names of seven different people who had been in town from the north country during the day of the murder. Five of them were Indians known to the townsfolk, but none of these had ridden a bay. The other two were whites, Caleb Elder and Victor Kitteridge.

Of the eight people who remembered Kitteridge being in

town that day, three thought he had been riding a buckskin, two remembered a hammerheaded roan, one thought it might have been a bay if it wasn't a chestnut. It wasn't very conclusive, but one of the axioms of law was the unreliability of memory and personal observation. Banner realized it was just the beginning of an infinitely painstaking job. But at least it was a start.

9

Banner ate at Tilfego's that night, and went to bed right after the meal, dead tired. He fell asleep immediately, but it seem ' only a second before he was awakened. He lay in the bunk, staring around him, with the sense of having been shaken. He was surprised to see dawn filling the room with a milky light. It did not seem possible he could have been asleep so long.

"Somebody belch big?" Tilfego asked.

"It wake you up too?" Banner said. He heard somebody calling from next door, something about an explosion. He sat up sharply, throwing off the covers.

"What you make?"

"I'm going to see about it."

"What for? Some railroad dynamite she blow up down by tracks. Those kids they are always get hold of it."

But something was working in Banner, an apprehension, a premonition, that would not let him ignore it. He dressed, slipped into his coat, even buckled on his Colt. Then he went outside. A few people stood in the squalid lane, a fat woman in a flimsy wrapper, a Mexican in nothing but greasy buckskin leggings.

"*Qué pasa?*" Banner asked.

"*No sé,*" the man said. "*Un explosión, al norte——*"

To the north? Banner found himself turned that way. The railroad tracks weren't up there. He went to the corral and saddled his chestnut, the premonition still tugging at him. He could hear Tilfego snoring again, from inside. He stepped into the saddle and turned down the street to Aztec, then up toward Reservation. Little knots of people were gathering on the corners, in their dressing gowns, their sleeping robes.

A thin trickle of them was moving up the street. A buggy passed Banner, going hard. He was almost to Reservation now, could see the crowd around the courthouse. Sam Price came running from the alley between Reservation and First, his nightshirt flapping around hastily donned pants. He had a six-shooter in one hand.

"He's not down there," he shouted. "Carey's starting a search of the houses now."

"Somebody said he got a horse down on Second," another man called. "He'll head north for sure. What the hell is that sheriff doing?"

Banner pulled up on the fringe of the crowd around the jail, saw Blackstrap Kelly, raised his voice to be heard above the gusty roar of his horse's breathing. "What happened, Kelly?"

The saloonkeeper turned a scarred face to him. "Somebody blew up the jail safe. Jahzini got out the hole."

Banner swung down and shouldered his way through the men. The splintery cedar door was wide open. There were more men inside, examining the blackened hole in the back wall of the office. The safe had been knocked over on its side by the explosion, the heavy door bent open like a piece of tin. Charlie Drake was down on his hunkers, pawing through what was left of the papers. He had drawn on his blue serge pants over his striped nightshirt, and a peaked hat still bobbed on his grizzled head. He gave a tremendous wheeze, coming to his feet. He had a few burned pieces of paper in his hand, and Wright's saddlebags.

"That's all I can find," he said. "The rest must have been burned up. I had a lot of exhibits on that Johnson case, too."

"You're wasting a helluva lot of valuable time," somebody said hoarsely. "Let's get after him."

"We'll get after him," Drake said. "As long as we don't know for sure which way he went, I ain't running off half cocked. We may have to be gone several days. Somebody can go get them Papago trackers for me right now. I can use a dozen men in the posse. I'll deputize the first twelve of you that come back with a horse and two spares, two five-gallon canteens, and food for three days."

There was an eddying shift around Banner as the men started going out. He stepped past Judge Prentice, speaking to Drake.

"That cigarette butt is gone?"

The sheriff turned around in surprise. "Hello, Lee. What cigarette butt?"

"The exhibit Dodge gave you Saturday."

"Oh." Drake wiped the wrinkled back of his hand across a ruddy nose, toeing at the mess on the floor. "I guess it is. This is all I found."

"And Wright's letter?"

"I told you." Drake held up the saddlebags. "This is about all anybody could recognize."

Judge Prentice irritably pulled his coat shut over his nightshirt. "I don't see how they got in to do it in the first place, Drake. It looks like willful negligence to me."

"I don't think you can blame Drake, Judge," Kelly said. "Somebody started a fight in the alley back of my place. They began shooting off a gun and yelling bloody murder. Drake was the only one on duty over here. He come running with his shotgun."

"Who was it?"

"I didn't catch 'em," Drake said. "The explosion came when I was out back of Kelly's. Time I got back into Reservation, whoever'd done it was gone. Jahzini was gone too." The sheriff waved the saddlebags at the breach behind the safe. "Jahzini's cell was on the other side of that wall. When they blew the safe it made a big enough hole for him to crawl out."

Banner began backing out of the room, into the crowd, getting his horse. At the corner of Aztec, just about to mount, Banner saw three men swing onto Reservation at the next corner. Each one had a saddle roll, a pair of canteens, and two spare horses. And one of them was Big Red.

Before the man could see him, Banner swung around into Aztec. He stepped aboard and kicked the horse into a run. He turned on Gayoso Street and headed eastward out of town. Beyond the last house on the Ganado Road, he pulled the animal down to a walk-canter-trot that kept the miles unraveling behind him without draining the beast completely. His mind was on Big Red, and the implications of that, but he was also calculating how much of a head start he'd have. It would take them twenty minutes to get the Papago trackers, in their camp west of the railroad station. Maybe another ten to deputize the men, to get the group organized. Half an hour. It wasn't much.

The sun was up now and the heat waves were beginning to dance along the buttes. He turned off on the Yellow Gap cutoff, went through the gap itself, rose to the higher land northward. Two hours later he was riding through the mesquite forest south of Jahzini's. The sun made glittering beads of the ripening mesquite beans. Its heat drew a rancid stench from the deep layer of beans that had dropped in a thousand former years to putrefy on the ground. Then the stench was behind, and he rode into the rocky benchlands. An hour of this brought him out of the rough country into the wash where the hogan stood, with the sweep of white sand shimmering pallidly in the sun and the bittersweet scent of woodsmoke tainting the air.

Cristina must have heard his oncoming horse, for the wickerwork door was pushed aside, and she stooped through and straightened, a slim figure in her blue velvet tunic and voluminous skirt. He checked the horse before her and spoke without preamble.

"Your dad's escaped, Cristina. A posse's after him. We haven't got a minute to waste. Is he here?"

"He isn't here, Lee. From my lips, that is the truth. How—how——"

"Somebody got into the sheriff's office this morning and blew up the safe. It knocked a hole in the wall. Your father got out that way. By a strange coincidence, the only evidence destroyed was the stuff I'd gotten which might have proved your father's innocence."

He could see the fear begin to shine in her eyes, as if she had started to sense what lay in his mind. "What are you thinking, Lee? Don't try to spare me."

"Big Red was there," he said. "One of the first to join the posse. Why would he be in town at this time? Hackett needs every man on roundup."

Her eyes grew darker. "My father is liable to get drunk. He doesn't understand all this, and he always got drunk when he was mixed up about the white men. He has friends all the way up to Corn River. If he gets hold of liquor——"

"That's what I figured too. He'll put up a fight if they catch him——"

"And they will shoot him." There was a dead sound to her voice, a fatalism that came from deep in her Indian heritage. "That is what you mean, isn't it? Hackett did this on purpose. He wanted my father to escape so they could kill him."

"It would clear things up for Hackett," Banner said. "Maybe he was beginning to feel the pressure. To be afraid of what I was turning up. This way the case would be closed quick. No court battle. No evidence turning up in favor of your dad. Just a posse, a fight, a coroner's inquest. The feeling of the people is still bitter enough so there wouldn't be many questions."

She frowned, shaking her head. Light shimmered down her glossy braids. "When Jahzini was in trouble before, he always hid with a friend north of the Corn River. One of the old warriors that never surrendered to your people. Few know where the place is. It is two days from Mexican Hat, pushing hard. I had better go with you. You could never find it alone."

He saw that the old woman had come from the hogan. A rising wind whipped her bayeta shawl across her seamed face. She seemed to shrink a little when Cristina told her what had happened.

"We will stop by one of my cousins," Cristina told Banner. "They will come back to take care of her."

He helped her saddle up. Then they rode. The last sight he

had of the old woman, she was still standing beside the door of the lonely hogan, the wind ruffling the shawl across her face.

Westward the benchlands began lifting upward till they reached a rim that ran northwest for miles and then petered off in ridges shaggy with another mesquite forest. There was no rancid smell of decay here, for the wind kept the rocky ground swept clean of fallen beans, and the scent of white blossoms lay sweet as honey on the clean air.

The sun rolled toward its zenith, turning the sky's turquoise bowl to an arch of blinding brass. Banner was sodden with sweat and giddy with the heat. The horses were stumbling and wheezing, and he knew they would have to stop and rest. They found a trickle of water in a narrow gorge and let their horses drink and drank themselves and then hitched the animals in the dubious shade of scrub oak growing on the ledges beside the stream. Banner settled onto the baked earth beside the girl, scrubbing with a neckerchief at the clammy mask of sweat and dust on his face. The oppressive heat of the ride had drained much desire to talk from them, but the question had been on his mind for some time now.

"Did you find out anything more at Chin Lee?"

She gazed somberly at the stream. "The women knew little. They said Adakhai was one of the really wild boys. He hates the white men like the old warriors used to. His father was killed in one of the fights over grazing trouble. They would not tell me much more. They said Adakhai had been south, and might have been through Yellow Gap on the day of the murder. I tried to speak with him the next day, but he had gone hunting again."

"I'm sorry I caused that trouble, Cristina. But I had to see the horse."

"It is not your fault. If you had waited, he would have gone the next day, and you would never have seen the horse anyway." She looked up at him, a wondering expression parting her lips. "When everything was happy, when the world was peaceful, I saw very little of you. How strange that it should take death and pain to bring us together. Will you come to me—as you go to Julia Wright?"

He almost smiled. Something in her eyes kept him from it. They were filled with the paradox of a child's naïveté and a woman's intuitive wisdom.

"Are you jealous of Julia Wright?" he asked.

The wisdom, the naïveté seemed to recede within her, leaving only a fathomless blankness.

"Why do you look at me like that?" he asked. "Did I say something wrong?"

"Would you say a foot separates us, Lee?"

He frowned, puzzled. Then he smiled wryly. "No more than a foot, certainly."

"A thousand years separate us, Lee."

"Cristina——"

"I saw your face up at Chin Lee when you stepped down among those people. They smell like wild animals, don't they? You were stepping down into the past. A thousand years into the past. That's the way you felt. A man cut off from all he knew, surrounded by people he could never understand."

"That has nothing to do with you."

"They are my people, Lee."

"They may be of your blood. But you've lived among the white man now. You speak our tongue, your mind works like ours——"

"How do you know how my mind works? Just because I spent a few years in a white man's school . . . Does your mind work like an Indian because you lived with us for a year? You proved it did not at Chin Lee. You violated everything I thought you had learned when you lived among us. They hated you, yet they gave you hospitality. You violated that. You did not even understand what it would do to Adakhai if he found you with that horse. You will never get his trust now."

"Cristina, please——"

She shook her head, eyes dropping. "It is no use, Lee. You showed me up there how impossible it is that our two races could ever understand each other. That thousand years will always stand between us."

"No!" He caught her arms savagely, angered by her dogmatic insistence. "Only a foot separates us. We can cross that right now."

He pulled her toward him, bent his head to hers. There was a silken warmth to her lips. It was a transitory thing, a hint of satiny passion. Then it was gone; she tipped her head back, pushed him away. He let her do it, for all his savagery was washed out of him by his own surprise at what he had done. There was a startled look to her eyes, like a child with her first real glimpse into an adult world.

He stared down into her face, trying to understand what had happened to him. Suddenly their whole relationship was changed. He had started out teasing her, as he had done so many times in the past, teasing her about Julia Wright, like a boy would tease a little girl.

But she was no longer a little girl. She would never be again. Not for him.

Looking down at her, still trying to define what was happening within him, he could not help smiling, his rueful quirk of a smile. She reached up to touch his mouth with the tips of her fingers.

"When I think of you, I think of that," she said.

She took her hand away suddenly, swiftly, as if from a burn. She stood up and turned around and walked to her horse. She stood there with her back to him till he got up and followed her and took her shoulders in his hands and turned her around. Her eyes were squinted shut and tears were running down her cheeks.

"Cristina, I didn't mean——"

"What didn't you mean?"

He gazed down at the piquant oval of her face, helpless before the turmoil of his own feelings. "I don't know," he said, in a low voice. What should a man mean, or not mean, when he suddenly realized that a girl had become a woman? He had recognized the physical change back there in the jail that morning, the first time he had really seen Cristina since her return from Carlisle. But it seemed to have saved its emotional impact till now. He shook his head wonderingly, still holding her arms.

"At least that thousand years is gone from between us now."

Her head came up, almost in anger. "You still don't see it?"

"Cristina, don't talk that way again——"

"You're right. I shouldn't talk. If you don't see it, talk won't explain."

She twisted away, toed her stirrup. Her skirts flared as she swung up. She wheeled the pinto on down the canyon. He went to his own horse and pulled the latigo tight and stepped aboard and turned to follow her. Her strange mood was something he could only partly grasp, and it left him with a deep sense of frustration.

10

In the afternoon they reached Cristina's cousins at Ta Lagai. They came out of the highlands again into the greasewood flats and the logs-stacked-up house. As soon as Banner and the girl appeared, there was a call from somewhere, and people began to pop up like ants swarming from the earth. Banner was surrounded by a cacophony of Navajo and English as they surrounded the horses, all talking at once. When an ancient headman had finally quieted them, Cristina looked at Banner.

"Did you understand? Jahzini passed here on his way north. He sneaked in without any of them seeing him and got hold of some liquor and a gun. All the young men have gone south to sell the wool. The women and old men couldn't keep Jahzini here and had nobody to send after him when he left by horse."

"Did I catch Drake's name?"

"Sheriff Drake and his posse got here by horseback an

hour after Jahzini left. The Papago trackers didn't have any trouble following him on north."

Banner felt himself settle deeply into the saddle. "Then we're too late."

She shook her head. "If Jahzini is going north of Corn River, I know a short cut between here and Turquoise Buttes that might get us there ahead of Drake."

She turned to tell the palsied old headman of her mother. He said he would send one of his wives to take care of her. They watered their mounts in the brackish sink behind the hogans, then they pushed on.

The heat became more intense, sucking moisture from Banner till he was drenched in sweat. Yet he felt dry as a husk. His eyes ached, his face felt flayed raw, he began to have the sensation of riding in a feverish stupor. The girl accepted it all with the expressionless calm that made these people seem so Oriental to Banner. It was one of the times when she seemed completely withdrawn from him; it brought him frighteningly close to a sense of that thousand-year gulf she had said separated them.

They topped Turquoise Mesa and rode westward for three miles along its rim and then saw the stain of dust against the steely northern sky.

"That is probably Drake," she said. "It looks like they are heading west. That means they have struck the river and are following it at a walk. If we cut straight through these bench-lands ahead of us, we might reach Moqui Ford before they do."

It was a cruel stretch, studded with lava that would have cut a horse to ribbons if a man didn't know the trail. They finally reached the ford. The water was sullen and brassy under an afternoon sun. The stain of dust against the sky was to their right now, coming toward them, and they knew they had beaten Drake. Cristina took one glance at what looked like the fresh tracks of a shod horse, lining through the sand toward the river. Then she led Banner into the water, slopping across three hundred yards of brazen shallows to the narrow strip of beach on the other side. A great sandstone escarpment rose beyond the beach, running up and down the river as far as Banner could see, ruptured by a single canyon, directly ahead of them. Cristina rode unhesitatingly into this.

It was a narrow gorge, a place of shadows, of silence. Sometimes it was so narrow it scraped Banner's legs. It twisted and turned, back-tracked and looped. Sometimes its bottom was so choked with mesquite and oak they had to dismount and lead their animals through. Sunset was turning the sky to a bloody stripe between the rocky walls far above them when they began to smell the stench.

A few yards on they found the dead horse. It lay on its side, already bloating, foam a yellow crust on its snout. Cristina stared down at it, compassion darkening her eyes.

"Jahzini must have run it all the way through this heat. He would never do a thing like that if he was sober."

"That foam's not dry yet. He can't be too far ahead."

They rode another half mile through the narrow chasm, crossing shale where the clatter of their hoofs ran before them and died to a soft rustle between rocky walls beyond sight. Then Cristina pulled to a halt, staring at the rim above.

"There is a foot trail up here to the mesas. It will take him a mile across them to the northern rim and then down again. It is the shortest way. I think he would use it. If we both go up here he might get away at the other end."

"Could we split up?"

"That's the only way. A half mile on, this canyon opens onto the desert. You turn west along the mesa rim for a mile to where that foot trail comes down again."

"Do you want me to go that way?"

"I had better. You couldn't find where the trail comes down. You'll have to leave your horse here when you go up."

Cristina looked at him for a last moment. There was a darkness in her eyes. Then she turned her horse and rode on into the canyon, into the shadows, out of his sight.

He hitched his horse to some mesquite and started climbing. It all depended upon whether they could find Jahzini up there before Drake reached them. It was talus slope, at first, treacherous going in his high-heeled boots. Twice he had to go onto his belly to keep from sliding back down. He squirmed over the lip at the top, with the rocks and debris rolling down the steep slope and making a small roar in the gorge.

He rose to his feet on a narrow ledge that shelved upward, switching back on itself, becoming a defile between outcropping rocks. It was steep, laborious going, cutting his hands, drawing a heavy sweat from him. He had to stop for a breath more than once, in the rocks, on the ledges.

In one of those pauses he looked down. The bottom was swallowed in shadows so deep he could not make out his horse. Then he felt his head jerk up in reaction. Had there been motion above him?

He could see nothing.

He began moving upward, for the first time realizing the full implications of what he might meet up there. Jahzini might start shooting without taking time to recognize him. Or, if he was too drunk, maybe Jahzini wouldn't recognize him anyway.

Banner had only seen the old man that drunk once or twice. Jahzini liked his *toghlepai,* but mostly he had only imbibed enough to give him a glow, to bring out the clownish mischief in him. Yet the pressures against him had been enormous these last days, things he didn't understand, couldn't cope with. There was no telling how much of a release he would seek.

Banner's eyes began to ache with the strain of trying to find something on the twilit rim of rocks. There was no movement above him. No sound. Nothing.

The ledge widened, fanned out through a studding of rocks that hung on the lip of the plateau. His breathing was loud and gusty. He neared the top of the cliff, his eye level lifted above the tops of the last rocks. He stopped.

"*Belinkana?*"

A sly, nasal, questioning tone to it. "American?" A cunning tone, matching the cunning light in Jahzini's eyes, in his blandly smiling face. He sat there like a paunchy, leering Buddha, in the rocks, with the *tusjeh* beside him, uncorked, lifting the reek of raw corn liquor into the air. The Remington six-shooter in his lap was pointed at Banner.

"Jahzini——"

The gun snapped up, stopping Banner short. Jahzini held it in both hands. Banner could see no recognition in the drink-glazed eyes.

"Belinkana?"

High and nasal. "American?" Like a child who had just learned a new word. Rolling it around the tongue. Savoring it.

Banner sought swiftly for the right words to say now, trying to avoid the verb forms that could put so many different, wrong meanings on his explanation.

"Jahzini, Hackett did this on purpose. Big Red is in the posse. They know you will fight. They want you dead, don't you understand? They want you dead——"

"Dead!"

The gun jerked as Jahzini said it. His whole body seemed to lift up, a wild light in his eyes. And then the small click.

Jahzini had cocked the gun. He was staring at Banner over a cocked gun. Banner felt the sweat break out on his palms. Had he made a mistake? Had he used the wrong form of the verb?

He knew he had to speak again. There was so little time left. He sought desperately for the right thing to say, knowing the slightest error of inflection, the smallest alteration in construction could put the wrong meaning into his words, probably the fatal meaning.

"Jahzini, you remember me. You remember Tsi Tsosi."

"Tsi Tsosi?"

"Yes. Yellow Hair. And Keet Seel. Remember the lion at Keet Seel? Who was it saved your life? You cut our palms. We mingled blood. We were brothers. Look at your hand."

Suspiciously, the Indian let that pass through his mind. It seemed to take forever. Then he let go of the gun with his right hand, stared bleary-eyed at the palm. The old scar was faint and white against the dirty brown skin. Slowly the Navajo's eyes raised. Just as slowly, Banner held his hand out, palm up. It bore a faint white scar too. Jahzini squinted to make it out in the last light of the dying day.

The gun seemed to lower a little. The effort of remembering etched the million wrinkles deeper into Jahzini's nut-brown face. The drunken cunning faded from his eyes.

"Tsi Tsosi?" he said wonderingly. Then he grinned, tentatively, and his voice was touched by all the chuckling warmth with which he had imbued the name when he had first called Banner Yellow Hair. "Tsi Tsosi . . ."

Banner knew a glowing triumph, and started to move toward the old man. Then he stopped. Jahzini's head had lifted sharply, his pinched nostrils fluttering like a horse testing the ⌐ir. The wild look was back in his eyes. They were staring ͺ͜ͺͻnd Banner.

And the young man could hear it now too. Down in the canyon. A hollow rustling. A far-off clatter of hoofs across shale in the canyon bottom. Then there was a shout from below.

"Jahzini, is that you?"

It was Drake's voice, coming from the depth of the gorge, echoing and re-echoing till a hundred men seemed to be shouting. It filled Banner with the impulse to turn. But the expression on Jahzini's face checked him. All the warmth, the memory that had started to wipe away the glaze of liquor was gone. The Indian's features looked shrunken with rage. The gun was pointed at Banner's chest, and the wrinkled thumb was clamped hard over the cocked hammer.

"Jahzini," Banner said. "I didn't bring them here. You've got to believe me. I didn't betray you——"

"All right, you old fool," Drake called. "We're coming up. Cut loose just once and we'll shoot you off that cliff."

The creak of leather, from below. The first rustle of climbing men, from below. The irony of it filled the young lawyer bitterly. He was skylighted on the rim, and the men down there thought he was Jahzini.

The gun was trembling in the old Indian's hand. Banner knew that one move from him would set it off. He was even

afraid to speak. He stared across its black bore, its glittering
sights, into those yellow-tinged eyes.

Then somebody started the first landslide. He must have
kicked a sizable rock loose, for it made a startling crash of
sound in the canyon.

"Belinkana———"

There was no question in it now. There was only exploding rage as Jahzini jumped to his feet, shouting it, and fired
down into the canyon.

In sheer reflex, Banner threw himself at the man, knocking
him backward. The shot was magnified a hundred times by
the acoustics of the chasm. A dozen guns must have gone off
below in the following instant. They sounded like a thousand
A hail of bullets took vicious bites out of the rocks wh...
Banner had stood the moment before. If Jahzini had been on
his feet he would have been cut to pieces.

Jahzini struggled to free himself from beneath Banner. But
the young lawyer caught at the gun, twisted it from his grasp.
The old man clawed him like a cat. Banner hit him across
the side of the head with the barrel of the gun. Jahzini went
slack beneath him.

The guns were still racketing from below, filling the gorge
with a gigantic roar. A ricochet screamed like a woman in
pain. The echoes multiplied it to the howl of a hundred
banshees. Deafened by the din, Banner crouched low over
Jahzini. He was trembling in reaction, realizing only now how
close he had been to death, realizing only now that Jahzini
had deliberately fired past him into the canyon.

Without raising up, he tried to drag the old man farther
back from the edge. There was furtive movement from among
the rocks. Banner jerked the gun up. Cristina crawled into
view. Banner let his pent breath out.

"I had to hit him," he said.

"I know." Her words were almost lost in the crash of guns.
"He fought you." She came closer, shouting in the din. "We
cannot go back to my horse. Those Papago trackers must have
known about this foot trail. They led Arles and another man

around to that end of it. I saw them reach my horse as I got to the top of the mesa. They will be coming up after me."

"Is there another way down?"

"A mile to the west. It is dangerous, but we might make it."

"And from there, how far to the nearest place we could get horses?"

"Ten or twelve miles to Kitteridge's place. We could lose our tracks in the Corn River. If they were not sure where we were going on foot we might make it to Kitteridge's ahead of them."

They pulled Jahzini back into the brush, trying to revive him enough to walk. He crouched on his hands and knees, shaking his head. Finally he looked up at Banner. The blow seemed to have sobered him somewhat.

"Bahagi," he groaned. "I have committed a great offense."

"You did nothing of the sort," Banner told him. "You fired past me, down into the canyon. I should have known you couldn't ever get drunk enough to shoot me."

"I thought you were an evil *he'inkana.* I thought you were Nayenezrani himself come to strike me down with all four of his lightnings."

"We've got to make a run for it, Old Black Ears. Can you stand?"

"Stand? I can fly. I am sober now. The wind cannot keep up with me." He tried to rise, swayed, would have fallen if they hadn't caught him. He shook them off, snorting disdainfully. "Let us go," he said. "Cry out when you grow tired and I will carry you on my back."

11

Somehow they made it down the treacherous, forgotten trail on the west end of the mesa. They knew it would be hard for the Papagos to track them at night, and in that lay their hope. They left a false trail leading north and then gained the Corn

River and turned south in its shallows. For the first few miles the old man showed a surprising stamina, slopping through the muddy water. He seemed to have recovered from the blow on the head. As Banner moved beside him, Jahzini chuckled roguishly and gave him a poke in the ribs.

"I should escape jail more often, if that is what it takes to see my white son again. I have missed those nights in the hogan. With Cristina gone away to school, there was no one I could tell the myths to."

"Those nights will come again. You must help them come. You must tell us what happened. You wouldn't talk when I first saw you in the jail, you know."

The old man nodded. "I know. I was all mixed up. They showed me Wright's saddlebags and said they had found them in my hogan and said I killed him. I was drunk when they found me and I couldn't remember anything anyway and I thought maybe I did kill him and couldn't remember it."

"But you didn't."

"No. Now I do not think I did. I was taking wool to town by wagon that day when I heard the shot in Yellow Gap. When I came upon Wright he was dead. It gave me great fear. I had fought with Wright over the land. His death would make great trouble for my people. The Army might be sent out and we would have war again. It was very bad. I wanted to run. I wanted to hide somewhere. I went to the hogan of my cousin."

"And got drunk."

"Sometimes just running is not enough. You run till you can run no more and still have not escaped. Like today. I could go no further and still they came. That is why I got drunk, I suppose."

"Never mind, Old Black Ears. You are with your people now."

"That is good. It gives me strength. If you grow tired we can sing *hozhoni* songs. They will make us holy and give us wings to our feet."

So they sang *hozhoni* songs as they ran, and because they knew it would help the old man, they sang the Lightning Song

and Pounding Boy's Song and the War God's Song and all
the old songs that Jahzini's people had been singing for hundreds of years when they set out upon a journey or started
off to war — as they ran.

But finally the old man began stumbling and they had to
slow down to a walk, and even the songs were too much effort.
Banner did not know what time of night it was when they
reached the forks in the river and left the shallows and made
their way into the broken country west of Chimney Buttes.
Then the old man stumbled and fell to his hands and knees in
the sand, his breathing shallow with exhaustion. When they
helped him up, he shook his head.

"It is a bad thing to have a father who will lie to you. I
really could not carry you on my back if you got tired. And
those *hozhoni* songs, they were for me. I was the one who
needed the wings."

Banner slapped him affectionately on the back. "You can't
fool me. I am onto your jokes. You pretended to be tired that
time when we were racing for the blankets, and I slowed down
because I thought I had beaten you, and you passed me up
before I knew what had happened."

A feeble roguishness lit the oblique glance Jahzini sent him.

"Ai," he said, giving Banner a sly poke in the ribs. "Who
has a son like Old Black Ears? I did beat you that time, didn't
I? You make me young again, bringing back the old days. Very
well, let us run some more."

"And sing some more," Cristina said. "Sing us the Clown
Song, like you used to."

"I cannot thump my belly to make a drum any more. It
seems to hurt me or something."

"I will thump my belly," Banner said. "You sing."

So they sang another song, moving across the broken land
in that unremitting, Indian dog trot, with Banner thumping
his belly and the old man chanting the Clown Song in a husky,
wavering voice. It helped for a while. Then the old man began faltering again, and they had to slow down to a walk, and
finally he fell again, and they had to stop and rest. Banner
lost count of the times they ran, the times they rested. He

thought the night would never end. He thought they would never make it.

But the dawn came at last, revealing Chimney Buttes on the horizon. And when the sun rose, they were in sight of Kitteridge's. His house was backed up against the wall of a mesa, a long adobe, tawny as worn buckskin, a crumbling pole corral lying in a jackstraw pattern against the land to one side.

Banner and Cristina were half carrying Jahzini now, each holding him up by an arm. He was stupefied with exhaustion, his feet dragging and stumbling behind, his head swinging slackly from side to side.

"Just cry out if you cannot go on," he mumbled. "I will carry you on my back———"

Banner saw the hammerheaded roan and half a dozen other horses in the corral. The roan began running along the fence and whinnying at their approach. Kitteridge opened the door before they reached it.

His gaunt frame seemed to stiffen as he saw them. His eyes widened with his first surprise, then squinted almost shut. The tiny scarlike lines of weathering formed about his pursed mouth, and he watched their approach with a suspicious withdrawal on his face, seamed and aged beyond its years by the sun and heat of this land.

"Let us get Jahzini inside," Banner panted. "I think he's passed out."

"I ain't harboring no murderer."

"He's not a murderer, damn you! Let us in. You'd help a dog if he was in this shape."

Reluctantly Kitteridge moved out of the way, and they staggered into the room, carrying Jahzini to a chair. When they got him into it, Cristina had to hold the old man to keep him from falling. The room was low-roofed, gloomy, with morning light sifting through the slotlike windows to cast pale stripes across the hard-packed earth of the floor. At one end were rude shelves and an estufa—the cone-shaped Mexican oven of adobe which was molded right into the walls at one corner. Kitteridge still stood at the door beside the heaped gear of a rawhide-rigged saddle, a pair of sweat-stiff saddle blankets, a Winchester in a scarred boot. Banner pulled the table across in front of Jahzini so he could lean forward without falling. When Cristina let him go he dropped his head into his arms. She took the other chair, leaning heavily against the table, her eyes blank with exhaustion. Banner, his eyes glazed with weariness, let a long gust of air run out of him.

"Now," he said. "We'll need three horses."

"The hell you will. I told you——"

"I'm trying to get Jahzini back to Mexican Hat," Banner said. Anger made his voice husky. "They set this up so Jahzini could escape. They wanted to kill him before this case came to trial."

"Is that so?" Kitteridge said cynically. He settled back onto his run-over heels, thumbs tucked into the beltless waistband of greasy jeans. "Who set it up?"

Banner hesitated, remembering what he had lost by telling Julia and Dodge. "I haven't got time to explain that, Kitteridge. But Jahzini's innocent. You've got to help me save his life. There's a posse on our trail now and they'll kill him if they get him."

"I ain't helping no murderer."

"He isn't a murderer, damn you——" Banner broke off, staring in frustrated anger at the droll cynicism in the man's long face. Kitteridge took his thumbs from his waistband, slouched indolently across the room to the spindled Mexican cupboard. From this he took a coffeepot, shook coffee into it from a sack. Then he shambled to the barrel near the rear door, dippered water into the pot, moved unhurriedly back to the estufa.

"Shouldn't of let you spoil my breakfast," he said. "If you want to get away from that posse bad enough to walk all this distance for my horses, you sure as hell won't let them catch you here, whether you get the horses or not. *Ipso facto,* Counselor?"

Banner's voice was pinched with restraint. "You won't give us the horses?"

Kitteridge set the pot on the coals. "I told you."

The restraint left Banner; his words exploded in a gust of anger as he wheeled toward the back door. "Then we're taking them!"

Kitteridge did not seem to move fast. He straightened and stepped toward the front. Cristina jumped from her chair, trying to block him. But somehow he was at the door before she reached him.

"No you ain't," he said.

At the rear door, Banner half turned, to see the man standing by the heap of rigging. He had pulled the Winchester from its boot. It was crooked in one elbow, pointed toward the lawyer.

"There ain't so much as a rope out in them corrals," Kitteridge said. "You'd have to come back here anyway. The halters are in this pile."

Cristina had stopped, halfway to the man. Now the look of her face altered subtly. Shadowed hollows appeared beneath her cheekbones, making them look sharp and high; her eyes took on a fathomless blankness. It was that expression of oriental fatalism Banner had seen before. She began to walk toward Kitteridge. He did not even shift the gun.

"I never shot a lady," he said. "But I'll sure as hell swipe the barrel of this gun across your head if you come any nearer."

"Don't do it, Cristina!" Banner's voice was sharp. "He means what he says."

Cristina stopped. A long breath left her. It made a hissing sound in the room. Banner stared at Kitteridge, tense with the effort of checking his foolish impulse to jump at the man. The frustration of it dug deep lines about his compressed lips.

"I always thought they misjudged you in town, Kitteridge. I'm beginning to believe they didn't."

"I mind my business. I expect other people to do the same."

"Why?" Banner asked thinly. "Are you running from something too? You've been here three years and haven't made a friend in the whole time. There's a lot of people in town who think you're on the dodge. What are you, Kitteridge? A thief? A murderer?"

A whipped look crossed Kitteridge's face, and he started to lean forward. Then he checked himself. Slowly he settled back. The expression drained from his features, until it was only that veil of cynicism, lying rancidly in his eyes.

"You're not in the courtroom now, Counselor," he said.

Banner hardly heard him. He did not know how long he had been looking at the gear beside Kitteridge. The yellow color on the saddle had been visible all the time, but his anger had blinded him to its significance. It came through at last. A yellow stain on the bottom of a stirrup. Clay. The bright yellow clay a man would pick up at Yellow Gap. It made Banner forget everything else for a moment.

"That's a little saddle," Banner said. "Was it the bay's?"

Kitteridge revealed his surprise. "What bay's?"

"The bay you gave to Jeremiah Mills."

Kitteridge's grin held no humor. "You think of the funniest things."

The man's sardonic insolence exasperated Banner. He felt his hands closing into fists. "That tree looks too small to fit any of the horses you've got here."

"The bay was a little horse. I'll get me another little horse."

"Then you haven't used that saddle since you rode the bay?"

"What's that got to do with anything?"

"A lot. Did you go through Yellow Gap the last time you rode the bay?"

The coffee started to boil. Its hissing was the only sound in the room. Kitteridge was studying Banner narrowly. When he finally spoke, his voice was ragged with disgust.

"Why should I want to kill Wallace Wright?"

"I'm not implying you killed Wright," Banner said hotly. "There was an eyewitness to the killing. We have every reason to believe he saw it from the rim of the gap. He came from up here and he rode a bay horse."

Banner saw the little muscles draw up about Kitteridge's mouth till it had a puckered look. Cristina was watching the man intently. The hiss of boiling water became a gurgle. At last Kitteridge spoke. His voice was like the rustle of wind through dry leaves.

"All of Mills's saddles were too small for that bay. He used this one for quite a while after I gave him the horse."

"Mills said you gave him the horse after the killing."

"He's a liar."

"You're saying you didn't see the killing?"

"A man that minds his own chores don't go around poking his nose into things like that."

"Damn you, Kitteridge, it isn't a matter of poking your nose in people's business. This eyewitness saw the whole thing by chance. You'd be saving a man's life. If you didn't talk, it would be the same as murdering Jahzini——"

"Save your howling for the jury, Counselor," Kitteridge said. "I didn't see any killing. I didn't see nothing."

Banner felt his whole body grow rigid in frustrated anger. He stared at the man, completely blocked by his impervious cynicism. It was in such antithesis to anything he knew, to all his own reactions, his intense enthusiasms, his ardent impulsiveness.

He started to run his hand through his hair, in that irritable habit. Then he remembered he had his hat on, and balled his hands to fists, jamming them in his pockets. He began to pace across the room.

"Isn't there anything that can touch you? They're set to kill this old man, shooting, or hanging, or however else they can do it. The man who saw that murder is the only one who can save him——"

"Looks like you're gettin' impatient," Kitteridge said. "It's true you ain't got much time left. That posse's had a lot of daylight to track you now. They might be riding up outside right now."

Banner checked his angry pacing. He knew the man was right. The trick of hiding their tracks in the river wouldn't fool the Papagos for long. One would go upriver, the other down. The one who had gone down would see where they had left the water. After that it would be simple.

The lid of the coffeepot began to clatter and dance, and Kitteridge glanced at Cristina. "Move it off, honey. It's fixin' to boil over."

The girl rose, going toward the oven. She picked up a dirty rag to use as a pot holder and bent over the coffee. It was then that she glanced at Banner. Just a passing glance. But there was something in her eyes. And the implications reached him. Was that what she intended? He looked at Kitteridge. Then he took a lunging step toward the man.

"Damn you, Kitter——"

"Stay there," the man snapped, jerking his rifle up.

For that moment it took his attention completely away from Cristina. She picked up the coffeepot and threw it.

The man reacted instantly, turning toward her motion. But he was too late. The top fell off as the pot struck him. The boiling water cascaded over his head.

His shout of pain filled the room. He dropped the rifle and staggered backward, hands clapped to his scalded face. Banner jumped to the Winchester, scooping it up. Kitteridge stood rigidly against the wall, hands spread tightly over his face. His breathing was a sobbing sound in the room. Banner gave the rifle to Cristina and turned to get the can of beef tallow on a shelf.

"Stay away from me," Kitteridge said. His voice was strangled with pain and anger.

"Don't be a fool," Banner told him. "You'll be scarred for good unless you get some of this on your face."

He had to pull the man's hands down. Kitteridge's eyes were squinted shut, his face intensely contorted. Banner put the grease on his cheeks in great gobs and rubbed it in gently. Cristina held the Winchester on the man, mouth pinched and tight.

"I am sorry," she said. "You forced us——"

"If you was a man I'd kill you," Kitteridge said. "I'd kill you right now."

"It was my father. You made me do it. I could not let them kill him. You must understand."

Kitteridge leaned back against the wall, drawing a thin, whistling breath between his teeth. "All right." He sounded weary, the bitterness drained from his voice. "So you couldn't let them kill him."

"You do understand? You don't hate me?"

"Hate you?" The man opened his eyes to look at her. They were watering and twitching with the pain of the burn. But there was no rancor in them. They merely looked tired. "No, honey," he said finally, "I guess I don't hate you."

Banner looked at him in surprise. It was the last reaction he had expected. He turned to put the can of grease on the table and took the rifle from the girl.

"I'd better hold him here while you saddle up, Cristina."

"That ain't necessary," Kitteridge said. "If you want the horses that bad, you got 'em."

"You disappoint me," Banner said. "I thought you were all vinegar."

Kitteridge took a weary breath. "Nobody's all anything, Counselor. Just get out of here before that posse shows."

"You'd better get a doctor as soon as you can."

"I don't need a doctor." The man turned to pace across the room, as if unable to stand still with the pain. He stopped by the fireplace, staring blankly at the wall. His voice had lowered till it was barely audible. "I don't need nobody."

Banner stared at his back with a new insight into the man. "I think that's where you're wrong, Kitteridge," he said. "I think you've needed somebody for a long time."

12

It was evening when they got back to Mexican Hat. They came in from the south, across the railroad tracks, through the Mexican district. Tilfego was not home, but they left their jaded horses in his corral so they could move with more secrecy into town. They went up the alley between Aztec and Central to Judge Prentice's house. But the place was unlit.

The only other possibility was that the judge was working late in his chambers at the courthouse.

It was a tense journey to the square and into the gaunt old building, but they were not stopped. Light showed under the judge's door. Banner knocked softly. Prentice's voice sounded muffled, asking them to enter. His swivel chair shrieked as he leaned back in utter surprise at Jahzini's appearance. Banner towered behind Jahzini in the doorway. Beneath the brim of his hat, dust tarnished the edges of his blond hair and lay like caked powder on his face. His eyes were red-rimmed and feverish, the deep lines of weariness about his mouth made him look older.

"He came back of his own accord, Judge. You've got to believe that. I brought him to you because you're the only one I can trust now."

The chair groaned more softly as Prentice leaned forward again, putting his hands on the desk, littered with the Manila-backed briefs of his cases. Then he rose abruptly, coming around the desk, shaking his distinguished head in a troubled perplexity.

"Sit down," he said. "You look all beat out." He went to the scarred highboy by the window and got a bottle of brandy and three glasses from one of the cupboards. While he poured the drinks and handed them around, Banner helped Jahzini into a chair. The old man was stupid with exhaustion and sat huddled over, gazing blankly at the floor. Banner could not relax himself, as drained as he was. He spoke tightly, swiftly.

"The posse can't be far behind us. Even if they don't trail us to town, Charlie Drake and some of them will be back here to tell you what happened. I want your word on something before they come. If you won't give it I'm taking Jahzini right back out, Judge."

Prentice smiled ruefully. "Don't put me on the spot, Lee."

Banner's voice crackled with the angry tension of fatigue. "I only want your word you'll put Jahzini on the first train out of Mexican Hat. Send him to the Territorial Penitentiary at Yuma till the date of his trial."

Prentice turned and walked back to the highboy, setting

the bottle down. He wheeled and moved to the window, and stared out into the soft summer night, his hands locked behind him.

"I know there's a lot of feeling against him. There's even been talk of lynching. But I doubt if it will come to that."

"You know what I'm talking about."

The judge was silent for a long moment. Then he took a reluctant breath. "All right. Talk has also been going around that you think Hackett had Wright killed. I asked your uncle about it. He said that was your theory."

"It's more than a theory," Banner said. "I turned two items of evidence over to the court which might have proven Jahzini's innocence. Doesn't it strike you as strange that they were destroyed in that explosion, while all the evidence against him was saved?"

"I've been thinking of that——"

"Thinking of it!"

Prentice turned toward him. "Take it easy, Lee. I know you're perfectly sincere in what you're doing. But I also know how impulsive you are. Remember how you lost the Farris case for your uncle by going off half cocked? Have you stopped to think what this has done to Henry? Not only his personal feelings for you, but his position——"

"Have you stopped to think what it's done to Jahzini?"

Prentice flushed, started to speak, checked himself with effort. He began turning back toward the window. Then the thud of hoofbeats came from the street, the faraway shout of a man.

"They're here," Prentice said.

"Judge, please——"

The man frowned at him, running a long finger thoughtfully over his silvery mustache. The heavy echo of boots ran down the outer hallway. Cristina came up out of her chair, hands clenched at her side. There was the rumble of voices outside, the door shook to a knock. Banner felt the tips of his fingers brush his gun. Prentice glanced apprehensively at Jahzini, then said:

"Come in."

Sheriff Drake was the first to enter, with Clay Hackett and Big Red and Blackstrap Kelly pushing in behind. Drake halted his gross bulk a couple of paces inside the room, staring at Jahzini, at Banner, with no great surprise in his red face. He settled himself heavily, emitting a wheezing breath.

"How do you like that?" he said, with weary disgust. "Chase all around the country and find them right back where we started." He seemed to settle against the floor, emitting a long, wheezing breath. "We tracked you to Kitteridge's. He said you was coming back here. I wouldn't believe him."

Anger made Hackett's prominent cheekbones stand out whitely, rawly against the sun-reddened flesh of his face. "That was you up on the cliff?" he asked Banner.

The lawyer ignored him, speaking to Drake. "Jahzini came back of his own accord." ·

"After trying to ambush us," Hackett said.

"He was drunk. He didn't know what he was doing."

"Well, we know what we're doing," Hackett said. "Charlie, slap those cuffs on him. He won't get away again."

Drake started to move. Banner took one long step that put himself between Jahzini and the sheriff. His eyes had that chipped-glass glitter.

"Don't get in the way again, Lee," Hackett said. "They can give a pretty stiff jolt to anybody that helps an escaped murderer."

Banner spoke to Prentice without moving his eyes from Drake. "Judge?"

Prentice had been watching Hackett closely. "How do you happen to be in the posse?" he asked.

"I wasn't," Hackett said. "There was a card game at Blackstrap's."

"I understand you were represented, anyway. Good of you to spare Big Red, right at roundup time."

"And Arles," Banner said.

Hackett turned sharply toward Banner, a biting anger filling his eyes. He had taken a quick breath while he turned, as if to speak. But he did not speak. Prentice was still watching him closely. As if feeling the man's gaze on him, Hackett closed his mouth and wheeled slowly back till he was looking at Prentice again. The narrow speculation in the judge's eyes changed the expression in Hackett's face. It was as if he deliberately masked his anger. It left his gaunt features wooden and enigmatic.

"So it's bad to join a posse now," he said. His voice was silk-soft. "Maybe you'd rather chase your murderers next time without one."

Drake shifted uncomfortably. "Now, Clay——"

"We didn't mean to criticize your public spirit, Mr. Hackett," Prentice said. He studied Hackett quizzically for another moment. Then he turned to walk behind his desk. When he faced them again, he was looking down at the litter of briefs, his lips pursed. "The feeling's bad enough in this town. After this little escapade it might get dangerous. I think we'd better send Jahzini to Yuma for safekeeping till the trial."

"And give him another chance to escape?" Blackstrap Kelly said.

"Not many men have escaped Yuma," Prentice answered dryly. He lifted his gaze inquisitively to Hackett. The man met his glance with veiled eyes, not reacting in any way. Prentice brushed a finger absently across his mustache, sat down. "I'll sign the order. You can wire Yuma for confirmation tonight, Charlie. I think there's a train at ten thirty-eight tomorrow morning. You can send a couple of your deputies to guard him."

As the pen began to scratch, Hackett turned to look at Banner. For a moment he let the anger show in his eyes again, naked and ugly. Then, without a word, he wheeled to the door. The room was filled with the jingle and clank of spurs, the hollow clatter of boot heels, as Big Red followed Hackett out. As they passed into the hall, the scratching pen stopped, and Prentice raised a brief glance to Banner. Then he lowered his head and began to write again.

Cristina was bent over her father, explaining to him in Navajo what had happened. His eyes were heavy-lidded, his face slack and heavy with fatigue. But he began to nod, frowning. When she was finished, he raised his head with great effort to look at Banner. He held up an arm, and Cristina caught it, helping him to stand. Then he shuffled over to Banner, putting his sinewy old hands on his shoulders, tipping his head back to see the lawyer better. He was smiling, and his eyes were suspiciously wet.

"*Shiye*," he said, patting Banner gently with both hands. "My son."

13

The next morning Banner boarded the train with Jahzini and two of Drake's deputies. Hackett had little power outside Navajo County, and Banner felt sure the man could not touch Jahzini beyond Flagstaff. So he rode that far, checking each passenger who got on, making sure that none of the cars held anyone remotely connected with Hackett. It was an uneventful trip, and Banner said good-by to the Indian at Flagstaff, returning to Mexican Hat on the next train, secure in his own mind now that Jahzini would be safe.

And again he set out on the process of elimination. It took him two days to finish questioning the people of Mexican Hat. No new suspects arose. Though the reports were confused and inaccurate, Mills and Kitteridge were still the only white men from the north country that had been seen in Mexican Hat during the day of the murder.

After finishing in town, Banner rode out to the trading post. Besides meaning to question Calico Adams, he had half hoped to see Julia. But it was after three o'clock, and school had already closed; Calico said Julia had already gone on her usual afternoon ride. Out of the trader's seemingly endless knowledge of the comings and goings of the Indians, the lawyer gained many facts which substantiated what he already knew. There had been no stranger on the reservation who might have come south through Yellow Gap during June. And though Adakhai had not been at the trading post since April, several Indians had seen him hunting in the country west of Yellow Gap on the week before the murder.

After leaving Calico, Banner rode north to begin his routine check of the remaining whites between the railroad tracks and the reservation. He reached Caleb Elder's about five.

The man was a big, taciturn cattle operator who had been Banner's rival for Julia two years ago. That old antagonism, and the trouble Elder had been having with the Indians, filled him with a hostility he did not try to veil.

But Banner told him that the trial would probably be in September, and that unless he cleared himself of any suspected connection with the murder he could be subpoenaed to testify, and would undoubtedly lose a lot of time from fall roundup. This made him admit that he had been driving cattle across the reservation to St. Michaels during the week of the murder. He gave as witnesses Joe Garry and Breed, whom he had met holding some Hackett cattle on the Rio Puerco. Banner would not accept them, and Elder included the priest at St. Michaels, to whom he had delivered the cattle on the day of the murder. Banner knew the man would not say this unless it were true, for it would be too easy to check. It completely obviated any chance of Elder being at Yellow Gap, seventy miles away, on the same day.

However, the fact that the two Hackett riders were holding Broken Bit cattle deep in reservation land was direct evidence that Hackett was violating the treaty, and Banner knew it would be a strong item of subsidiary evidence for the defense. So he prepared a statement, including the names of Joe Garry and Breed as witnesses to Elder's claim. Elder was reluctant to sign until Banner convinced the man that this would free him of any further connection with the murder.

The trail back to the Ganado Road cut across a vast, broken country, and Banner free-bitted his horse through the soft dusk. He wound into a cut, red with crumbled sandstone, puckered with the mounds made by kangaroo rats. He emerged from the mouth of the cut and crossed a sandy flat to Parker's Sink, the only water hole between Elder's and the railroad. It was surrounded by a thick stand of willows and cottonwoods, ragged and browning with summer. The brackish water had a silken gleam, through the trunks, and the horse nickered eagerly. It was answered by another nicker. Banner pulled up sharply at the fringe of the trees.

Two riders were already watering their animals at the sink. One of them was Julia Wright, a handsome figure in her riding habit of dark green suède, a pork-pie hat tilted saucily on high-piled hair. The other one, sitting slackly on a hammerheaded roan, was Victor Kitteridge.

There was a long space of awkward silence. Then Kitteridge's saddle groaned as he shifted his weight.

"Seems like everybody's out riding tonight."

"Seems like," Banner said. He gigged his horse over to the water hole, nodding a sober greeting to Julia. "Did you get your three horses back, Kitteridge?"

"Your Indian boy brought 'em back all right."

"How's the face?"

"No uglier'n usual."

"It didn't seem to leave any scars."

"Take more'n that."

"You don't seem mad."

"Bygones."

"Then maybe you'll tell me about the bay now."

"No."

"When they hang Jahzini, will you come to see it?"

Julia stiffened in the saddle, her face going white. Kitteridge showed no reaction. He sat slack on his horse, his cheeks hollow, his eyes squinted with that barrier of sardonic cynicism.

"I'll be dragging," he said.

He gathered up his reins, nodded to Julia, heeled his horse around, rode out through the trees. Banner was watching the small changes of expression pass across Julia's face.

"Did you know him, back in Denver?"

She flushed. "I told you I didn't. I stopped here to water my horse. He was coming back from Ganado."

"A man saw your father murdered, Julia. I've narrowed it down to three possibilities. Kitteridge is one. If you know him, I need your help the worst way. I'm hoping time has healed your grief enough so you can see this thing in its proper perspective——"

"Oh, stop it," she said bitterly. "Do you have to go on hurting everybody——"

"You know I don't mean to hurt you."

"Then why don't you stop? It's not only me. Can't you see what you're doing to Henry? It used to be I couldn't go into town without seeing your uncle out there on the corner, talking with some friends. Now he's never there. Do you know why? He's up in his office. He's hiding, Lee——"

"Julia——"

"He's the laughingstock of the town. You've made a circus of this thing. Running all over the country with that old Indian. Sending half the town out after him ready to shoot on sight and then showing up with him right in Prentice's chambers, meek as a lamb. Can anybody take Henry seriously with his own son turning on him like that? Everybody's come to look on you as practically his son."

"I can't help it. Do you think I'd turn on Henry if there was any other way? Don't you think it's tearing my insides out to see him cross the street to avoid me?"

He stopped, breathing heavily. She turned her head sharply aside, squeezing her eyes shut to keep the tears from coming out.

"Oh, Lee, why does it have to be this way? I'm so mixed up. You're right. Time has made me see things differently. I still want to believe Jahzini killed Dad. I want to hate him for it——"

"But you can't," he said. "Admit it."

"All right"—she shook her head savagely—"I admit it, I admit it."

She put her hands over her face, her shoulders began to tremble with her sobs. He stepped over to her horse, holding up his arms.

"Julia," he said, softly, persuasively. "Julia."

She looked down at him, face stained with tears. She shook

her head, turning away once more. He could still see her throat working.

"You would have come down to me before if you'd really relented," he said.

"I've relented. I've admitted I couldn't just let Jahzini hang, if there was any chance of his innocence. What more can you ask?"

"Things have changed," he said.

Her throat stopped working. "I suppose they have," she said in a low voice.

"Hackett?"

"Don't be a fool."

"You've seen a lot of him lately."

"It isn't Hackett. Can't you leave it at that?"

"Then it's just that once you would have come down to me, and now you won't."

He stared up at her, searching her face, filled with the poignant sense of having lost touch with something. But he could not quite define it, was almost afraid to explore it further. He took a ragged breath.

"Then you'll help me with Jahzini," he said. "You'll tell me about Kitteridge."

"Lee, I don't see what possible connection——"

He reached up to catch her hand. "I've checked at the post office. Ed tells me that in the three years Kitteridge has been here he's gotten one letter, from Denver. If you knew Kitteridge up there you've got to tell me, Julia. I can't seem to reach him. He knows that if he saw the murder he could save Jahzini's life by testifying. But he won't admit anything."

"Maybe he actually didn't see the killing."

"I can't cross him off till I'm absolutely sure. If he did see it, Julia, what's keeping him from admitting it? He must have some powerful reason. The same thing that's kept him so lonely down here, so suspicious. Is it something in his past?"

She gave that savage shake of her head again. "If it was, could you ask me to betray him?"

He tightened his grip on her hand. "If you don't tell me, I'll have to wire the district attorney in Denver. I'll have to

give him a description of Kitteridge, the date of Kitteridge's
arrival here. I'll ask him if anyone is wanted in Colorado
who would fit the description."

Her voice was barely a whisper. "You wouldn't."

"I'm trying to save a man's life, Julia."

She looked away, biting her lip. He couldn't count the
emotions passing across her face. But one by one they washed
out, disappeared, until only defeat was left, slackening the
pouting shape of her lower lip, deadening the light in her
eyes. She took a deep breath, and finally spoke.

"I did know Kitteridge up in Denver." Her words were
flat and toneless. "He was Victor Morrow then. You probably
remember the case."

"The Morrow-Ware Land and Cattle Company." Banner's
eyes were wide with surprise. "About five years ago, wasn't it?
One of the biggest swindles in the Southwest. As I remember, the chief bookkeeper was the only one they caught. Shef-
field, or something."

"Shefford," she said. "His testimony led to Morrow's indictment. Morrow escaped before they could jail him, came
down here, changed his name to Kitteridge. But he didn't
have anything to do with the swindle. It was Ware who
engineered the whole thing, with the bookkeeper's help."

"But the grand jury didn't even indict Ware. He got off
with a clean slate——"

"Of course he did. He framed Morrow. As general field
manager for the company, Morrow only got into the office
twice a month. He had no idea how Ware was pyramiding the
stocks or appropriating the company funds. They made him
the goat. Shefford falsified the books to make Morrow seem
responsible. But something must have slipped, and Shefford
was caught."

"Then why didn't Shefford expose Ware and get a chunk
of his term knocked off for turning state's evidence?"

She shook her head. "I know that would be the logical
thing. But Shefford was playing for bigger stakes. Morrow
did have access to the books, but they probably let him see
only innocent figures. As he remembers it, though, even those

figures didn't turn up at the trial. The only thing we could figure out was that Shefford had kept two sets of books. The falsified ones, which made Morrow seem guilty, and which turned up at the trial, and the real ones, which nobody ever saw."

"Why would Shefford do that?"

"Because the real ones would prove Ware's guilt," she said. "Shefford was keeping them as sort of insurance against Ware. If Ware could frame Morrow he could frame Shefford too. Maybe he did."

"And you figure that while Shefford might get a couple of years off his sentence by turning state's evidence against Ware, he'd gain far more by sitting out his term and then holding those books over Ware's head."

"Ware must have made a couple of hundred thousand on that swindle. He'd certainly pay to keep Shefford from turning the real books in."

"It sounds logical," Banner muttered. "But if those real books would prove Ware's guilt, they might also prove Morrow's—Kitteridge's innocence."

"Don't you think I've told Kitteridge that a million times?" she said bitterly. "I spent weeks talking with Shefford, trying to get him to admit the truth, to tell us where the real books were. It was no use. But I'm convinced I'm right."

"And you really think there's a chance Kitteridge could prove his innocence?"

"I know he could, Lee. It would just take someone who knew how to work, someone with more connections than I had. There are other angles besides the bookkeeper. Ware disappeared shortly after the trial. A couple of years later we got word that he was separated from his wife, that she was living somewhere in Kansas. I even tried to follow that down. I ran out of money . . ."

She trailed off, close to tears again. She was stooped in the saddle, her head hanging, all the spirit drained from her.

"I always wondered what lay between us," he said.

She looked down at him, frowning intensely. Then she shook her head. "No, Lee, you're wrong. I knew Morrow had come down here and changed his name to Kitteridge. When Dad got a chance to transfer to the Navajo Agency, I asked him to do it. I don't know what I expected. Maybe I still hoped to help Kitteridge clear himself; maybe I had some fool notion that we could go on, even though he couldn't clear himself. I was wrong both ways. He's so changed, Lee, so bitter; not the man I knew in Denver at all. It took me a year down here to finally admit it to myself."

"And that was where I came in?"

She nodded slowly. "About that time. You were so different from Kitteridge, you have no idea what it meant to me." She glanced at him quickly, apprehensively. "Don't think I was using you merely to forget Kitteridge. What you and I had would have happened whether I'd known Victor or not. It was good, Lee. Maybe I still wasn't completely over Kitteridge. Maybe that's what you felt between us. But it isn't between us now, Lee. Whatever I had with Kitteridge up in Denver is over."

He studied her face somberly, and his voice was dark and wondering. "Is it, Julia?" he asked.

14

It was in his mind all the way back to Mexican Hat. A dozen different thoughts gnawed at him, a dozen different emotions. And none of them would become clear. He didn't know yet whether he believed Julia when she said she and Kitteridge were through. He didn't think she knew herself. He didn't even know what he felt for Julia now. Hurt? Jealousy? Bitterness? It was all running through him, rising up poignantly for a moment, fading away. Yet it answered nothing, left him no clear course.

In this frustrated confusion he reached Mexican Hat. The bright hardness of burning sun was gone from the streets. The buildings etched a broken silhouette of rooftops and false fronts against a moonlit sky. Kerosene torches flared from a score of wooden overhangs, dappling the rutted street with miniature lakes of yellow light. At Reservation and Aztec he could not help looking up at the windows above the general store. The peeling gilt letters were barely legible on the dust-filmed panes, lit by one of the torches. Henry Dodge, Counselor-at-Law.

But there was no light in the office, and Banner knew that his uncle was probably eating at Blackstrap Kelly's. Remembering what Julia had said, Banner knew a painful need to see the old man, to straighten things out between them. He saw Tilfego's buckskin yawning at the hitch rack before Kelly's, and swung his own animal into a slot between two horses.

He got off and stepped up to the sidewalk. Over the tops of the batwing doors he could see a thin evening crowd lined up at the Brunswicke bar, a few scattered diners at the tables near the front of the room. Tilfego sat near the wall, a plate of tortillas before him. As Celestina maneuvered her jiggling bulk past him with a tray, he reached out to pinch her on the hip.

Banner saw his uncle, then, sitting at a corner table. He started to push through the doors, but something about the man's posture checked him. The white-haired lawyer sat stiffly in his chair, facing the wall. His meal was only half finished, his glass of beloved port untouched. But he was not eating. One of his hands was gripping the edge of the table so tightly that the tendons stood out in bluish ridges. It struck Banner how many of the men at the bar were looking at Dodge. There was derision in their drink-flushed faces, and a couple of them were grinning broadly. With a faint sickness, Banner realized he was looking at something that must have been going on for some time.

The two Hackett riders Elder had seen on the reservation stood at the far end of the bar. Joe Garry was a short, broad-girthed man, his mud-colored eyes turned to a sleepy indolence by heavy lids. Breed was taller, with a slouching, stoop-shouldered way of standing. Beneath his greasy horse-thief hat, his face held a hollow-cheeked balefulness.

"Hey, Henry," Joe Garry called. His voice was slurred with drink. "Give me the latest. They tell me you don't have enough evidence to convict Jahzini. You just sent Banner out to raise all this ruckus so you wouldn't have to prosecute."

A general laugh went up from the men at the bar. Banner saw the artery in Dodge's temple throbbing, saw the deep red flush of his face. But his back was to Garry, and he did not turn to answer the Hackett rider.

"Leave the old man alone," Tilfego said. "His supper you are spoiling."

"We're just asking him the latest." Garry laughed.

"Yeah," Breed said. "What about that, Henry? I hear the Indians are going to run one of their men for district attorney. If they can murder the agent and get away with it, they figure they can do anything."

Banner saw Dodge's body begin to tremble faintly. Hot with anger, the young man pushed through the batwings, starting to speak with Garry and Breed. But the scrape of Dodge's chair checked him once more. The old man had pushed it back, and was rising. He turned without looking at Garry, and started to walk stiffly toward the door.

Then he saw Banner.

He stopped, eyes wide with surprise. A corner of his mouth twitched. Banner moved swiftly between a pair of empty tables.

"I've got to see you, Henry."

The flush of anger remained in Dodge's face, but a strange, pleading look filled his eyes, like that of a man clutching at his last straw. "You mean you're ready to admit you're wrong about Jahzini?"

"No, but we can't go on like th——"

"Then we have nothing to talk about."

Dodge's face was so set it looked frozen, and he started to go around Banner. The young man tried to grab his arm.

"Henry——"

Dodge jerked free. It unbalanced him and he stumbled into a chair, almost upsetting it. Half a dozen of the men at the bar began to laugh, and Joe Garry shouted again.

"Why not take the buggy whip to him, Henry, like you used to?"

One hand on the table, Dodge wheeled toward them. His neck was swollen with choleric anger, the pulse in his temple looked as if it would burst. His mouth was open, and he seemed about to say something. Instead, he only made a strangled sound of rage. Sending a last, torn look at Banner, he wheeled and stamped out.

"Looked like the old mossyhorn was goin' to bust a gut." Garry laughed. "You oughtta have more respect for your uncle, Lee. You're both shysters under the skin."

It brought laughter from the whole line at the bar. Banner spun toward Garry, eyes like chipped glass in a face turned gaunt with intense anger. But he felt a hand on his arm, and Tilfego's bland voice came through his anger.

"Toss the slack out, Lee. Let them ride you and every man in town you have to fight."

Banner stood rigidly, staring at the crowd, trying to gain control of himself. He realized he couldn't blame them, really. Julia had been right. He had done this to Henry.

He shook his head helplessly, allowing Tilfego to guide him to an empty space near the front end of the bar. In the back-bar mirror he could see men still watching him from the tables and the faro layout. Joe Garry put down a silver dollar for his drinks and turned toward the front door, followed by Breed.

"The drunker that Garry he gets the sleepier he looks," Tilfego muttered.

"I hear you had a job with the Army," Banner said. It was an effort for him to speak.

"Some Zuñi," Tilfego told him. "Steal a couple of horse or something. Me and some soldiers from Fort Defiance we track him. Up around Chaco Canyon. No shooting. No girls. No fun."

Blackstrap Kelly stumped along on the other side of the bar till he was in front of them. He put his hairy hands flat on the gleaming mahogany and waited, staring unwinkingly into Banner's face.

"What you like?" Tilfego asked.

"How about some of that Old Kentucky?" Banner asked.

"All out of it," Kelly told them.

"Make it beer then."

"All out of that too."

Banner took his foot off the worn rail, straightening up. "What have you got?"

"Nothin'."

"You make it pretty clear, Blackstrap."

"It hurts my business to have you in here. But I wouldn't serve no Injun lover anyhow. It's you oughtta be strung up, after letting him escape like that."

"He didn't escape. They took him to Yuma———"

"I'll believe that when Charlie Drake's deputies get back."

Joe Garry stopped before passing Banner. "What's this about the deputies? I hear Jahzini tried to escape at Flagstaff and they had to shoot him down."

Banner wheeled to him. "Don't be a fool. I rode as far as Flagstaff with———"

"Don't take it so hard, Lee." Garry's greasy jowls were flushed with drink, his eyes were almost closed. "You're the one to crow now. They tell me your uncle has started scrambling around the country hisself. Like a rooster with his head chopped off. You're collecting so much evidence there won't be any left for old Henry."

Tilfego grabbed Banner's rigid arm. "Cut it out, Garry," he said.

"What the hell." Garry chuckled. "Lee knows all the latest news. Don't he, Breed?"

"Tha's what they tell me," Breed said.

"Give me the latest, Lee. They say you was building up such a case for Jahzini that Henry knew he couldn't win if it reached court. He blew that safe open hisself so the old Indian could escape———"

Banner hit Garry.

It smashed the man backward into Breed and then he twisted off and fell to the floor. Breed had been thrown back into the bar. He recovered with a violent lunge, slapping for his gun.

"Stop it," Blackstrap said.

Breed's whole violent movement halted with his hand on his gun. Slowly, he turned to Blackstrap Kelly. The saloon-keeper had a sawed-off shotgun resting on the bar.

"I don't want no killing in my place," he said. "Get out of here. All of you."

Garry got to his feet. The drink was knocked from him. He stood before Banner, swaying faintly, his eyes muddy with a seething anger. Then he turned around and pushed his way through the batwings. Breed followed, in his slouching, saddle-bound walk, his hand still on his gun. Banner waited till he saw them both cross the sidewalk and drop off to their horses. Then he went out through the doors with Tilfego.

The kerosene torches on the edge of the overhang splashed their smoky yellow light across Garry, standing between two animals at the rack. He seemed to be tightening the cinch on his paint. But the light caught the whites of his eyes turned obliquely toward the sidewalk.

"Can you see me as well as I can see you?" Tilfego asked softly.

Garry went on tugging at his latigo, without answering. But he was plainly visible in the torchlight, while Banner and Tilfego stood in the black shadows beneath the overhang. Garry must have realized the advantage that gave them, because he finally tossed his reins over the paint's head and swung aboard. He held the fiddling horse, waiting for Breed to mount, looking sullenly into the deep shadows shrouding the Mexican and Banner. Finally he spoke.

"You made a mistake, Banner. Twenty men ride for Hackett. Every one will just be waiting for you after they hear about this."

He wheeled his horse out and spurred it into a dead run down the street, followed by Breed. Banner moved to the edge of the sidewalk and put his hand against one of the peeling cedar poles that supported the overhang. He was looking down the street after the receding drum of their hoofbeats, but his mind was hardly on what Garry had said.

"I didn't know what I was doing," he said. "It happened so fast I didn't know what I was doing."

"Because you still love the old man and you been work so hard you are jumpy as the jackrabbit," Tilfego said. "And I am glad you hit Garry. The hell with him."

Banner put his weight tiredly against the post. "It's true, then. Julia told me. I guess I hadn't realized it. I'd seen it, but I hadn't realized it. I've made Henry a laughingstock. Did you see his eyes that last time he looked at me? Like I stabbed him or something."

"Is something you cannot help," Tilfego said softly.

Banner shook his head, broad shoulders stooped. "Maybe I'm wrong, Tilfego. Maybe there isn't really an eyewitness. Maybe I'm doing all this for nothing."

"You cannot give up now."

"I can't go on hurting Henry this way. He was right. I'm too impulsive. Get an idea and I jump. Don't care who I hurt or why. All I can think of is myself——"

"You are not think of yourself. Everything you do is for Jahzini."

"Just because we find a few tracks out at Yellow Gap. Just because an Indian boy has a bay horse. It's got to be more, Tilfego. I got mad at Henry for not seeing it my way. But now I'm beginning to doubt myself. I can't go on hurting him this way. If something doesn't break soon——"

He broke off, realizing Tilfego was not looking at him. He raised his head, following the man's gaze, out into the street. At first he thought it was Joe Garry returning. Then the rider pulled into the flickering light. There was the wink and glitter of silver jewelry. There was the rustle of voluminous skirts. There was the hair, making a coal-black frame for the piquant oval of her face.

"Cristina."

She pulled her mare to a halt, unsmiling, staring at him

with a strange tension in her face. Before he could step out to aid her, she swung down.

"I thought you'd want to know about Adakhai," she said. "Two of his people passed our hogan this afternoon with the news. They told me Adakhai had disappeared. Over a week ago he left by horseback for a hunting trip up near Navajo Mountain. He was going to stop at Tonalea and get his cousin. But he never got there. Some of the young men from Chin Lee tried to trail him. They lost his trail."

He stepped into the street, staring down at the troubled darkness of her eyes. "Eight or ten days isn't so long for a hunting trip that far north."

"But he did not appear at Tonalea. His cousin is still waiting there. A bad feeling is among his clan at Chin Lee. A fear."

Tilfego was beside them now, his eyes squinted thoughtfully. "Hackett know you thought Adakhai was the eyewitness?"

Banner turned to him. "Yes," he said reluctantly. "Hackett knew."

They were all silent. The horse snorted. The kerosene torch spat softly. Tilfego moistened his lips before he spoke.

"I was pass by the roundup camp of Hackett on my return from army job. Arles and Big Red they was not there. A Mexican hand he say they been gone many days."

Banner was watching Cristina. Her lips were parted—so ripe for such a delicate face—and the luminous fear in her eyes seemed to grow deeper. Slowly, heavily, Banner asked:

"Would they know that country up there?"

"Arles would," Tilfego answered. "Remember when he was a kid? He kill a man in Tucson. He hide out around Navajo Mountain for two years. Then he hook up with Hackett and Hackett have the influence to get a self-defense ruling on it."

Banner's voice was dull with defeat. "I don't want to believe it."

"You put Jahzini out of Hackett's reach," Tilfego said. "This is all Hackett has got left. Without an eyewitness, you do not have a case."

Banner was staring beyond Cristina. "How could we ever do it?"

"A man he leave sign," Tilfego said.

"But the trail's over a week old. And even the Indians lost it."

Tilfego looked hurt. "You are give me the insult."

Banner shook his head. "I couldn't ask you to do it. If it's true, if Arles and Big Red are really up there——"

"Leave me out of good fight and I never call you *amigo* again." Tilfego chuckled. He jingled coins in his pocket. "I will not go back to work till this he is spend anyway. You do not have to ask me. I volunteer."

The girl's skirts rustled softly. "I will go also."

Banner shook his head. "We can't take you. No telling how long it's going to be. Just tell us where the Indians lost the trail and anything else you can think of."

She hesitated, as if about to protest. Then, with a little shake of her head, she said: "They followed it as far as Dot Klish. You know how to find that. In the land beyond is where Adakhai's people lost his trail. It is sand country, and the wind had covered his tracks."

She stopped, gazing up into his face, and he knew there was no more she could tell him. He nodded, saying:

"We'll start right away."

"Thank you, Lee. I must get back to my mother now." Her eyes clung to his a moment longer. Then she turned to Tilfego, putting her hand on his arm. Banner saw Tilfego's eyes widen. They held an indefinable, luminous expression. "You are very good," Cristina said. "It is my wish that more people realized how good."

She smiled up at him, a fleeting little smile, and then started to turn away. Banner held out his hand.

"Cristina."

She faced back quickly, almost breathlessly. "Yes?"

He stared down at the soft oval of her face, turned to burnished copper in the flickering lights. "Nothing," he said awkwardly. "We'll let you know as soon as we get back."

She seemed to understand. The smile came again, briefly, shyly. "Thank you, Lee."

Her skirts whirled and rustled as she swung up on the horse. She heeled it around, sent them a last look, and rode down the street. Banner finally turned to see that Tilfego was still staring after the girl with that shining look yet in his eyes. Banner grinned.

"You didn't ask her to marry you," he said. Tilfego did not seem to hear him. Banner put a hand on the man's beefy shoulder. "Tilfego?" he said.

The Mexican jerked a little, then turned. *"Si?"* he asked blankly.

Banner frowned wonderingly at him. "Don't tell me."

The man scowled. Then his gaze dropped to the ground; a sheepish grin came feebly to his face. "Why not?" he asked. "Can the clown I be all the time? Everybody think is big joke. Tilfego the feelings he does not have." The grin faded. *"Chilipiquines.* That is all the girls are to him. Chili peppers. Ask them all to marry him? What a comedy." His voice sounded thick. "Love today, leave tomorrow. All the time a new woman. What a rodeo——"

He trailed off. He looked up, until he was staring down the street, though Cristina was out of sight by now. "Well," he said, almost inaudibly, "maybe they are right."

All the humor was washed out of Banner. "Did you ever tell her?" he asked softly.

"I would not give her the insult," Tilfego said.

"It's strange," Banner said. "I've known you most of my life. Yet I don't think I've really known you till now."

Tilfego's primitive face colored with embarrassment. He looked at Banner, trying to grin. *"Qué barbaridad,"* he said.

"Yes," Banner said. "What a barbarity."

15

They left before dawn the next morning. They rode north in a hot wind that seemed to be sweeping the world clean. The sand blew into their faces all day and all night and they had to stop every half hour to clean out the clogged nostrils of their horses. They passed the Corn River and they passed Moqui Buttes and then the desert was broken by the patchwork welcome of the Hopi fields, corn, beans, squash, peach orchards, lying green and cool and soothing to the eye. And on the horizon were the villages with the exotic names, Meonkopi, Oraibi, Misongnovi, clinging to the same mesa tops they had occupied when the white man first came to this land.

North of the Corn River, north of the Hopi villages, farther north than Banner had ever been before, they began to ascend the Shonto Plateau.

Near the end of the second day they reached the tributary gorge called Dot Klish by the Navajos for the blue clay in its walls. Erosion had eaten out all the sand around the clay, leaving a labyrinth of weird blue shapes that covered the walls like twisted gargoyles waiting to pounce. The wind was still blowing. It had sifted three feet of sand into the bottom of Dot Klish. Banner pulled his animal to a halt, settling wearily in the saddle, his voice muffled by the neckerchief tied over the lower part of his face.

"No wonder they lost him here. He might as well have walked in water."

Tilfego's eyes were squinted almost shut against the stinging sand. "If they trail him this far, it means he come into this canyon. So he has got to leave it somewhere. He come from Chin Lee? That means he travel west. He was go to Tonalea? She is north. So he leave this canyon by either the west or the north."

They knew the canyon only ran a few miles, east and west.

But that was a lot of ground to cover when you were looking for sign. They made camp at its east end, leaving the horses there so they would not obliterate any of the marks left on the land. Then, on foot, they began their search. Slowly, painfully, inch by inch, foot by foot, yard by yard, they studied all the ground adjoining each exit through the north wall of the canyon. When daylight failed, they returned to their camp and ate and slept. They were up before dawn, eating again, waiting for the first light again.

They worked through the forenoon, sweating under a brazen sun, faces whipped raw by the wind-blown sand. By late afternoon they were only a mile up the canyon, working on the fourth exit, a tributary gully washed through the clay by centuries of erosion. It was a rocky gully, and one of the boulders rose like a jagged tooth from the sand covering the bottom. Tilfego squatted over the rock for ten minutes, giving its glittering surface a minute inspection.

"Lee," he said. Banner waded through the sand to him, staring down at the rock. He could see nothing. He squatted to get a closer look at the spot to which the Mexican was pointing. Still he could see nothing. "The little hole," Tilfego said. "Something chip it out."

At last Banner made out the tiny pockmark in the rock, hardly bigger than a pinhead. He was filled with a great sense of helplessness. It was so tiny, so insignificant. It could have been made by the wind, by some animal. It looked fresh, but it could be a month old. Yet he had seen Tilfego's uncanny faculties at work before, and knew it would be wrong to let the man see his doubts.

The tributary gully cut through the wall in a northwest direction, and the Mexican started working his way down its sandy bottom. Banner followed. Inch by inch. Foot by foot. Yard by yard. With the sun dying and the light failing and night coming again. But just before dark Tilfego found it. He stooped over a bench of sandstone, wet his finger, rubbed it across the surface. Then he looked at Banner and Banner went to him. It was a chip of granite no larger than the head of a pin, glittering like a miniature jewel against the coffee-colored finger.

"A horseshoe could have chip it out back there," Tilfego said. "It could have caught in the nail, be carried this far, be knock out again. Will do?"

"Will do."

Night again. Dinner again. Sleep again. Up with dawn and eating a cold breakfast and into the tributary gully with the first light of the sun. Working along the twisted walls and in the bottom where the sand was piled high as a man's knees. For a mile they worked; for half a day they worked without finding another sign. Then the gully petered out and opened up and they were faced with a vast plain, cloaked densely with creosote, stretching away as far as they could see in every direction.

"If a man he went through here he had to brush against that creosote somewhere," Tilfego said. "You start one side, I start the other. Cover all the ground in between and meet in the middle, out there."

It was a heartbreaking job. Again sand had drifted across the ground beneath the bushes, covering any tracks that might have been made. The bushes were knee-high, for the most part, and Banner had to squat all the time. His clothes were sodden with sweat, his back ached, he was dizzy with the intense heat. They met in the middle without having found anything.

"Damn it, Tilfego, maybe that was some animal we're tracking. It might have been a year ago. Why don't we go on to Tonalea and ask if they saw him?"

The Mexican chuckled. "His own people do that. Cristina she tell you. You are tracking now, *amigo.* Is not sit down and turn to page ten and find the rule. I have spent a week looking for one sign."

"But we haven't got the time. If Big Red and Arles are on his tail, we haven't got time."

"You tell me a better way, *amigo?*"

Banner drew a weary breath, shoulders sagging. "All right. What now?"

"Same thing."

Same thing. Bending their aching backs to the task again, studying the creosote and the greasewood and the cactus till their eyes burned and began to lose focus. No telling how much later it was that Banner found the cholla, stout-trunked, short-branched, covered thick with glistening spines that could stab like a dirk. Banner called Tilfego. The Mexican came through the bushes, careful not to break any foliage.

"Does it look like that joint's been torn off recently?"

The Mexican stared at the healing end of the branch, chuckled, clapped Banner on the back. "A tracker you are. The spine she catch in something and pull the whole joint off." He glanced behind them. "Is almost due north from gully. We go in same direction. Somewhere that spine she drop off."

Half a mile on they found the cholla spine, broken, lying in an open patch of ground. A triumphant grin tilted Tilfego's eyes into that oriental mask.

"Finally we know this he is man. There is nothing around here the spine could have brush off on. The man broke it when he pull it from his horse, or his saddle leather. Will do?"

Banner could not help his husky laugh. "Sure as hell, will do."

They had their direction now, and they clung to it. They got their horses and moved northward. They found more sign on the brush, but soon it got patchy, and finally ceased growing altogether, and they found themselves on the edge of a sand flat that stretched beyond sight. They camped there that night and started hunting the next morning, and after half a day Tilfego admitted there were times when the land hid all from a man. So they had to gamble. They moved on north across the sandy wasteland. They had used up all the water in their canteens by now, and came across no new water holes. By noon Banner's throat was burning, the horses were spooky and wild with thirst. Yet they pushed on, for they had only the one hope left—that it was the Indian's trail they were following, and if he could make it they could.

In the late afternoon a great escarpment rose before them. And in the towering rock wall, farther to the north, was the knife-blade crack of a canyon. They turned off their course toward it. Distance was deceptive, and it took them till sunset to reach the escarpment.

There was soft earth about the entrance of the gorge. It had recorded the imprints faithfully. They had been made by an unshod horse. Its right front hoof left the mark of a squeezed frog.

The two men stared down at it for a long time. Then their eyes lifted, met. Banner shook his head, voice husky with wondering triumph.

"I knew you were the best tracker in the world, but I've got to admit this is one I didn't think you could pull out of the hat."

Tilfego laughed hoarsely, slapped him on the back, and they gigged their jaded horses into the rock-walled chasm. The sky was a tortured thread of turquoise above them, striped with crimsoned cloud banners. Against this the circling birds were silhouetted darkly. Banner pulled up, when he saw them, for they were buzzards. He looked at Tilfego, felt something tighten in his chest. Without a word they heeled their fretting animals into a sluggish trot. A few hundred yards on, the canyon formed an elbow turn. Rounding it, they came in sight of the dead horse.

They startled the feeding buzzards. The birds rose into the air with a funereal whir, a ghastly squawking. The smell of putrefying meat almost gagged Banner. But there was enough hide left on the carcass to tell its original color.

It was the bay.

Reluctantly, Tilfego stepped off his horse and walked toward the carcass. He began grimacing with the stench and shaking his head from side to side. But he forced himself to stand over the dead animal, studying the signs.

"She fell hard." He pointed to the earth at one side. "There is where Adakhai he hit and roll and get to his feet."

He began to follow the tracks. They led up a talus slope to a ridge of cap rock. Here he stopped, beckoning Banner to bring the horses. Banner gigged the animals up to him. They were snorting and fiddling constantly, blowing nervous little whinnies out of fluttering nostrils.

"What do you think?" Banner asked.

"I think somebody they shoot. His horse instead of Indian. He run up here. I could try to follow his sign. But an Indian on foot is the hardest thing in the world to track. You can see here. One minute are moccasin tracks. Next minute the earth she swallow him."

"What else can we do?"

"Look at our horse. Crazy for water. Smell it somewhere near."

"I guess you're right," Banner said. "If Adakhai had been without a drink as long as we have, he couldn't make a run for it on foot without water. So you think we'll find his sign at the sink."

"Not find his sign, even if he go there. But if they are follow him, their sign we will see."

They let the horses have their heads, knowing the uncanny faculty of thirst-crazed animals for finding water, even at a great distance. The beasts led them unerringly down the twisting gorge. The towering escarpment must have been the east wall of a great mesa, for soon they reached the western mouth of the canyon, cut into another skyscraping wall of rock, and rode out into rough benchlands of rusty sandstone. The mesa was not far behind them when Tilfego reined his horse in. His head was lifted and his splayed nostrils were fluttering, like some animal testing the wind. Banner had seen that before.

"Now listen," he said. "Not out here. There isn't a human being within a hundred miles. There can't be."

Tilfego asked angrily, "Do not these horse know when there is water near?" He thumped his chest. "Then Tilfego he know when there is *chilipiquine* near."

"All right. So you know. We haven't got time to look for them——"

"Tilfego he always has time. I look around, I sniff the air, I turn the corner. Hola! Chili peppers."

"Tilfego, this may mean a man's life!"

The Mexican settled sullenly in the saddle. He stared uncomfortably about him at the land, wiping a thumb across his bulbous nose. Then, pouting like a child, he grunted.

"Very well. No *chilipiquines* today."

They wound on through the broken branches, with the horses fighting to break into a run. Finally they reached the lip of a dropoff and looked down into the shallow valley ahead, where the lake lay like a piece of turquoise sky dropped into the coals of a dying fire. Banner had never been here before, but he recognized it as Red Lake, named for the ruddy sandstone surrounding it. As the horses broke into an eager scramble toward the water, Banner saw the sagging Studebaker wagon at the edge of the water. An old Navajo, wrapped to his chin in a blanket, sat on the seat. The horses had been unhitched and led to the lake. Standing beside them was the figure of a girl.

"What I tell you?" Tilfego thumped his chest. "I never miss. I look around, I sniff the air——"

"All right, you old horse thief," Banner said. He had to grin at the man's childish triumph. They could not hold their horses, so they let them run right into the water and drink their fill, before trying to talk with the Indians. When Banner's animal had finished, he rode over to the wagon, stepped off, loosened the cinch. The girl had brought her team back to put them in harness again, and after the formal greeting was over, Banner asked them where they were from. She said they were from Tonalea. Her grandfather had dreamed of bear during the summer, and was very sick. Banner knew one of their beliefs held that the bear was wholly evil, and that anyone dreaming of it, or mistakenly eating its meat, would die unless the animal's spirit was exorcised. Patients were usually cured by the ceremony of the Mountain Chant, and that was why the girl and her father were traveling south. She said a Mountain Chant was to be held near Yellow Gap.

Banner asked her if she had seen any men during the journey, an Indian, or two white men. She said her grandfather had seen something last night. Banner spoke to the old man.

The Indian started a quavering oration about the spirit of the bear coming to carry him off and the holy young man with his sacred arrow coming to fight the bear. The girl went around to hitch up the traces on the other side. It took Banner a long time to pin the old Indian down to the fact that the only people he had seen were the ones in his dreams.

Disgustedly, Banner turned around. The girl was not in sight, and Tilfego's horse stood ground-hitched and empty saddled a few feet off. Banner heard a giggle from behind the covered wagon. He walked around the tail gate. The Mexican was rubbing noses with the girl.

"Tilfego."

The man looked up in surprise, then grinned at Banner. "That is the way the Digger Indians do it, *amigo.*"

"These people don't know anything. We've got to go on."

"A Zuñi tell me. He say he learn it from a Digger Indian."

"Tilfego."

Pouting, wiping at his nose with a thumb, the Mexican walked back to his horse with Banner. They led the animals to the lake again, and while Banner filled the canteens, Tilfego began hunting for sign, following the shore eastward. He was a small figure in the dusk when he finally stopped, hunkering down. Banner drove the horses to where the Mexican had stopped.

"Adakhai?" he asked.

"I tell you we would not find his sign, even if he was here," Tilfego said. He pointed to the prints. "These are two shod horses. See the left hind shoe on this one. Sharp edges. Nails nice and clear. Want to bet?"

"On what?"

"That she is a new shoe. That a week ago she was change for a shoe with three nails gone."

"You mean Arles?"

"I mean Arles."

They followed the tracks of the shod hoofs northward, through a broken country, a country of giant mesas, of tortured canyons, of dusk that was rapidly thickening into night. When it grew too dark to see they ate supper. When the moon came up they started again. For a great urgency was pushing them now. The tracks at the lake were days old, according to Tilfego's estimation. And the signs on the land were telling him the story.

Nowhere could they find Adakhai's trail. But Arles and Big Red would not have gone farther north unless they were following the Indian. And if Tilfego could not find Adakhai's trail, the other two men certainly couldn't. There was but one logical answer. Arles and Big Red were following the boy himself rather than his tracks. Adakhai was hiding his sign in an attempt to throw them off. But he was on foot, and they were ahorse, and though he had been able to keep out of their reach, he had not been able to get out of their sight.

This knowledge filled Banner with a sick foreboding. It could not last long, that way. It drove the two of them, when the moon rose, to follow the tracks of Arles and Big Red through the night, until the moon died and there was no more light. At dawn they were on the trail again, with Navajo Mountain in sight far ahead, lonely and serene in the desert solitude.

The sun rose. Sweat made a clammy paste of their clothing. The weariness of the sleepless hours behind bore them down in the saddle like an overpowering weight. And still they pushed ahead, with Tilfego reading the story on the land.

Here Arles and Red had stopped, had held their horses in the cover of twisted juniper. Adakhai must have holed up across the canyon, in the rocks over there, and kept the white men off with his gun, for here in the sand were two spent bullets. And then the Indian must have started running once more, for the two horses had bolted suddenly from their cover. And the white men had shot at Adakhai, for here were more spent slugs, of different caliber than the first.

And then Tilfego found the dark spots.

In a twisted section of the canyon, in among the red fir and scrub juniper choking the narrow gorge, Tilfego pulled his horse up, staring down, and finally got off. Banner could see the stains against the bone-white sand, like faded rust. Tilfego squatted there a long time, running his finger over the ground.

"Blood," he said. "Days old. He was hit bad, to lose this much. He cannot go much farther. I think we hitch our animals here. Whatever we find, it will be close ahead."

16

They left their animals and took their Winchesters and worked their way slowly through the brush-choked canyon, finding more spots of blood in the sand. Then the canyon broadened, its walls receding into great broken benches.

And high on those benches, on the west side, were the buildings. They were of adobe and rocks, ancient, crumbling, so close to the earth in hue and texture that they seemed to have grown from the land. In countless places their walls had fallen in, and the rubble supported the smashed ends of fallen beams, immense and smoke-blackened.

They were the same kind of aboriginal cliff houses Banner had seen at Chaco Canyon and Canyon de Chelly, deserted by their makers centuries before the white man had come to this country. The stains of dried blood led up through the benches and into the buildings, while the prints of the two shod horses continued on down the canyon, disappearing around a turn. The picture was plain to Banner.

Adakhai had taken refuge in the cliff houses. Like a wounded animal, unable to run any longer, he had found a hole to crawl into where they couldn't get at him. And they were down in the canyon somewhere, keeping the boy up in the ruins till he died of his wounds, or starved to death. Banner's face grew gaunt with a slowly deepening anger. All the sly humor was gone from Tilfego's eyes too. His voice had an ugly sound.

"Those *chingados*."

Then they did not speak for a space, gripped in the musty silence of the ancient place, a silence so intense it almost hurt. Banner studied the canyon with slitted eyes, trying to decide where Arles and Big Red were. There was not much cover on the sloping, broken side of the canyon opposite the cliff houses. They had probably taken up their watch in the ruins along the bottom. Above these ruins were two more levels of buildings, and high above the top level, beneath a deeply over-hanging cliff, was one lone, circular structure.

"Looks like one of those kivas these people used to wor-ship in," Banner said. "It's the most logical place for Adakhai to be. They couldn't reach him from above. That cliff hangs clear over it. And he's got command of the whole canyon be-low him."

Tilfego nodded. "The bloodstains they lead up that way."

"How long do you think they've been here?"

"Sign pretty old. Broken brush already healed. Many days."

"Then we can't wait any longer. No telling how bad off Adakhai is. Another night up there might finish him." He pointed to a series of steps built into one of the walls. "That stairway leads to the second level. If I can get up there I'll be above Big Red and Arles."

"You forget the Indian. He is liable to shoot you just as quick as them. He can see you even on that second level."

"Not right back against the wall."

"You are guessing."

"All right, so I'm guessing. I'll take the chance. It's almost dark already. We haven't got time to hunt around for an-other way."

Tilfego shook his head. "Henry is right. Always jumping in without a look——"

"So I'm always jumping in. If you don't want to——"

Tilfego slapped him on the back, grinning broadly. "Slack up, *hombre*. Who would like you any other way? Is what make you Lee Banner. Go ahead and jump. I am right on your back."

Banner could not help grinning, sheepishly, his quirk of a grin. He studied the buildings a moment longer. He looked at Tilfego. The Mexican nodded. Banner lunged out into the open.

There was thirty feet of bone-white sand between the brush

and the walls. He was halfway across when the shot cracked. It came from the kiva, high above. He saw sand spew up five feet to his right.

Before it had settled, another shot smashed. This came from the ruins at the bottom of the canyon, but it went even wider. Then the steady crash of Tilfego's Winchester blotted out all the other firing, and Banner had reached the wall.

Crouched here, he was cut off from Adakhai above, and from Arles and Big Red in the canyon. Ahead of him a flanking wall was molded in to steps that led to the roof of a building. And from the roof was another stairway that led to the bench above. He would not be exposed to Adakhai till he reached that roof. But as soon as he left this wall, Arles and Big Red would have a shot at him. The knowledge brought clammy sweat to his palms.

And what if he did gain the bench? Maybe he was mistaken. Maybe there was no cover from Adakhai up there. Maybe——

What the hell!

He sucked in air and jumped out and ran for the steps. There was one shot, from the direction of Arles and Red. It ate a piece of adobe from the wall behind Banner.

Then Tilfego's gun was going again, filling the canyon with an awesome din. Banner didn't know whether Arles or Red were firing any more. He only knew that he had reached the stairway and was scrambling up the narrow steps and jumping onto the roof.

It was one of the few roofs left intact, but it almost gave way beneath him, and the instant he reached it Adakhai's gun smashed from the kiva above and kicked earth out of the roof a foot from Banner.

He ran on across the trembling roof and started up the second tier of stairs. He was out of sight of the white men now. Tilfego had shifted his fire to the kiva, and was keeping Adakhai down.

Then the top step crumbled beneath Banner.

He felt himself falling and threw himself in a wild dive for the lip of the bench just above. He reached it, sliding across it on his belly. At the same time Tilfego must have run out of bullets. The echoes of the shots rolled down the canyon, wrapping themselves in the muffled cloak of distance, dying. The silence came while Banner was still sprawled on his belly on the edge of the bench.

And then, like a thunderclap, Adakhai's first shot.

He felt the smash of a blow against his foot and didn't even know what it meant, because he was rolling, flopping over and over like a fish out of water, with the gun crashing again and again from above, until he came up against the wall of the buildings on that second level. He lay there, cut off from Adakhai once more, gasping, drenched in sweat.

He felt no pain in his foot and saw that the bullet had only knocked the heel of his boot off. He got to his hands and knees and then stood up against the wall, chest swelling in its need for air.

The Indian had quit firing. It was silent. So silent, after all that din, that his ears hurt. He began to work his way swiftly down the front walls of these buildings toward the north end of the canyon. He passed doorways so low he would have had to stoop double to get through. His feet crunched through shards of pottery that had been broken hundreds of years before. Finally the long adobe wall angled out toward the edge of the bench and brought him abruptly into sight of the man below.

It was Big Red, crouched on a roof top, behind the parapet formed by an extension of the wall. He was not looking for Banner. He was watching Tilfego.

The Mexican must have figured Banner was in a position to cover him by now. He had run across that stretch of sand and was beginning to work his way through the lower level of the city.

In that first moment, Banner saw him duck across a courtyard, run into a long passage, pass through its end. It opened into a roofless room. Tilfego hesitated at the end of the passage, then darted into the open.

"Tilfego——"

Banner's warning shout was cut off by the blast of Big

Red's gun. Banner saw Tilfego halt in surprise, look vainly for a man he couldn't see, then wheel and run for the doorway from which he had come. Banner saw Big Red pump his lever and knew the man couldn't miss this second time. He swung his own gun around till the dark blot of Red's body covered his sights, and fired.

The man shouted in pain and flopped over. The weight of his great body hitting the flimsy roof made it collapse and he fell through with it. Tilfego gained the safety of the doorway and checked himself, wheeling back.

"Arles," Red shouted. His voice sounded muffled. "They broke my arm. Come and get me, damn you. They broke my arm."

There was scurrying movement below Banner which he could not see. He heard husky cursing. Tilfego took a chance, knowing Banner was covering him now, and scuttled once more from the doorway, crossing the courtyard. Banner moved on down the bench, keeping in the shelter of walls that would protect him from the Indian above. Finally the buildings ended, the bench ran around a point where the canyon turned, cutting Banner off from Adakhai's sight. Then the bench became a shelving trail that led down into the canyon.

Banner could hear them running down below, the rattle of rubble underfoot, the crunch of that broken pottery. There was a wild whinny from a horse, somewhere within the ruins. He stopped, trying to place it. The frantic beat of hoofs filled the canyon. He heard Tilfego calling him, and answered. The man appeared in a few moments, coming from a black doorway.

"You save my neck on that one." The Mexican grinned. "Must have hit one of them good. He left his rifle."

"They're through, then," Banner said. "They must know they can't do anything with one of them wounded." He moved close to the point, staring up at the corner of the high kiva.

"You cannot go up there," Tilfego said. "He shoot you as quick as them. You know these bronco Navajos. They hate any white man."

Banner moved closer to the point. "If he's still losing blood another night might kill him," Banner said. "We've got to get him now, Tilfego." He raised his voice. "Adakhai? *Tsi Tsosi. Dancahas, shichi handsi.*"

There was a protracted silence, then the answer came, a feeble cry in the thin air. *"Chindash."*

"What you say?" Tilfego asked.

"I told him I was Yellow Hair, asked him how bad he was hurt."

"What he say?"

"Go to hell."

Neither of them spoke after that. The silence of the gorge was tomblike. Night was settling velvety darkness into the canyon. Banner was trying to think of the right words. It was so similar to that time with Jahzini, wanting to say so much, knowing how to say so little, acutely conscious that the slightest mistake in verb stem or inflection might put a completely wrong construction on the words. A man could think he was talking about saving his friend and he'd be talking about killing him. It was that treacherous. Finally he began to talk, telling Adakhai that they only wanted to help him, that they had chased away the men who had done this to him, that he would probably die if he stayed up there much longer. Then he stopped and waited for the answer. For a long time he waited, in the velvet darkness, in the musty silence. There was no answer. Finally Tilfego snorted disgustedly.

"Is how much good the talking does with them."

"Then we'll have to go up there," Banner said. "The only way is right through the buildings. You couldn't get down on the kiva from above. That cliff hangs over too far."

"Do not be loco. They would have get him if it was possible."

"They didn't have to take a chance," Banner said. "All they wanted him to do was die, and they could wait for that. I want him to live. And I can't wait. We haven't got much time before moonrise. You cover me from below. Don't shoot to hit him. Just try to keep him down while I'm in the open spots. If he's lost much blood he's weak as hell. And you can't shoot very straight when everything's weaving in front of you."

He handed Tilfego his rifle. He turned to go back up the trail, around the point, against the front walls of the buildings on the second bench, which hid him from the kiva above. It was so dark he could see but a few feet in front of him. Everything was shadowy and unreal. The smell of ancient decay, musty, powdery, seemed stronger.

He could not find any more outside stairways to the next level. But he found a notched beam in a room, and knew it was one of their ladders. He finally made out the hole in the ceiling, a vague square, only faintly lighter than the blackness of the roof. The beam was almost too heavy to lift. He finally got it up, and leaned it slantwise against one corner of the hole.

It was a precarious climb. The beam threatened to roll beneath him at any moment. He finally reached the hole, lifted himself through onto the roof. His foot hit the tip of the notched beam. He heard a crunching sound; the corner of the hole gave way and the beam fell with an echoing crash.

Before the sound was dead there was a wild yell above him. A gun made its smashing detonation. He heard the bullet strike the roof somewhere to his left. He was completely exposed here, with the wall of the kiva ten feet away, and no cover between.

He had that moment of choice, with the impulse running savagely through him to drop back down through the hole.

Then Tilfego's gun began to clatter from down below. It was too dark for the Mexican to see the kiva, but he must have been firing at the position of Adakhai's gun flash. Banner heard bullets chopping into the wall of the kiva.

He lunged to his feet and headed in a wild run for the round building. Adakhai fired again, but Tilfego's gun was still going, and would give the Indian no time to aim. It was so dark that Banner made only a shadowy impression of a target anyway. And he reached the wall, throwing himself up against it, panting heavily.

Tilfego's firing ceased abruptly. Again it was the echoes,

rolling down the canyon, dying. Again it was the silence, like a palpable pressure against Banner.

The Indian was right above him now, on the roof of the kiva, behind the parapet formed by the top of the wall. In order to shoot Banner, he would have to poke the rifle over the side. And Banner would see it against the sky.

It was the only way Banner could get him. The wall was about seven feet high, and he could reach the edge with his hands, standing on tiptoes. But it would be suicide to try and get up onto it. He had to bring the boy down.

Deliberately, he sucked in a deep breath and exhaled in a noisy gust. He heard a faint scraping from above. His body stiffened.

Then he saw it, skylighted above him. Like a thin strip of darkness, barely darker than the heavens. He lunged up, knocking the rifle aside as it went off, grabbing it in both hands and throwing all his weight against it. He heard the wild shout.

Adakhai must have held on too long. He plummeted down on Banner. The lawyer had that last instant to throw himself from beneath the Indian. But the thought of those wounds flashed through his mind. He let Adakhai strike him, cushioning the fall.

It drove him to the ground, knocked the wind from him. He caught at the Indian's flailing arms. Adakhai rolled over and began fighting immediately. It caused them to flop over and over down the slope leading to the top of the buildings below. Banner saw one of the Indian's hands slap at his belt, saw the flash of a knife.

He was not caught off guard this time. As they rolled out onto the roof, he was beneath. But he lunged up with both hands and caught the man's arm as the Indian raised it to strike. They were still rolling and Banner came on top, throwing all his weight against the arm.

It twisted Adakhai's wrist back on itself. He shouted in pain. The knife slipped from his hand. Banner tried to keep the Indian beneath him, but he held onto the arm too long. With a tigerish lunge, Adakhai flopped them over again, and

Banner could not release his hold soon enough to stop himself from going under. Then Adakhai tore his wrist free and his hands found the white man's throat.

Banner's eyes swelled in their sockets with the pressure. His head was smashed against the roof. With the Indian straddling him, he fought to tear the sinewy hands free, battered wildly at the catgut muscle of the arms. But he came against the same savage strength he had met at Chin Lee. His head seemed to be bursting with the pressure. The night spun about him. He struck up at the boy's face and could not reach it. In a last desperate effort he twisted against the throttling hands and drove a blow for Adakhai's belly. He felt his fist sink deep, heard the explosive gasp torn from the Indian.

It jerked the hands off Banner's neck, unbalanced Adakhai in that moment. Banner heaved him over and sprawled on top. He let his whole weight sag down onto the Indian and lay there, gasping, drained. For a moment Adakhai was too spent to struggle.

Then, in a new burst of savagery, he tried to fight free. Banner caught his arm, twisted it around into a hammerlock.

"Do not struggle, you fool," he said in Navajo. "We come to help you. We made your pursuers leave by horseback. Can't you understand that?"

"Tlish bizedeigi, yishi," Adakhai gasped, still fighting. "You are the spit of a snake. I swear it."

The Indian's struggles grew gradually weaker, however, and finally he stopped, unable to tear free, lying slack beneath Banner. His wounds had started to bleed again and Banner was soaked with blood.

"Tilfego," Banner called. "I've got him. Bring a rope."

Tilfego had to get the rope off the horses, and he led them back to the ruins on the lower level. Then he brought a coiled dally up and they tied Adakhai hand and foot.

"Is helluva thing to do with wounded man," Tilfego said.

"It's the only way we can keep him quiet," Banner said.

Adakhai lay on his back, staring at them balefully. In the moonlight he looked like a wild animal. His hair was matted and dirty; the bones stood out so whitely in his gaunt face that it looked like a skull. There were two wounds. The one in the shoulder was clean. But when Banner unwound the dirty strip of buckskin from the boy's thigh he saw that the leg was badly swollen.

"He'll die if that blood poisoning isn't stopped," Banner said.

"You mean dig the bullet out?" Tilfego shook his head. "If you do that and he die you have every Navajo on reservation after your scalp."

"He'll die if I don't do it. Maybe you'd rather not be involved."

"Don't be a burro," Tilfego said. He pulled his bowie. "You can use my knife."

They built a fire and heated the blade till it was red. The boy made no sound. His body lunged up just once when the blade entered. From then on he lay rigid, his eyes open, staring at the sky, the sweat running off him till it drenched the earth of the roof beneath him. Banner finally got the bullet out, and sank back, as sodden with sweat as the Indian. Tilfego brought him the water he had boiled, and while Banner cleaned the wound he sent the man after as much prickly pear as he could find.

In fifteen minutes Tilfego came back with a hatful of prickly pear paddles. Banner pounded them to a pulp between two rocks and mixed them with water till they were paste. He put this poultice on the boy's wounds, binding it with his neckerchief and strips of blanket.

"Jahzini taught me that," he said. "The prickly pear will draw the pus out like nothing you ever saw." When he was finished, he went over and sank down on the parapet of the wall, utterly played out. "I feel like I've run a hundred miles," he said. "I sure as hell wouldn't want to be a doctor."

"What you need is a quart of coffee," Tilfego said. "Let's get the boy down into one of these houses and then I'll fix something to eat."

They carried the boy as gently as possible down one of the wall stairways and into a room that was still intact. Then Tilfego built a fire and fixed coffee and heated tortillas and

made a stew from some of their smoked meat. The Indian
would not eat, and Banner did not want to force anything on
him in his weakened condition. They spent the night sleeping
and watching in shifts. At breakfast, the Indian still would
not eat.

"We've got to get him to a doctor," Banner told Tilfego.
"You can get a wagon at Tonalea. You can at least get it part
way down that gorge, a mile or so from this place. Bring a
couple of men with you and a stretcher, and we can carry him
out to the wagon. It should take you three or four days in
all. We can hope he'll be strong enough for a trip then."

"Anything you want me to leave?"

"All the coffee. That bottle of whisky. Food for at least
four days. And that pack of cards you always carry."

Tilfego frowned. "They will do you no good. This is one
man you cannot make the friends with."

"We'll see," Banner said. "They don't call him The Gambler for nothing."

17

A little while after Tilfego was gone, the boy began to get
delirious. He thrashed around and fought the ropes, and Banner could not keep the blanket on him. Then he stopped sweating and began to shudder with chills, whimpering like a lost
puppy. Banner threw all the blankets on him and finally he
started sweating again. It lasted all day and by the time the
boy finally dropped into a deep sleep, Banner was trembling
with tension and fatigue.

He went to sleep himself and did not wake up till the middle of the night. The boy was still sleeping and Banner walked
out onto the bench which overlooked the ruins below. It was
a weird ghost city in the moonlight. As he was staring down
into its depthless shadows, he thought he saw a faint motion.
He stared for a long time, waiting to see it again. Nothing
happened. He went back inside and got his rifle and took it

outside again and sat down against the wall. Arles was in his mind.

He saw nothing more, however, and finally fell asleep sitting there and was awakened by the first daylight. It showed him nothing but empty ruins below, and he went back inside. The boy was conscious, lucid again, watching him from eyes black with hate.

Banner made some ash cakes from meal and water and fried them in the pan with bacon. Then he put the coffee on and let it boil till its fragrance mingled with the rich odor of crackling bacon. He saw Adakhai lick his lips.

He put the fryingpan beside the Indian, poured a cup of coffee. *"Ko adi yil,"* he said. "You may eat."

The Navajo closed his eyes; his lips became a thin line of defiance. Banner sat cross-legged beside him and took one of the cakes out of the pan, putting a strip of bacon across it, eating. He finished his portion of food and coffee and went out on the bench again, spending fifteen minutes in a search of the canyon. Still he could see nothing. When he went back in the cakes and bacon still lay uneaten in the pan beside the boy, cold and congealed in their own grease. Banner wrapped them in a piece of buckskin, scoured the pan with sand. Then he sat down against the wall and got out Tilfego's cards and began idly shuffling them. He saw the boy's glance run involuntarily to the pasteboards.

"I'm pretty good at cooncan," Banner said. "Never been beat in Mexican Hat." No answer. He began to play solitaire. "Maybe poker's your game. I bet I could beat you. In the past I played with Jahzini. You would like him. It is a wonderful thing when a Navajo will take in a *belinkana* and treat him as his own son. I remember one night it was so cold I thought I would die. Jahzini gave me two extra sheepskins. I did not know till the next morning that they were his skins, and that he had no more——"

"You lie!" It was torn from the boy. His face was contorted. "No Navajo would take in a white man!"

"Would I know the story of the Emergence if I had not lived with your people?" Banner asked. "I remember it well.

Jahzini was a wonderful story teller. It is told that there were four worlds, one above the other. There was a great flood in the underworld, people were driven up by the waters. First Man and First Woman brought with them earth from the mountains of the world below. With this they made the sacred mountains of Navajo land. To the east they placed the sacred mountain Sisnajinni. They adorned it with white shell and fastened it to the earth with an arrow from the War God's bow——"

"They fastened it with a bolt of lightning——" Adakhai broke off suddenly, staring angrily at Banner. He settled back, his eyes sullen. "You know. You just wanted me to talk."

Banner looked down at the cards so the boy could not see his eyes. He had not forgotten about the bolt of lightning. But he said, "Jahzini told me a long time ago. The details are not all clear. So they attached Sisnajinni with a bolt of lightning. And to the west they placed the sacred mountain Doki-oslid. They adorned it with haliotis shell and fastened it to the earth with a moonbeam——"

"A sunbeam."

"Yes. A sunbeam. I remember now. And when they had finished putting down all the sacred mountains the holy songs were sung. Jahzini used to sing the Mountain Song to us. He was a wonderful singer of songs." Banner leaned back and closed his eyes and began to chant.

"Piki yo-ye, Daichl nantai Piki yo-ye, Sa-a naral [Singing of the Mountain, Chief of All Mountains, thither I go, Living forever, blessings bestowing] . . ."

He sang all the verses, almost forgetting Adakhai; forgetting where he was, because it was bringing back those half-forgotten nights when he had sat with Jahzini in his hogan, when he had sat with the old man, listening to him sing these ancient chants, transported in space and time by the old Navajo's mystic incantations, as only a child could be transported, until he was one with the gods, coming up through the hollow reed from the underworld, seeing Haliotis Maiden and Twilight Youth, riding with the Sun God on his turquoise horse, or his silver horse . . .

When Banner was finally finished, there was no sound in the room. He did not open his eyes for a while. When he did he found the Indian watching him with a strange expression on his face.

"How you sing." It was barely a whisper, from Adakhai. "I could almost believe you had our blood."

"I have." Banner held out his hand so the Navajo could see the scar on his palm. "Jahzini and I became brothers. It was after I saved him from a mountain lion. He cut my palm and his palm and we clasped hands."

The boy did not answer. But he continued to watch Banner. The balefulness did not return to his eyes. Banner went over and heated the coffee and cakes and bacon again and set them before the boy once more.

"Perhaps you would like to eat now. If you are too weak, I will help you."

"I am not weak."

"You will be if you don't eat."

Adakhai looked at the coffee. At last he rolled on his side and picked up the cup. He spilled some, lifting it to his lips. But Banner knew the boy's pride, and made no move to help.

The effort of eating left the boy weak and listless. Banner changed the poultices and found that some of the infection had been drawn out. In the afternoon the boy went to sleep. Banner went out onto the bench to watch. The canyon lay simmering and lifeless under a scorching sun. It was not so bad in the daytime. He could see anyone who approached. But the closer it got to night, the more restless he grew. With dusk falling, he went back inside. The boy was awake. His eyes were like dim coals in the gloom of the room.

"You think those others are still about?" he asked in Navajo.

"I thought I saw something last night."

"Why did they want to kill me?"

"One of them is the man who murdered Wallace Wright.

He thinks you saw him kill Wright. If you told, he would hang for it."

"And you saved my life."

"I will not lie to you. I had a selfish reason. You know it. I want you to tell if you saw the murder. It will save Jahzini's life."

"You are helping Jahzini because you are his friend. But you are not my friend."

"Only in your own heart am I not your friend," Banner said. "My heart has no hatred."

The boy turned restlessly to one side. "White men killed my father. I vowed I would not forget that."

"If an Indian killed your father, would you hate all Indians?"

Something that was almost surprise shone in Adakhai's eyes. Then he veiled it. Banner built a fire for supper, letting the Indian think it over. When they were eating, he asked Adakhai how Big Red and Arles had known where to find him.

"Some Navajos from Chin Lee went down to the trading post on horses," Adakhai said. "I do not think they would betray me knowingly. They must have passed through Hackett's cattle camp and made mention that I had just left by horseback for Navajo Mountain."

Banner poured the coffee. "I guess Arles knew the country well enough to figure you'd come up here by way of Dot Klish."

Adakhai nodded. "They waited for me at Dot Klish. They shot at me there and missed me. From Dot Klish there is no trail on north. A man may go any way he wishes."

"That is why your own people did not know where to look for you."

"I suppose so. I ran for Zuñi Canyon. But the two *belinkana* got on the rim above me there and shot again. They hit my horse. After that, I tried to lose them by hiding my tracks. But they kept me always in sight. With my gun I prevented them from getting too close. Then, back there in the

canyon, one of them hit me. I had been up here many days
when you came. I would have been dead by now."

Banner scoured the pan after they had eaten and then sat
down to begin idly shuffling the cards again. The more levels
upon which he met Adakhai, the more chance he would have
of winning his confidence. Any Navajo was a passionate gambler. That one would be named The Gambler indicated it
was the breath of life to him.

Banner nodded at the knife they had taken from the boy.
"That is a beautiful weapon."

"Those are cannel coal beads in the hilt," Adakhai said. "I
won it from a chief."

"I have five dollars," Banner said, taking the silver from
his pocket. He saw the Indian's eyes begin to glow. It was
much more than the worth of the knife. Then the Indian lay
back, shaking his head. Banner smiled thinly. "When I go to
Mexican Hat I will say that The Gambler has been mis-
named," he said. "From now on they will know him as Old
Squaw."

"Tchindi!" With an explosive oath, the Indian lurched up
on an elbow, staring hotly at Banner.

"I have two Mexican dollars also," Banner said, adding
them to the others.

The Indian stared at the little stack, winking in the gloom.
There was a varnished look to his eyes. Banner picked up
the knife and tossed it to him. The Indian stared down at it,
the temptation working through his face.

"Cooncan?" Banner asked.

The Indian dropped off his elbow, but remained on his
side, breathing shallowly. Finally, suspiciously, he said,
"Poker."

Banner shuffled again, let the Indian cut, then dealt. Adakhai studied his cards, then pushed the knife out between
them. Banner had a pair of tens. He put two dollars beside
the knife.

"Will that call you?"

"Yes. I'll have two cards."

Banner dealt the Indian a pair, drew three himself. He

didn't get another ten. After glancing at his new cards, Adakhai took off his bow guard and added it to the pot. Banner put in another dollar.

"Call you."

Adakhai showed two pairs, kings high. Banner put down his two tens. Without changing expression, the Indian pulled the knife, the bow guard, the three dollars back to him. Banner passed the deck over. Adakhai revealed a smooth skill in shuffling, despite the awkward position imposed upon him by his wounds. As the Indian dealt, Banner found his eyes going to the man's *bizha,* which hung from his belt by a thong. It was the personal fetish every Navajo carried. For a gambler it was a piece of turquoise, because Noholike, the gambling god, had always been made successful with it.

For its deep religious significance alone, turquoise was of great value to the Navajos. Banner had known men to trade a horse for a single turquoise. The fact that it represented a man's personal fetish made it doubly valuable. Banner felt sure that if he could win it, the boy would gladly pay any price for its return. Even to telling if he had seen Arles kill Wright.

"You opening?"

Banner glanced up to see the Indian watching him narrowly over the tops of his cards. Banner picked up his hand, saw a pair of queens, opened with a dollar. The game went on, lasting long into the night. When they finally quit, the Indian had won Banner's money, his ten-dollar Stetson, and the silver belt buckle.

Adakhai was more cheerful the next morning. After breakfast his eyes kept going to the cards, and when Banner suggested playing another game, the Indian accepted eagerly.

It went back and forth, as it had the night before. Banner won his money and his hat back, lost the money again. They ate lunch. After lunch they played again, and Banner lost his Winchester. The Indian's gambling fever was running high. He didn't bother to veil the varnish of excitement in his eyes when he won. He was dealing, when Banner got the hand.

It was three kings, an eight, and a four. The right draw

would give him a full house. He found his eyes lifting to the Indian's *bizha* once more. He realized this might be the time.

"How much is my shirt worth to you?" he asked.

The Indian glanced at the stack of seven dollars. "A dollar."

"I'll open with it."

"Raise you a dollar."

"How much for my boots?"

"Four dollars."

"Then they'll raise you a dollar."

"I'll raise another dollar."

"How much are my pants worth?"

"A dollar."

"I'll call you with them," Banner said. "And I'll take one card."

He discarded a four. The Indian dealt to him, then dealt himself a pair. Banner picked up his card. It was an eight.

Sitting there, looking at his full house, he could feel the blood pounding at his temples. It was hard to keep his face expressionless. But he could not help thinking of the *bizha* again. He knew it was within his reach now.

"I'll open with my hat," he said.

"I have bet all the money. Will the rifle and my bow guard raise you?"

Banner nodded, studying the Indian's face. He could not believe the man would have gone along this far on a bluff. Adakhai had not been playing that way. Then the Indian held a good hand. Was it good enough to carry him all the way to the *bizha*?

"My clothes are all in the pot," Banner said. "Will my revolver raise you?"

"I'll take it. Will the silver buckle off your belt and my bracelet raise you?"

Banner's mouth felt dry. His palms were sweating. He knew this was the moment. He might well be gambling for Jahzini's life.

"All I have left is my horse and saddle," he said. "I'll raise you with both of them."

He saw the light go out of Adakhai's eyes. Slowly, the Indian lay back. "I thought you were bluffing and would not risk them," he said in a low voice. "I have nothing with which to call your bet."

"You have your *bizha.*"

Banner saw surprise widen Adakhai's eyes. Then the Navajo masked it, the sullen woodenness returning to his face. "I would not bet my *bizha* against the wealth of three men. It came to me in a vision. I dreamed that Noholike came to me and said that if I would go to Bead Spring I would find the *bizha* for which I would be named. I found this torquoise. From that day on my name was changed from Slim Man to The Gambler, and I have been invincible."

"You mean you are going to let me take this whole pot without a fight?" Banner asked.

The expression had been gathering slowly in the Indian's face. It looked close to pain. He shook his head, without answering.

Banner said disgustedly, "What power can your *bizha* have if you fear to wager it? If you let me have the pot now, how will you ever be invincible again? How can they call you The Gambler when you are afraid to gamble?"

The Indian came up onto his elbow, eyes smoldering. The breath passed through him, sibilant with anger, as he stared at Banner. The lawyer waved his hand at the pot.

"With the horse and saddle, it must be worth three hundred dollars. What will your people think when they hear you did not have the courage to gamble for such wealth? They will laugh behind your back. They will change your name to Man Without Heart."

Banner could see the combination of pride and gambling fever gnawing at the Indian. His mouth began to work. His face was flushed. At last it was too much for him. He unfastened the turqoise. Holding it in his palm, he looked down at it.

For that instant, the anger, the bitterness, the pride were washed from his face. His eyes grew dark with all the primitive beliefs and superstitions and fears bound up in the *bizha.* It did something to Banner. He had realized objectively how much the fetish meant to Adakhai. Now he felt it emotionally.

It was as if the fetish was his own. It was as if the warp and woof of his life had been bound up with that bit of turquoise for as long as he could remember. The relationship had no comparison in the white man's world, except, perhaps, his belief in God. The realization of the immense value of the *bizha,* the crushing possibility of its loss, was borne in on Banner with all its overwhelming ramifications.

He felt like a fool. Dodge was right. Always going off half cocked. He had made the same mistake at Chin Lee. Knowing enough about the Indian's reactions to use them against him, but not taking the time, not going deeply enough into them to see what the end result would mean to the Indian.

Could he really use the *bizha* to force the truth about Yellow Gap from Adakhai? Or would he gain nothing but the Indian's undying enmity by winning it? He searched Adakhai's face for the answer. And as the Navajo put the turquoise down and raised his eyes, with the intense bitterness returning to his face, Banner had his answer.

He knew he had only one chance left. The Indian had called his bet. It was Banner's obligation to show the first cards. His only hope was that the immense strain of the moment would blind Adakhai to custom.

"What have you got?" Banner asked.

The Indian hesitated. Then he turned his hand over. All he had was two pairs.

Banner put his full house on the floor, face down. "You win," he said. "Your *bizha* is truly invincible."

The Indian stared blankly at Banner for an instant. Then, with a whoop, he flopped over, clawing for the turquoise. Holding it tightly in his fist, he gazed at the heap of loot. Then he laughed. Banner had thought him incapable of humor. But he laughed. Like a child he laughed, all the dour impassivity gone from his face. Too elated to question Banner's hand, he lay back weakened by his effort, still laughing.

"You are lucky you did not wager that beautiful yellow hair. I would have had to scalp you."

Banner smiled, picking up his cards and shuffling them into the deck. "It is as I told Tilfego. They do not call you The Gambler for nothing."

18

Tilfego came back with the wagon the evening of the third day. Banner saw them moving down among the ruins and waited for them on the bench. Tilfego and a pair of Indians climbed up the precarious tier of steps molded into the wall and gained the bench. The Mexican introduced the Navajos as Hosteen Red Shirt, a half-breed trader from Tonalea, and Running Man, Adakhai's cousin. They all stooped through the low door and crowded into the room. Tilfego stared blankly at the heap of loot beside Adakhai. The Indian grinned broadly, thumping Banner's saddle.

"Kad xozozo nza yadolel . . ."

"What he say?" asked Tilfego, as the Indian rattled on.

"He says I'll continue to live in peace as long as I gamble like that." Banner grinned. "He says I must come up to his hogan at Chin Lee and we will have another game. He says he won my horse and my saddle and all my clothes. He says you will have to loan me some money when we reach Tuba, unless you want me to walk home naked."

Tilfego's eyes tilted up till he looked like a Chinaman. Then the grin broke into a laugh and he threw his head back and let it shake the rafters. The Indians were laughing too. Adakhai lay back on his pallet and laughed till he was too weak to go on.

"I never think I see this," Tilfego said. "Like you been pardners all your life. How did you make it, Lee?"

"There's some willow saplings for stretcher poles down the canyon," Banner said. "I'll tell you while we chop them down."

As they stooped out through the door, Tilfego turned to

Banner, squinting against the glare of the sun. "If he feel like this toward you now——"

Banner shook his head darkly. "I haven't gotten him to tell me whether he was at Yellow Gap yet."

Tilfego's humor was washed from him. Then he snorted, clapping Banner on the back. "Never mind. You cannot expect the miracle overnight."

They got an ax from the wagon and chopped down a pair of saplings and lashed a blanket between. Then they carried Adakhai down into the canyon and out to the wagon. Tilfego and Banner rode as far as Tuba with the wagon, where there was a doctor. Tilfego had to loan Banner all his army money to get a ratty Navajo pony and some old clothes and boots. They impressed upon the Indians the necessity of keeping Adakhai hidden from Hackett till he was well. The Indians assured them Adakhai would be kept safe, and they took their leave. It was two days back to Mexican Hat. They arrived late in the evening.

Tilfego wanted to see Celestina, so Banner left the man at Blackstrap Kelly's and went on down to the two-room adobe on the Street of the Beggars. He was too tired to want much supper and made a pot of coffee and drank it with some cold tortillas he found in the cupboard. He was thinking about bed when the knock came at the door.

It was Ramirez, the husband of Dodge's cook, a furtive little man with an immense black mustache. He told Banner he had seen Tilfego at the saloon and had known they were back. He said he had word that Dodge wanted to see Banner as soon as Banner returned.

Banner thanked the man, and stood motionless in the doorway after he had left, a warmth flooding him. He knew Dodge's pride. The old man wouldn't send for him unless he was willing to admit he had been wrong. Maybe he had heard from the Indians about Adakhai's disappearance. Suddenly Banner could contain himself no longer, and he shut the door behind him, walking swiftly down to Aztec.

A deep nostalgia filled him with his first sight of the house in which he had spent so many years. The windows made yellow slots against the dark adobe, the recess of the front door lay in black shadow. There was no answer to his knock.

He tried the door. It was not locked, and he opened it, pushing it ajar, stepping into the penetrating reek of Dodge's cigars. But the room seemed empty. He let his hand slide off the doorknob and took another step inside, calling:

"Henry?"

There was a faint sound from behind him. He started to wheel. The man came from behind the door and struck him on the back of his head before he was all the way around.

It drove him to his hands and knees. For a moment he swam in the shock of it, barely able to support himself. He made some feeble effort to move, but the scuffle of boots, the clank of spurs was all around him. His arms were grabbed. He was dragged heavily over to the high-backed chair by the fireplace and lifted into it, and his arms were twisted around his back and tied. Vision was returning. The vague shapes of men gained identity. Arles stood by the front door. He had shut it again. The six-shooter was still clubbed in his hand.

Hackett towered before Banner, black-haired, black-eyed, a bitter vindication deepening the grooves in his narrow face. Joe Garry stood by the ivory table, his hands tucked like horny claws into his sagging shell belt. Rope burns, fresh and healed, made livid tracks across their sinewy brown backs.

Banner leaned his head sickly against the high back of the chair, drawing a breath between his teeth. His voice shook with pain and anger. "Where's Henry? What've you done with Henry?"

"Don't worry about the old man," Hackett told him. "He's probably on the train by now. Some will to make out in Flagstaff. Ramirez didn't know about it. When I told him Dodge wanted to see you, Ramirez thought it was straight from the horse's mouth."

Banner squinted his eyes against the throbbing pain of his head, glance shuttling to Arles and Garry. "Not using Big Red any more?" he asked thinly.

"Never mind."

"Maybe he got hurt or something."

"I said never mind!"

It came sharply from Hackett revealing his first anger. His restless shifting made his spurs clank. When he spoke again, his voice sounded edgy.

"So you think Adakhai saw the murder."

"Do *you?*"

A little flutter of muscle ran across the gaunt angle of Hackett's jaw. "Where is he?"

"I don't know."

Hackett's cheekbones began to stand out whitely, rawly, against the buckskin color of his face. Arles moved from the door, reversing his gun.

"I could make him talk," he said.

"Now, listen, Lee," Hackett said. "We understand each other. You know why I want Adakhai."

"To kill him?"

"Nobody's going to get killed. We'll just get him out of the country till the trial's over."

"Then they'll hang Jahzini. One of them dies either way."

"I'll see that Jahzini isn't hanged."

"Maybe you'll let him escape again so you can put Big Red and Arles in the posse to kill him."

"Damn you, Lee"—Hackett's voice had risen close to a shout—"I didn't have anything to do with that."

"I thought we understood each other."

Hackett was bent toward Banner. His right hand was fisted. Arles was watching with an avid light in his eyes. Finally Hackett slapped his hand savagely against his leg.

"All right. We do understand each other. I'm in this too deep to back out now, Lee. I won't stop at anything to make you talk."

"I think you would have tried to get me killed a long time before this if you thought you could get away with it," Banner said. "But you'd lose the whole game then, Clay. I've raised too much stink. It would point the finger right at you to get rid of me that way."

"Nobody talked about killing, Lee," Hackett said.

He walked to the ivory-topped table. He opened the cigar

box and took out one of the long black smokes. He bit off its
end, grimacing at the bite of the tobacco. Joe Garry lit it for
him. Then Hackett came back to Banner, rolling the cigar to
make it draw. His eyes began to water and he had to take the
cigar out, shaking his head.

"How can he smoke these damn things?"

Banner's eyes were half shut. "Maybe it takes a man."

Hackett spat. "This isn't for jokes, Lee. You're in it up to
your neck. You've pushed me against the wall and you'll wish
to hell you'd kept yourself out of it before I'm through."

"I think Wallace Wright had you against the wall a long
time before this."

"You know he did. If they move me south of the railroad
again I'm through. I've fought for this all my life and no damn
sanctimonious fool like Wright was going to break it up for
me."

"He was only trying to protect the Indians," Banner said.
"If you'd let them alone you would have been all right."

"You know that damn railroad land isn't anything. There
isn't enough water on it to keep half my stock alive. The
sheep have cut all the grass off." Hackett's spurs set up their
clanking again as he wheeled to pace across the room, gestur-
ing savagely with the cigar. "It was just a damn sop they threw
us, hoping we'd knuckle under. But the association had a bill
up to open that southern reservation for homesteading. In six
months they would have given our land back to us——"

"*Your* land *back* to you?"

Hackett wheeled on him. "Damn right. Who opened this
territory? You wouldn't have a railroad if it wasn't for cattle.
You wouldn't even have any town. We build a country for
you and you try to take it away from beneath us——"

"Are you trying to convince me, or yourself?"

Hackett stopped pacing. His head lowered and he stared
dourly at Banner. Then he came back to the chair.

"All right. You just poked a sore and the pus had to come
out. I shouldn't have wasted the time on you." He began to
draw on the cigar till its end glowed cherry-red. "You know
you can't take this, Lee. I guess you've got as much guts as

the next man, but you can't stand up under something like this. We've got all night. You'd better tell me now while you've still got your face."

Banner stared at the glowing tip of the cigar. A fear welled up in him—he could not deny it—a fear of pain that came from the animal depths of him. He felt his fingers curling up behind the chair.

"I don't know where Adakhai is," he said.

Hackett drew a breath, a thin little breath. Garry wiped one hand across the dirty belly of his shirt. Arles's boots made an avid scrape against the floor.

"In his eye," he said. "Put it in his eye."

Hackett was looking into Banner's eyes. His glance slowly dropped to Banner's cheek.

"Hold his head."

Garry stepped to one side of Banner. The lawyer tried to jerk aside, tried to overturn the chair. Arles jumped forward and stopped that. Garry caught Banner's long yellow hair, jerking his head against the back of the chair. He cupped his other hand under Banner's chin, thumb and forefinger digging deep.

"One more chance, Lee."

"I don't know."

Hackett started to bring the cigar down to Banner's face. Then there was a sound from the rear, the creak of a door, the heavy tattoo of boots on the hard-packed earth of the floor.

"Conchita?" Dodge called. "Why'd you leave all the lights on in front? I thought you was going home early. I got to talking with Prentice and missed that damned train——"

Hackett, Arles, Garry—all three of them—wheeled toward the back door as Dodge appeared there. The old lawyer halted, his hair gleaming snowily against the black shadows behind him.

"What the hell?" he said. Then he began to come across the room in a stiff, stamping walk. "Hackett, what in the johnny-hell are you doing?"

Arles raised his gun. Henry Dodge took a last step, staring at it, then stopped. He lifted his gaze from the weapon to

Hackett's face. Then he looked at Banner, holding out his hand helplessly.

"Lee——"

"Get him out of here," Hackett said.

Arles put his gun in his holster to step toward Dodge and grab him, and Garry followed. Dodge swung away from them, fighting wildly. One of his flailing arms caught Arles across the face, knocking him away. Then he wheeled the other way, tearing free of Garry's hands, and lunged at Hackett, his old man's anger flushing his jowls. Hackett tried to jump back. But Dodge caught his arm, clawing at the cigar.

"You can't do this, Clay," he shouted. "Not in my——"

Hackett's blow cut him off, striking the side of his neck and knocking him heavily to his knees. Again Hackett tried to back off and free himself. But Dodge's face was against his stomach, and his clawing hands caught Hackett's belt. Hackett kicked him in the belly.

Banner felt himself shout and lunge up against his bindings. The kick doubled the old man over with a sick cough, and knocked him violently backward. He crashed into the marble-topped table, upsetting it. The Sandwich lamp smashed against the floor, and the smell of raw camphene flooded the room.

In the sudden darkness Banner writhed savagely to free his hands. He could hear Dodge making sick, retching sounds in his effort to get a breath.

"There's another lamp somewhere by the oven," Hackett said. "Light it up."

There was the stumbling sound of boots, a curse. Finally light blossomed at the other end of the room, revealing Joe Garry bent over the lamp on the *banco*. Banner could feel his wrists bleeding, but he was not free. The overturned table had kept Dodge from being thrown completely flat, and he sat in the wreckage, leaning heavily against it. His face was the color of parchment. He was still making the retching noises.

"You damn old fool," Hackett said. "If you'd gone to Flagstaff this wouldn't of happened."

"Hackett"—Dodge almost gagged on the words—"what is it? What is it——"

"I guess you'll find out now," Hackett said. "I'm through wasting time."

He put the cigar in his mouth, drawing on it till the tip began to glow again. Dodge cried out and tried to rise. But the effort cost the old man too much. With a low moan of pain he fell back against the table and slid down till he lay flat, one arm thrown across the broken drawer that had fallen out. Hackett had not even turned toward him. The man took out his cigar and held it in front of Banner's face.

"Tell me where he is, Lee."

Banner stared fixedly at the glowing point of light. The sweat slid down his face, filling his mouth with the taste of salt. Arles and Garry were watching tensely.

"All right, Lee," Hackett said.

"If you do that to my boy, Hackett, I'll shoot your belly out."

It came from Henry Dodge. It checked Hackett, with the cigar so close Banner could feel its heat. Slowly, he turned to look at Dodge. The old man still lay on his side. But in his hand was the old Dragoon Colt he had always kept in the drawer.

"Back away," he said. "Drop that cigar and back away."

Hackett's face was dead white. His black eyes were pinpoints of rage. As he started to take a step backward, Arles made a vicious motion to Dodge's right. Dodge turned and fired.

The shot was deafening. The bullet plucked Arles's tall hat off and carried it halfway to the wall before it dropped. Arles stood transfixed, his hand gripped around an undrawn gun.

"Next time it'll be your head," Dodge said.

Arles removed his hand from his gun. Hackett dropped the cigar. Dodge grasped the edge of the overturned table and pulled himself to a sitting position. The pain of the kick was still stamped into his waxen face. Banner saw that the heavy gun trembled faintly in his hand.

He picked up a shard of glass from the broken lamp and crawled over behind Banner, still aiming the gun at the men, and began to saw at the ropes. When they dropped off, Banner stood up, rubbing at his wrists. He took the Colt from Dodge's hand. The old lawyer got to his feet with difficulty, worked his way around the chair and lowered himself into it.

"Shall we put them away?" he said. He drew a wheezing breath. "We've got a dozen counts. Trespassing. Assault and battery——"

"Is that what we want them for?" Banner asked.

Dodge looked up at him, then looked at Hackett. Finally he said, "No, I guess it isn't."

"You'd better go, then," Banner said.

The intense rage was dying in Hackett's face. Without speaking, he walked to the door. The clanking of his spurs stopped there. He waited till Arles and Garry went out past him. He was looking at Dodge all the time. There was a thin venom in his voice when he spoke.

"They would have called you judge," he said.

"The hell with that," Dodge said. "All I want is my boy back. Touch him again and I'll kill you myself, Clay. I swear I will."

It failed to bring any more anger to Hackett. He stared at them a moment longer, with that dour expression accenting the gaunt shape of his cheekbones. Then he wheeled and walked out.

Banner went to the door, watching the three men walk up Aztec toward Courthouse Square, where they must have left their horses. Finally he turned back to Dodge.

"Want me to get the doctor?"

Dodge shook his head. "Nothing broken. I just can't take it like I used to. Maybe a drink."

Banner stuck the gun in his belt and went over to the spindled Mexican cupboard, pouring two glasses of Dodge's wine. Turning back with them, he saw that Dodge had been watching him all the time. The old man took the glass, raised it, still holding Banner's eyes.

"Here's to it, son. It should have been a long time ago."

Dodge drank, lowered the glass with a husky exhalation of pleasure. Then he stared at the floor, chin sunk against his chest. "What did they want, Lee?" he asked.

"They wanted to know where Adakhai was. They think his testimony would convict Arles."

"Then that Indian really did see the murder?"

Banner shook his head, frowning. "I don't know yet. There are still two other possibilities. I don't know whether Hackett is aware of them or not. Kitteridge and Mills are still on my list."

Dodge got out of the high-backed chair and went over to his leather armchair, dropping into it. Grimacing, he propped one shoe on his knee, began untying it. Banner saw the pain the effort caused him and went over and knelt before the old man, finishing with the laces, pulling the shoe off. Dodge leaned back with a pleased sigh.

"Thanks," he said. "Ain't had anybody to do that in a long while. Conchita won't let me go stocking-foot. Thinks I'll catch cold . . ." He trailed off as Banner unlaced the other shoe. There was a brooding expression in Dodge's eyes. "You were right, weren't you?" he said. "I'm getting old. And when a man gets old he gets afraid. He's worked so hard. Wanted something so bad. He sees it just within his grasp. Knows it's his last chance——"

"Please, Henry." Banner pulled off the other shoe. "You don't have to; I understand how it was."

"Yes, I have to," the old man said. "I'm glad you wanted to be a lawyer so bad, Lee. You can appreciate how I felt about that judgeship. All my life I'd wanted that spot on the bench. I guess I'd begun compromising for it a long time ago. Letting Hackett become one of my biggest constituents was a compromise. He was starting to trade pretty sharp even then. I told myself it was politics." He shook his leonine head. "But I just couldn't believe he'd kill."

"A man will do a lot of things when he's desperate," Banner said. "Do you think he'll try to get Arles out of the country?"

"Wouldn't do him any good if you've got an eyewitness. The man's testimony would convict Arles no matter where he is, and Hackett with him." He shook his head. "It's a crazy stalemate when a murderer can walk right in your house and you can't do a thing to him. I guess they're just as blocked, though. Hackett can't move till he's sure if we have the eye-witness." The bed of wrinkles grew deeper about his faded blue eyes as he studied Banner. Finally he said, "What can I do, Lee?"

Banner was still on his knees, and he raised his face to Dodge. Slowly a grin spread his lips, and he clutched the old man's knee. "I know we can lick 'em now," he said. They were silent a moment, inarticulate with the embarrassment of men too close to emotion. Then Banner rose and wheeled to pace across the room. "Wasn't the district attorney at Denver an old schoolmate of yours?"

"D. H. Pine. We almost got expelled for writing a parody on Blackstone."

"You can help then, Henry," Banner said. He went on to tell him how Kitteridge was really Victor Morrow, of the Morrow-Ware swindle. He told how Julia had known Kitteridge up there and was convinced of his innocence. "I guess you'll remember Shefford was the bookkeeper. He must have planned to get off clean with Ware, but something slipped up. Julia thinks he made two sets of books, though. The real ones, which never appeared, and the falsified ones, which proved Morrow guilty."

"Why would the real ones never turn up?"

"Shefford planned to use them against Ware, in case Ware didn't come through with his share of the money."

The old man nodded. "Been done before. If the real books proved Ware's guilt they'd be the best things in the world to hold over his head. It would be why Shefford didn't turn state's evidence against Ware too. His term's almost up now. If Julia's right, he'll be waiting to get out and force Ware to come across."

"Do you think there's an angle?"

Dodge leaned back in his chair, scratching one stockinged foot with the other. "If it's set up the way Julia claims, here's what I think. Pine being a friend, I followed that case closely. Ware got off clean, but the papers had a lot about what a high liver he was, a big spender. It's been close to five years now. I'd bet a box of my best cigars Ware hasn't got any of that money left. Few of those swindlers ever hold onto what they get, particularly if they're that kind. If we could prove to Shefford that Ware was broke, Shefford wouldn't have any reason for holding those books out. He'd surely be willing to turn state's evidence to get the rest of his sentence knocked off."

"Julia said Ware and his wife were separated. She was living in Kansas somewhere."

"I did a chore for the Pinkerton division manager in Kansas once. He'd find her for me if she was there."

"And she'd certainly know if Ware had spent that money. Do you think Shefford would believe her?"

"She might even have proof. And if she doesn't, I'll get it."

Banner stared at him. Then he turned and walked moodily to the fireplace, looking down at the dead ashes.

"We're talking as if we had all the facts. The whole thing's supposition. How do we know Julia's right? Maybe Kitteridge is guilty. Maybe I'm just going off half cocked like I always did, Henry. I've hurt you enough already. I don't want to suck you into something foolish again——"

"Don't talk nonsense." Dodge got up out of the chair and padded over behind him, clapping him on the shoulder. "It takes somebody like you to get anything done. If you hadn't gone off half cocked in the first place we'd all be sitting around on our rumps right now, thinking Jahzini was guilty. I *want* to go off half cocked, son. I don't want to be old or afraid any more. If Kitteridge is your witness, we'll find out. We'll damn well find out!"

19

It was August now, with the thunderclouds banked in threatening tiers along the horizon, spilling their rain on the land almost daily, tainting the mornings with the pungent scent of dampened greasewood. Dodge had gotten leave of absence from Prentice to go north, since Jahzini's trial was not set for several weeks yet, and Banner was left to handle the myriad details of the old man's private practice.

There were wills to change, a theft case before a justice of the peace, a brief to draw up on an inheritance contract. Banner kept the office open in the morning to receive those of Dodge's clients who still had enough trust in the old man to come.

But through it all, Banner did not forget his primary allegiance to Jahzini. And the second day after Dodge's departure, he rode out to the homestead of Jeremiah Mills.

When he reached the cutoff to Yellow Gap and gained the higher ground he saw the two riders on the Ganado Road behind him. Wariness squinting his eyes, he rode into the cover of twisted juniper and watched. As they approached the fork in the road, he saw the Broken Bit brand on the near horse. It was Joe Garry in the saddle, his broad-girthed figure trembling faintly to the unremitting trot of his black pony. The man with him was Breed.

Banner felt the savage thinning of his lips as they passed the cutoff and rode on down the Ganado Road in the direction of Hackett's outfit. Only when they were out of sight did he turn on north.

Beyond Yellow Gap the jade-green sacaton grass was so high that it kept up an incessant whisper against his stirrup leathers. He crossed washes turned crimson by Indian paintbrush and rode through draws swimming with the scent of purple sage. It was a time of year whose beauty had always uplifted him before. But he could not get Joe Garry and Breed out of his mind, and doubled around several times to check his back trail, without finding anything.

Mills's land was on Puffwillow Creek, five miles from the Gap. It was crisscrossed with the crumbled remains of canals built by the ancient peoples who had been here before the Indians, and Mills had dug out sections of these ditches leading from the creek to his alfalfa acreage. Banner followed the winding wagon road through canals filled to the brim with the recent rains till he found the farmer on high ground near the creek, jamming a crude head gate back into place in his brush-and-timber dam. The man straightened at sight of Banner, wiping sullenly at his brow with a grimy bandanna. No matter how much he sweated, his furrowed face always looked dried out.

"Afternoon, Mills," Banner said.

The man looked up at Banner, eyes squinted against the sun. Then he gave another angry swipe at his face with the bandanna, turned to walk heavily down the bank of the canal toward his house. Banner gigged his horse after the man, catching up with him.

"Looks like this rain is going to pull your crop through."

For a space, Banner thought the man would not answer this either. He continued to walk down the bank, tall, gaunt, stoop-shouldered. But he was too much a farmer to remain silent on that subject. At last he spat into the canal, grumbling at Banner.

"Thought I'd make me some money on it this year, but I can't find a cattleman who needs it."

"Not when they can graze on Indian pastures free."

Mills turned to glare at Banner, rubbing angrily at the back of his sun-reddened neck. "If you come up here to make trouble, you might as well ride on."

"I just thought I'd tell you that I saw Kitteridge," Banner said. "He says he gave you that bay before the murder."

This stopped the man. He wheeled to Banner, anger swelling his chest, lifting his whole body for a moment. Then he clamped his lips together, wheeled, and walked on toward his house. Banner saw that his wife had come to the door. Clara Mills was as stooped, as gaunt as her husband. Habitual worry pinched her brow into feathery creases, chronic fatigue formed deep hollows in her cheeks.

"Baby's cryin' again, Jeremiah," she said, tugging the tow-cloth wrapper listlessly around her shoulders. "Can't you git the doctor?"

"What with?" Mills said irritably. "He won't take no more alfalfa for pay."

"I'll get the doctor," Banner said, "if you'll tell me what you saw at Yellow Gap that day."

At the door Mills wheeled back again. Before he could speak, Joe Garry stepped around the corner of the house. He had a six-shooter in his hand.

"Just sit still, Banner," he said. "Breed's behind you with a gun."

Banner turned involuntarily to see the half-breed walking from the cover of ragged willows that topped the high creek-bank. He held an old fifteen-shot Henry across one hip.

Garry stopped in front of Mills, a head shorter than the towering farmer, just as broad through the shoulders. "Where's the Indian?" he asked. "We been waiting for this. Where's Adakhai?"

Mills stared blankly at him. "What are you talkin' about?"

"You know. That's what Banner's here for. Get aside and let us through. We'll find him ourselves."

"Don't let 'em in, Jeremiah," Clara said, from behind her husband. "They ain't got no right. Not with the baby so sick."

Breed walked up by the wall of the house, still holding his rifle pointed at Banner. "Maybe you like some cattle they stampede through the alfalfa," he said.

A squinted look drew Mills's eyes almost closed. "You wouldn't do that. I couldn't stay here without that crop."

"Then let us in, damn you," Garry said.

Mills's great shoulders seemed to stoop even more. He turned aside slowly, staring at Garry. Breed was right next to the door now, with the rifle. Garry passed between him and Mills, to go in. But Clara barred the way, her eyes glowing with anger.

"You can't go in there. My baby's sick——"

With a curse, Garry whipped his gun across her face. She reeled back with a sick gasp of pain.

"Garry!"

It came from Mills like the roar of some animal in pain. The man tried to wheel back and meet it, but Mills struck him with an echoing crack of bone on bone. It smashed the short man back into Breed, as Breed tried to swing his rifle around. Before either man could recover, Mills lunged into them, hitting Garry again, an awesome blow that knocked him free of Breed and carried him up against the house so hard the whole building shuddered.

It had given Banner time to pull his gun. As Breed staggered free, swinging his rifle up, Banner called his name. The man checked his whole motion, knowing what it meant, becoming rigid as a statue, with his rifle still pointed at the ground.

Mills had jumped after Garry, catching him against the wall before he could fall, hitting him again. It doubled Garry over, and Banner thought he had been broken in two. Clara staggered from the door, one hand to her bleeding face, and caught her husband's arm before he could strike again.

"Jeremiah," she pleaded, putting her whole weight on him, "you'll kill him. You'll kill him!"

For a space of time Banner couldn't measure, Mills held Joe Garry against the wall, slack as a sack of wheat. The farmer was breathing thickly; the muscles beneath his shirt rippled and knotted like the stirring of great snakes across his back. At last he released Garry, and stepped back. The man slid down the wall to a sitting position, chin sunk on his chest, face viscid with blood. Mills stared stupidly at him, then at his wife. She was looking up into his face with a shining look in her eyes, a mixture of fear, of awe, of something close to pride.

The kids had clustered in the doorway now, elfin little figures in their tattered clothes. There was a barefoot girl with tousled hair the color of corn, maybe three years old, and a boy about the same age, round-eyed, open-mouthed. There was an older boy, maybe ten, the first one to gain the courage to move out of the doorway, his eyes wide and awe-struck in his freckled face.

"Gosh, Pa," he whispered. "I ain't seen you whup a man like that since I was a little kid."

Mills looked around at him. The blank rage was gone from the farmer's eyes now. A realization of what he had done deepened the seams around his mouth. His eyes moved furtively from his boy to Breed. His shoulders began to sink.

"Put the rifle down, Breed," Banner said.

The hatchet-faced man sent him a venomous glance, then dropped the Henry on the ground. Garry lifted his head, groaning with pain. He tried to straighten, wiped feebly at the blood and dirt on his face. Banner jerked his gun at Breed, and the man went over to help Garry get up.

Once on his feet, Garry sagged heavily against the wall. Banner thought he was going to be sick. At last, however, he moved away from the wall, swaying heavily. He wiped more blood from his face with the hairy back of one hand. Rage gave his eyes that sleepy look. His voice shook when he spoke to Mills.

"You won't be on this land tomorrow," he said.

Mills held out his hand, started to speak, but Garry turned away. He looked savagely at Banner, then stumbled by him, toward the willows, where they had probably left their horses. Breed glanced at his rifle on the ground.

"Leave it there," Banner said.

The venom filled the man's face again, but he followed Garry. Mills watched them go, his shoulders sinking. At last he turned dead eyes to his wife.

"You better start packing."

She caught his arm. "No, Jeremiah——"

"You know what Hackett will do now. They'll trample the alfalfa, they'll burn us out. If we're here, they'll just as soon shoot us as not."

All the life seemed drained from his face as he shambled into the house. The kids scurried from his path, round-eyed and frightened. Soundless tears formed silvery tracks in Clara's worn face.

"Did you see him when he hit Garry?" she asked.

"I saw him," Banner said gently.

"That's what he used to be," she said.

"If it isn't completely dead in him, maybe we could give it back to him," Banner said. She turned, a wondering look in her eyes. He asked, "Was Jeremiah really here all that day of the murder?"

She locked her hands together and looked down at them. "It would save Jahzini's life, wouldn't it?"

"Yes."

Her eyes squinted shut; she shook her bowed head. "No. Jeremiah wasn't here all day. He went into town."

"Did he ride the bay he got from Kitteridge?"

"I can't remember that." She looked up, a plea in her face. "I really can't——"

"I believe you," he said. He frowned at her a moment. He was thinking of the statement he had gotten from Elder. It had been at the back of his mind for a long time. Now he saw why. He saw how he could use it. "What if we put Hackett in such a position that he couldn't touch you?" he asked. "Does your husband still have enough guts left to be worth saving?"

She reached up and caught the lapels of his coat, voice fierce. "Of course he has. If he had a chance, just one chance. You saw what he could do——"

He gently removed her hands from his lapels, and went around her into the house. Mills had thrown the tattered blankets off a bed and was rolling up the straw tick.

"Mills," Banner said. "In my saddlebags is a statement signed by Caleb Elder. It proves beyond doubt that Hackett is using reservation land for his cattle. If I turn this statement over to the railroad, they'll revoke Hackett's lease. It would finish him north of the tracks."

"Then why don't you do it?"

"Because that still wouldn't pin the murder on Arles. What we *can* do is hold Elder's statement over Hackett's head. He won't dare touch you——"

"Don't try to swindle me into another deal," Mills said bitterly. "I ain't gettin' my kids burnt out again——" He glanced bitterly at the children. "There used to be five of 'em."

Clara had come in to stand beside the baby's crib; her voice sounded husky. "It was the Johnson County War. The cattlemen were driving out the nesters. Jimmie got caught under a rafter when it burned through and fell. Jeremiah tried to save him. He couldn't."

Banner moistened his lips, checked for a moment. Then he forced himself to go on. "That won't happen again. I know Hackett, and I know what he wants up here. He couldn't stand to lose those railroad leases. They're his foothold north of the tracks. If you quit now you'll be running all the rest of your life. You had a chance here. This was your third year of alfalfa. That land's ready for money crops."

"He's right, Jeremiah." Clara spoke in a pinched voice. "Where will we go? What will we do? We haven't got a cent."

The man shook his bowed head stubbornly. "No—no——"

"Are you running for their sakes, or yours?" Banner asked. This brought the man out of his apathetic defeat for a moment. His head lifted, his eyes reflected a feeble anger. "Why don't you ask your kids what they think?" Banner said. "What will they remember? A man that was always running, a man that never had the guts to stay and fight for what he's won. Ask them, Mills. Look at them."

For a long time Mills refused to turn. But the three children by the door had their eyes fixed solemnly upon him. The baby began to whimper. As if moved by a force outside himself, Mills finally turned. The older boy tried to meet his father's eyes. But a vague embarrassment clouded his freckled face; he lowered his glance. Banner saw it bring the flush of deep shame to Mills's face.

"Is that what you want them to remember?" Banner said.

Mills was breathing shallowly, like a man in pain. His fists were clenched and his face was dull red in the gloom. He spoke with great difficulty.

"What do you want me to do?" he asked.

It was a long ride to Hackett's down through Yellow Gap, eastward along the Ganado Road, across the brackish waters of the Rio Puerco. Finally they reached the sprawling adobe hacienda Hackett had bought from a Mexican in the early years, on the high bluffs overlooking the river. Lights winked out of the darkness; the dogs began to bay.

Long ago some Mexican blacksmith had hammered an iron
wagon tire into the shape of a broken bit and hung it from
the high crossbeam above the gate. It creaked mournfully in
the wind as Mills and Banner rode beneath it. The hounds
flooded about them, yapping at their heels, and shadowy
figures began moving from the open bunkhouse door. Adakhai had won Banner's own Winchester and six-shooter, and
Banner was using the old Dragoon Colt Dodge had kept in
the ivory table, and one of Dodge's Winchesters. He bent to
pull the .30-.30 from its boot and laid it across his pommel.
Mills did the same.

Then the front door was flung open, and Clay Hackett's
swaggering broad-shouldered body was silhouetted in its
lighted rectangle. "Who is it, Red?" he asked loudly.

Banner saw the shadowy figure of Big Red halt near the
steps, towering above the others, and he rode boldly up to
them, rifle pointed at the redhead's chest.

"It's Lee Banner, Hackett," he said. "I've got my gun on
Red. If anybody starts anything he'll get it first. And Mills can
shoot you out of that door just as quick."

There was a general stir among the loosely grouped men.
Banner felt his fingers close tightly around the Winchester.
But none of them tried to change his position. Banner was in
the light flung from the door now, and he could see Big Red
staring up at him in sullen anger. The man's right arm was in
a sling, and a dirty bandage covered it from wrist to elbow.

"What's on your mind, Lee?" Hackett's voice was sardonic.

"I want to read you a paper." Banner fished Elder's statement from his pocket. The light was hardly enough to read
by, but he almost knew it by heart now. When he had finished, he looked up at Hackett. "I guess you know what
would happen if the railroad got hold of this, Clay. It proves
beyond a doubt that you're grazing on reservation land. The
last thing in the world the railroad wants is trouble with the
Indians. That's why they put that clause in all their leases that
any rancher grazing beyond the limits of the checkerboard
sections would automatically revoke his lease. Once the thing
got started it would snowball. A dozen witnesses could be

found who had seen your cattle up there. A hundred. Maybe the railroad's already heard rumors. But nothing could be proved. This isn't any rumor. You know what it can do to you?"

For a moment, the only sound in the dooryard was Hackett's acerbic breathing. At last he spoke, his voice guttural with restrained anger. "Why show it to me?"

"Because you're going to leave Mills alone. You're not going to touch him, or go near his house again. If you do, if so much as one of your men does, this goes to the railroad."

Garry's voice rose angrily from the group. "Don't let him bluff you, Hackett. I told you Mills is in with Banner. He knows where that Indian is too. We ought to burn him out tonight."

"It's no bluff, Clay, and you know it," Banner said. "You're going to leave Mills alone. I want an understanding on it before I leave."

Hackett's spurs set up their inevitable clanking as he walked across the porch to one of the poles supporting its overhang. Banner could not see his face. It sounded as if he was drawing in his breath through clenched teeth. It seemed a long time before he spoke.

"All right, damn you," he said at last. "You've got your understanding."

He wheeled around and walked inside, slamming the door after him. Banner stared after him a moment, then jerked his gun at Big Red.

"Walk ahead of us down the road."

Nothing happened on the way out. They could hear the stirring of men, their restless talk, but nothing happened. When they were beyond the fences, Banner released Red. The man stepped to the side of the road, letting them pass, the smoldering anger dimly visible in his face. They rode silently back to the Yellow Gap cutoff. Here Mills reined up, sitting heavily in his saddle, shaking his head.

"I never thought you could do it. Face Hackett on his own ground that way. Do you think he realizes that you know Arles killed Wright?"

"He knows I know," Banner said. "Does that prove the power of Elder's statement?"

"Won't Hackett try to get it?"

"He may. But he's smart enough to realize I won't carry it around on me. And he's got more important things to get."

"You mean Adakhai?"

Banner leaned toward the man. "Mills, it's either that Indian or Kitteridge or you. Now tell me. Did you see that murder?"

Mills pulled his reins up so hard his horse danced away from Banner. He slacked off, letting it settle down. His neck sank stubbornly into his shoulders and he shook his head.

"No," he said, "I didn't. I swear I didn't."

Banner shook his head disgustedly. "Tonight didn't mean a thing to you. You're still afraid."

"Who wouldn't be, damn you!" It came from the man in a subdued anger. "Whoever saw the killing would have to testify in court, wouldn't he? With Hackett's killers just waiting to cut him down. If Hackett had Wright killed he certainly wouldn't hesitate to have the eyewitness killed." He settled in the saddle, voice lowering darkly. "And his kids with him——"

"Then you did see the killing!"

"Damn you, I didn't! How many times do I have to say it? I'm just telling you, that's all. You're asking too much of a man. Any man. Admitting he was the eyewitness would be signing his own death warrant. And letting his family in on it too, probably."

Banner's eyes grew empty in defeat. He realized he had expected too much too soon. "Forget it," he said. He stared into the soft night, then asked the man, in a subdued voice, "What about now? You're at the crossroads, Mills. Are you going to leave, or stick it out?"

Still stooped in the saddle, Mills gazed down the road. Then his shoulders seemed to lift a little, and he swung in the saddle, looking up toward Yellow Gap.

"I guess I'll be going back to my place," he said.

20

After that it was the waiting. The rains came almost every day and turned the streets of the town to a muddy bog, and then the sun shone and baked it hard as cement. The scent of wet greasewood hung like syrup in the early morning air, and the smell of hot dust swept up out of the simmering deserts in the afternoon. Through Cristina, Banner heard that Adakhai was healing satisfactorily and would soon return to his people at Chin Lee. The young lawyer had the feeling that he had done all he could with Adakhai, and Kitteridge, and Mills, and that now all he could do was wait.

August passed, and the time set for the trial drew near. There had been no word from Dodge, but that was his way. Banner knew he would write when he had something definite. Over a week after Banner had ridden with Mills to Hackett's, Clara Mills came into town. It was about ten in the morning, with the threat of rain lying humidly on the air. He was in the office, in his shirt sleeves, when someone knocked. Clara entered when he opened the door. She was smiling; the hollows in her cheeks seemed to have lessened. After a first shy greeting, she told him eagerly:

"First time I been in town since that day. Jeremiah's working in the alfalfa. I got some shopping to do, but I just had to see you before anything, Lee. I just had to thank you for all you done."

"Hackett hasn't showed up, then?"

"Not a sign. And Jeremiah's got a buyer for the alfalfa. It's all because of you, Lee. We can't thank you enough. You should see how much Jeremiah's changed already. I wouldn't believe it. He's carryin' on like he did ten years ago. More alfalfa in that south forty, a new room on the house."

He smiled his quirk of a smile. "That stoop gone from his shoulders?"

She caught his hand. "A lot of it has. Every new day takes some more out. Every new day makes him realize a little more that he can stand up to Hackett now, that he hasn't anything to fear if he'll only stick. I been talkin' to him, Lee. I been tryin' to make him see how he's got to tell if he saw Wright killed. Maybe he ain't the man he used to be yet, but it's comin' back. Sooner or later he'll come up to taw. If there's anything to tell, he'll tell." Her voice grew grim. "I'll see to that."

"You give me new hope, Clara," he said.

She pulled her tow-cloth wrapper around bony shoulders. "I got to get on with my shoppin'."

"I'll see you downstairs."

He put his coat on and walked with her to the sidewalk. She took her leave and he stood there on the corner, reluctant to return to the confinement of the office. He became aware of Sam Price's boy running down the street. He came up to Banner, panting heavily, holding out an envelope.

"Si said you'd give me a dime for this. Just came in on the telegraph."

Banner found ten cents for the boy, ripped open the envelope with a sudden excitement.

DENVER, COLORADO
AUGUST 24, 1891

TO LEE BANNER

GOT LINE ON WARE'S EX WIFE. SHE HAD LETTERS FROM WARE PROVING HE HAD SPENT ALL THE MONEY. SHEFFORD BROKE WHEN HE SAW THEM. TOLD US WHERE TO FIND THE REAL BOOKS AND TURNED STATE'S EVIDENCE AGAINST WARE FOR LENIENCY. BOOKS PROVED MORROW'S INNOCENCE. PINE GETTING INDICTMENT QUASHED AGAINST MORROW. DON'T NEGLECT YOUR BLACKSTONE.

UNCLE HENRY

Banner realized his hands were trembling. He felt a flush of triumphant excitement fill his face. Stuffing the telegram in his pocket, he went to the hitch rack, knocked the reins loose, threw them over his horse's head, and swung aboard. He wheeled the animal around and put him into a gallop down Reservation. Before he reached Yellow Gap, however, he realized he could not go to Kitteridge alone. It was Julia's right to be along when he delivered this. It might help resolve things more quickly.

So he went on to the school. It was past noon when the buildings rose over the flat horizon. He passed the trading post and saw a dusty horse standing hipshot before the agency living quarters. It puzzled him, but he trotted on to the school building. In the long room a score of Navajo children were sitting in orderly fashion at the crude desks, reading, writing, staring solemnly at the simple arithmetic chalked on the blackboard.

"Where is your teacher?" Banner asked.

One of the older boys stood up, not looking at Banner, reciting it like a catechism. "White man he come to house by horseback at a trot. Teacher-woman she go walking fast to see him. Tell us our lessons to do until she come back walking."

Going back to the living quarters, Banner saw that the ratty bay by the door had Kitteridge's Flying Bar brand. He hesitated before knocking, oddly reluctant to see Julia and the man together again. Then his lips thinned angrily and he put his knuckles to the door.

Julia answered. Her full lower lip was stiff with tension, and anger made kindling lights in her great dark eyes. Banner saw Kitteridge sitting on the couch within the gloom of the room, smoking a cigarette. With sight of Banner, the man rose slowly, a network of fine wrinkles springing up about his narrowing eyes.

"Well, Counselor, come after some more horses?"

Banner found all the eagerness swept from him. He glanced at Julia, wordlessly pulled the telegram from his pocket. He saw the flush leave her cheeks as she stared at it. Then she stepped back to let him in. He walked over and handed the telegram to Kitteridge, still not speaking. Kitteridge read it with narrowed eyes, his lips pressing tighter and tighter. Slowly the blood left his face till the saddle-leather flesh was white as parchment. When he had finished he crumpled the telegram in one fist, viciously, and turned burning eyes to Banner.

"What kind of a fool do you take me for?"

Banner's lips parted in surprise. It was not the reaction he had expected. "You know Dodge wouldn't send anything like that unless it were true."

"The hell I do!" Kitteridge flung the crumpled telegram from him. "You damn shysters. Rigging up something like this. Did you think this would make me tell if I saw anything at Yellow Gap? Do you think I'm a complete fool?"

He wheeled and stalked to the conical adobe oven at the end of the room, staring down into the gray ashes. He took a last draw on his cigarette. It made a savage, sucking sound in the room. Then he flung it into the ashes.

In the meantime, Julia had picked up the telegram and read it. She went over behind Kitteridge, speaking in a voice low with restraint. "This must be true, Vic. I know Dodge went up to Denver. He wouldn't say this unless it was so. You know that. His worst enemies would take his word on anything. You are free, Vic."

It seemed as if he would never turn around to face her. It seemed as if there would never be another sound in the room. At last, however, he wheeled. There was a hollow-eyed expression on his face. It was like that of a little boy, a lost little boy. All the sardonic mockery, the impenetrable cynicism was emptied from his eyes. He stared at Julia, and then walked across the room and sat down on the couch again, looking blankly at the wall.

"Free?" he said.

"Free as any man," Banner said. "You can stop hiding up there in the hills. You can make friends. You can come down out of your hole——"

"And tell you that I saw who really killed Wright." The thin edge was back in Kitteridge's voice.

"That's what kept you from telling, wasn't it?" Banner asked. "The fear that your true identity would be found out if you got mixed up with the law."

"Yes, Counselor. It was."

"Vic," Julia said sharply. "Don't go back to that. Can't you see how much Banner and Dodge have gone through for you? And then you act like this."

"For me?" he asked cynically.

"All right. So they had their reasons. What's the difference? They've given you back something you could never have gotten alone in a million years——"

"Slack off, will you?" Kitteridge bent his head, running rope-scarred fingers through his thinning hair. Then he rose, to pace savagely toward the fireplace. "How can I trust them? I've been framed once, by my best friend. How can I trust anybody after that?"

"Vic," Julia said. "It's not a frame-up. You can take my word on it."

"*Your* word!" He wheeled on her, bitter-eyed. "Why should I take your word? How did Banner know who I really was in the first place? You're the only one who could have told him. I might as well put you in the same boat as Ware. My best friend and my woman——"

"Vic, don't be like that." She went to him, tried to grab his arm. "Maybe I told, but I knew they only wanted to help you——"

"How did you know?" He tore loose, pacing back toward the couch. "I'm not going to be caught short again, Julia! I've put in five years of hell because I trusted someone I'd known since I was a kid. I'm not going to be jammed in a corner again, understand?" He wheeled on them, almost shouting it. "Understand?"

They both stared at him, neither answering. Banner heard the distant roll of thunder outside. His face grew dark and somber.

"It would take courage to testify against Arles," he said. "Maybe I made a mistake. I thought that indictment was the only thing that kept you from telling what you knew."

For a moment Kitteridge's eyes were blank with anger. Then, with palpable effort, he masked it off with his sardonic cynicism.

"Maybe you did," he said. "Maybe you made a mistake about everything. *Ipso facto,* Counselor?"

He picked up his hat off the couch and walked out.

Julia went halfway to the door after him, and then stopped, helplessness in her face. Banner did not move. His first anger was gone, leaving a hollow defeat at the pit of him. Julia turned toward him. Anger had replaced her helplessness. She was biting at her underlip, her heavy breathing swelled her breasts.

"I thought I knew him. Even the way he'd changed, I thought I knew what he was really like underneath. But now——"

He shook his head in deep discouragement. "I've run into the same thing with Mills, Julia. Maybe we expect them to change too soon. It's been five years for Kitteridge now. A man can't switch back in a minute. You could see the shock it was. I'd need time to think it out."

She came to him. She reached up to touch his cheek with the tips of her fingers. It was a cool, satiny pressure. The anger seemed to have left her. Her voice was low, throaty. "I wish——"

He waited for her to go on. When she didn't, he asked softly, "You wish what, Julia?"

She stared at him with a luminous darkness in her eyes. Then she wheeled and walked over to the couch, facing away from him.

"Nothing," she said.

He studied the bowed line of her shoulders, sharing her helplessness. "I guess I'll be going," he said.

21

Henry Dodge got back on September the eighth with a letter to Kitteridge from the Denver district attorney, and one from the foreman of the grand jury, and a half-dozen Denver newspapers headlining the story of Morrow's innocence and of

Ware's arrest in New Orleans. They had printed a picture of Morrow as he had been five years ago, and Banner could understand how Julia had loved him. In the picture, he was a different man. The thinning hair Banner knew was a handsome black mane; the cynical sun-faded eyes were bold and laughing.

Dodge and Banner rode up to Kitteridge's together with the newspapers and the letters. But the house was empty, and the horses were all gone. Knowing a deep fear that the man had fled, Banner got Tilfego to hunt for him, giving the Mexican the newspapers and letters in case he found Kitteridge. It took Tilfego three days. He returned with the news that he had come across the man with his cattle on the north fork of the Corn. Apparently the man was not running away, but the newspapers and the letters made no appreciable change in him. It left Banner with nothing but a deep discouragement as the day of the trial arrived.

It was the twelfth, and Jahzini was to get in from Yuma that morning. Banner and Dodge had an early breakfast and walked up Aztec to the courthouse. The streets were already teeming with life. A crowd of prospective jurors was talking and smoking restlessly on the courthouse steps; more men were gathered in little groups along the picket fence. As Banner reached the corner of Aztec and Reservation, he could not help looking eastward, toward the desert. Dodge stopped beside him, lighting a cigar.

"Which one are you looking for, son?"

Banner shook his head helplessly. "I don't know. Maybe I've been a fool, Henry. Maybe none of those men saw it—"

Dodge cut him off, grasping his arm. "There's still time, Lee. I don't think any one of those three men are the kind to let a man die, after what you've done for them."

Banner hardly heard him. He felt his whole body lift up. The sound of voices, of husky laughs, of scraping boots seemed to die about him till he was standing in a void, staring down that street. He could feel Dodge's hand tighten on his arm.

"Who is it?" the old man asked. "My eyes ain't as good as they used to be."

"I can't see yet. One rider, leading an empty horse."

Banner realized the cessation of sound wasn't in his mind. Every man in the crowd had seen it now. The silence was an eerie thing, gathering weight, exerting pressure. Then Banner felt the tension washed out of him on a husky breath.

"Who is it, son?" Dodge asked.

Banner's voice had a dead tone. "Cristina."

Sound began to stir again, like the rustling of autumn leaves in a wind. Cristina was a block away now, riding down the center of the street. Someone gave a catcall, another man shouted an obscene joke at her. She looked neither to right nor left. She had a silver comb in her black hair. She wore her best blue velvet blouse and skirts of black wool. She sat motionless as a statue on the horse.

Then Caleb Elder's voice rose mockingly from the crowd behind Banner. "Hear you've taken the Injun lover back in your office, Henry. Is this the squaw you're goin' to hitch up with now?"

A jeering laugh rose from other men, and Banner could not help wheeling savagely toward them. Dodge caught his arm.

"Put some slack in it, son. You're going to get a lot of that from here on in."

The chipped-glass look filled Banner's eyes. Slowly he wheeled back till he was facing Cristina again. She rode up to them and reined in and stepped off. A flush showed through the sun-tinted copper of her cheeks; her eyes were black and depthless with anger.

"Never mind them," Banner told her gently. "They don't count."

"I didn't even hear them," she said stiffly. "I was told my father would be in on the ten-fifteen."

"We were just going to meet him . . ." Banner trailed off, frowning. His attention had been so fixed to her that he had not realized what horse she led. It was his own chestnut, saddled and bridled. For the first time a faint smile came to her lips. She handed him the lead rope.

"Adakhai came past my hogan by wagon last night. He left this gift for you."

Eyes filled with wonder, he stepped over to the chestnut. The horse nickered and tried to nuzzle him. He could not help chuckling. Rubbing its satiny nose fondly, he spoke to Cristina.

"It's hard to believe Adakhai would do this. He won it gambling. You know too well how they feel about that."

"It is what gives it so much meaning," she said. She was searching his face, an intent look in her eyes. "He told me he wanted to see you again. He said his hogan is your hogan whenever you come to Chin Lee. It is something I never would have believed."

Banner held out his hand. "If he'd do this——"

His voice died as he saw the darkening of her eyes. Sunlight made a quicksilver shimmer across the top of her black hair, with the shake of her head. "He did not tell me whether he saw the murder at Yellow Gap," she said.

The eagerness fled Banner's face, leaving it somber, older. She came close, caught his arm.

"Perhaps he must think it over longer. If anyone could give him reason to tell, you did. You did more with him than I thought possible for any white man to do. This proves it. That he should give you such a gift, after hating the whites all his life. That he should call his hogan your hogan. How did you do it, Lee? It couldn't have been merely that you saved his life."

He shook his head. "It was a lot of things, I guess. I think the gambling must have been part of it. Did he tell you about the *bizha?*"

"Yes. He said you knew such great defeat that you put your cards face down on the floor and surrendered completely."

"I'm still wondering if I did right," he murmured. "I know how much that *bizha* meant to him. I thought that if I could win it, he would do almost anything to get it back, even tell me if he was at Yellow Gap——"

"No!" She broke in angrily, shaking her head. "Its only value is in the power it gives him in gambling. Of what value would it be if he lost it that way? He could not bargain for it. You would have gained his undying hatred. He would never have told you what you want to know. How could you misjudge him so?"

"That hand I put face down was a full house," Banner said. "He was so excited at winning that he didn't question it. He only had two pairs."

The anger left Cristina's face in an instant. He saw her eyes widen and grow luminous with surprise, with realization. "Lee." Her voice had a breathless sound. "You could have won."

He nodded soberly. "I realized in the last moment what a great mistake it would be."

Her lips were parted and she was frowning and shaking her head from side to side and staring into his face as if seeing something there for the first time. "I have been wrong," she said. "It is I who have misjudged you. Only a man who understood us could have realized that. No wonder you could change Adakhai so."

"Are you thinking," he asked gently, "that perhaps there aren't a thousand years between us, after all?"

For a moment longer she stared up into his face. Then she turned away, toward her horse, as she had when he had kissed her out there on the desert. He could see the agitated breath stirring her shoulders. When she finally spoke, her voice was so low he could hardly hear it.

"Perhaps I am like Adakhai," she said. "Perhaps I too must think it over."

Banner stood looking at her back, wanting to do something, to say something, he didn't know exactly what, yet held from anything by the watching men. Finally Dodge cleared his throat.

"Sounds like that's the whistle. We better get up to the station."

Banner took the reins of his horse, and Cristina turned and moved up beside him and they walked together down the street, running the gamut of veiled comments, of curious stares, of open insults. In front of Price's Mercantile was a growing crowd of Indians, sitting stolidly on the curb or squatting in the shade against the wall. The ruddy mahogany of their faces, the bright silver of their jewelry, the vivid blues and reds of their blankets made a barbaric splash of color against the earth-colored buildings.

"Didn't know Jahzini's clan was so big," Dodge muttered.

"They are not all my people," Cristina said. "A Mountain Chant is being held east of Yellow Gap to cure a man who dreamed of bear."

"I think we met him up by Red Lake," Banner said. "He was very sick."

"Many of these people came south by wagon to attend the ceremonies. That is why Adakhai came."

"And the only reason," Banner said bitterly.

Cristina's chin lifted. "I have faith that Adakhai will not let my father die. I saw how you changed him, Lee. If he is the one who can save Jahzini, he will come."

The train was half an hour late, and there was little time for greetings when it finally arrived. Sheriff Drake and three deputies hustled the old Indian through the crowds to the courthouse. Banner saw Arles and Big Red lounging beneath the façade of Blackstrap Kelly's drinking beer. Red's arm was no longer in a sling, but a dirty bandage still showed beneath his cuff. As Banner pushed through the throng behind Jahzini, climbing the steps to the courthouse porch, he could not help turning to look over the heads of the crowd, down Reservation, toward the desert. He heard the heavy clank of spurs to his right, and Hackett's brittle voice.

"You really don't expect anybody to come in, do you?"

Banner wheeled sharply to meet the man's black eyes. The biting mockery in them made him lean forward. "Hackett——"

"Yes, Lee?" The man's humorless smile grew broader.

Banner settled back, forced himself to turn toward the door. He saw Dodge waiting for him, and stepped up beside the man. Dodge put a hand on his shoulder.

"Good boy," he muttered. "Just hang on tight."

By the time they reached the rail, they saw that Jahzini had been seated at the defendant's table with Cristina. She had brought him some paper bread she'd made the day before, blue as turquoise from the cedar ashes baked into it, and the old man was grinning like a kid at a picnic as he munched it. Prentice soon came from his chambers, his black robes giving him a towering, impersonal dignity, and the bailiff opened court. The first juryman was called.

He was James Wentworth, who ran the feed barn on Aztec, and who did a lot of business with Hackett. It was highly possible that he was under Hackett's thumb and would constitute a threat to Jahzini if he got on the jury. Dodge tried to establish this fact, without success, and finally turned the challenging over to Banner with a helpless gesture of his hand. Banner stepped up to the jury box.

"James Wentworth, isn't it true that on June the twelfth of 1889 you had a quarrel with the defendant?"

"I—I don't quite recall."

"He was going home drunk and ran into your barn, knocking off a door. You threatened to take your shotgun to him if he ever came down that street again?"

"That isn't true. I——"

"You're under oath, Wentworth. I have signed depositions from two witnesses to the incident. Shall I have them subpoenaed?"

"No, but I——"

"I submit that this man be rejected for prejudice he might have against the defendant."

Judge Prentice waited for Wentworth to protest. When the man did not, he nodded frostily. "Sustained."

"Step down," the constable intoned.

Frowning, snorting self-consciously, Wentworth walked out, and the next man was called. He could not be proven prejudiced, and was accepted. The third man was Seth Masters, a small cattleman south of the tracks who had lived off Hackett's bounty for years.

"Seth Masters, isn't it true that your father was scalped by Indians?"

"Damn right."

"Isn't it true that on a dozen occasions you've been heard to say that the best Indian was a dead Indian?"

"I never said exactly——"

"You're under oath, Masters."

"Well——"

"I have witnesses to these instances, your honor. I submit that Seth Masters be rejected as unfit for prejudice he might have against Jahzini as an Indian."

"I don't think the witnesses are necessary, Mr. Banner. You may step down, Mr. Masters."

When court was recessed for lunch, only three jurymen had been chosen. Dodge met Banner at the gate, wiping a handkerchief around the inside of a limp collar and grinning broadly.

"I never seen anybody hang it up like this. How'd you ever dig up so much dirt about this town?"

"I've been going through your old briefs for the last three weeks. You've got fifteen years of testimony in there, Henry. It's like the whole history of this town. If Jahzini isn't going to have an eyewitness, he's going to have a fair jury."

As they pushed their way through the sweating, clamoring crowd to the door, Banner saw Julia standing behind the last row of seats. He knew a leap of hope, and elbowed his way quickly to her.

"Have you seen him?" he asked. "Has he come?"

She shook her head, eyes squinted almost shut to check the tears. "I waited at my place till the last minute. I thought he might——" She shook her head. "I haven't seen him since that day. I'm beginning to wonder if you weren't right. Maybe it wasn't the indictment that kept him from talking. Maybe he just doesn't have the courage."

"Now, Julia——"

"It's true, Lee. Remember what you said, about Kitteridge still standing between us, about me not even realizing it? I thought maybe you'd struck the truth. I thought that telegram would answer it for me, would bring him back to what he used to be, and I'd know. But now it's even worse. Someone who doesn't even have the backbone to speak up in something like this, who would let an innocent old man die. How could I love a man like that?"

He patted her helplessly on the shoulder, lips compressed, unable to say anything that might help her now. He finally left her and went bleakly out through the crowd. He saw Hackett and his men trooping into Kelly's for lunch. He knew that Dodge's cook would have a meal waiting, but he had no appetite. He could not help turning down Reservation, staring out toward the desert again. It seemed as if all he had put his faith in was crumbling about him. At last he became aware of Tilfego, pushing his yawning buckskin through the thinning knots of people. The man reined in beside him, wiping the sweat from his lips with the back of one hand.

"Which one you look for, Lee?"

Banner shook his head helplessly. "I've almost given up, Tilfego. If one of them was going to come, he'd surely be here by now."

"I been wait out in those hills by the Yellow Gap cutoff, like you ask. Nobody he come down from the north. But something is happen I think you should know. Breed and Joe Garry they are waiting there too."

"That's one of the things I was afraid of," Banner said. "I'm helpless. I should be out there too, but I've got to see that Jahzini gets a decent jury." He looked up at Tilfego. "Will you go back? Don't take any chances. If our eyewitness comes, just give him some kind of warning before Breed and Garry can get to him. Will do?"

The man grinned broadly. "Will do."

Banner watched him thread his way back through the crowd. But somehow it didn't quite fit. He couldn't understand why Arles would stay in town. It was his neck more than anybody's. Perhaps it was to allay suspicion till the last moment.

Banner hunted up Ramirez, the husband of Dodge's cook, and asked him to mingle with the crowd at Kelly's and keep an eye on Arles and Hackett's other men. If any of them left town he was to tell Banner immediately. Then Banner returned to the court.

Though all the windows had been opened, the room was still oppressively hot, filled with the thick odor of sweating men and stale cigar smoke. Most of the crowd had removed their coats and were shrugging irritably at shirts turned clammy by perspiration. Wiping at his red face, the bailiff reopened court, and the choosing of the jury went on.

By four o'clock Banner's voice was husky from the constant questioning, his back ached, he had a throbbing headache from the heat. He had just finished questioning a juror and had returned to the table when he saw Ramirez beckoning him from the gate. He went to the rail and bent over so the man could whisper in his ear.

"Joe Garry he come into Kelly's, talk with Arles and Big Red. Then all three they get Hackett and ride out of town."

"Thanks, Ramirez."

Banner hardly heard his own answer. He turned back to the table, sick with the implications of it. Then, swiftly, he slid into the bench beside Cristina, whispering in her ear.

"Tell your father he's got to pass out. Something's come up and I've got to get out of here. Tell him he's got to faint."

She frowned intensely, then whispered to her father. Banner saw the old man's face go blank with surprise. Then that clownish look Banner remembered so well began to tuck in his eyes. He grinned mischievously at Banner.

"*Shiye,*" he said, in a chiding way. "My son."

For a moment Banner thought he did not understand. Irritably he bent to whisper in Cristina's ear again. Before he could speak, Jahzini's head lolled back and he slid out of the seat to fall limply on the floor. There was an immediate stir in the courtroom; the bailiff ran over to squat beside the old man, and Prentice began pounding with his gavel. Banner stood up, shouting to be heard over the babble of voices.

"Your honor, I request that the court adjourn for the day. The strain has been too much for my client. He could not possibly go on any longer."

"Sustained," Prentice said. "Bailiff?"

The bailiff popped up like a jack-in-the-box. "Hear ye, hear ye, hear ye. This honorable court is adjourned till nine o'clock tomorrow morning."

22

Banner pushed his chestnut unmercifully all the way to Yellow Gap. He had left the court in a rush, without even taking time to explain to Dodge or Cristina. The sense of urgency in him was too great. At the cutoff, he turned north. The sun was dying in the west, flooding the rough benches with a sanguine light, turning the shadows crimson in the bottom of the twisting gorges. He saw the pockmarks of fresh hoofprints in the sand. Then, sliding down a steep cut into a broad wash, he sighted the horse.

It was Tilfego's animal, cropping peacefully at a patch of buff sacaton. Banner pulled up beside the buckskin, finding no signs of violence. Yet the reins were trailing, unhitched. He gathered them up and led the horse on northward, through the gathering twilight. It filled him with a sick sense of guilt that he had sent the man out there. He reached a plateau and was running the animals through its mantle of curing grass when he heard the cursing from the benches ahead.

"*Chingados*, I hope they get the *corajes, que padrotes*. I hope they get worse than the *corajes, que rumberos, sin ver-güenza*——"

"Tilfego!"

The cursing stopped. The man's immense sombrero and moon face were visible above the edge of the dropoff. His blank surprise turned to a broad grin and he struggled up through the notch till he was on the plateau.

"*Hombre*, what luck, what happiness! If Carlotta I was not marry tomorrow I could almost marry you. I was watch for man from the north like you say. I think I know where Joe Garry and Breed they are. But they get around behind me and start shooting. My horse he spook. I get in arroyo. They kill me I think if other man he do not come."

Banner bent sharply toward him. "What man?"

Tilfego shook his head. "Him I could not see. But they go down in canyon after him. They shoot."

Banner's voice was tight. "Then it must have been our man, Tilfego. How long ago?"

"Hour, maybe two. The shooting sound like they chase him off to the east."

"Then they must have holed him up somewhere," Banner said. "Joe Garry came in to get Hackett and the rest of his crew."

"Maybe we can follow the trail," Tilfego said.

It was not hard for Tilfego to find the tracks. They led away from the Yellow Gap cutoff on one of the dim cattle trails that wound tortuously through the rough and twisted land to the east. But night came, with its blackness, and slowed them down to a snail's pace. At last Banner halted, in a narrow wash.

"We'll never catch them going this slow," he said. "We've got to take a chance, Tilfego. Where would a man run to, around here?"

"All flatlands beyond. Not much cover a man could take."

"Then there's only one possibility. The Navajos are holding their Mountain Chant east of Yellow Gap. It can't be too much farther. If that was Adakhai they saw in the canyon, wouldn't it be logical for him to seek refuge with his people?"

Tilfego nodded. "I know where the Indians they build the big corral. Pretty near the trading post. We can reach it in hour."

They forced their horses through the night, keeping to the direction they had already been taking, leaving the benchlands and coming into the vast sage flats. And finally they saw the ruddy glow of the great fire, far ahead, and then the immense corral, built of cedar boughs, piled eight feet high, with only one opening, toward the east.

The Mountain Chant was one of the most important ceremonies of the year and the Navajos had been gathering for

days, camping around the chosen spot. Now most of the
throng was within the immense corral, but a small crowd still
eddied back and forth around the gate, and latecomers were
constantly passing through the deserted cookfires and tents
and wagons.

The Indians had worn their best clothing and all their
jewelry for the annual ceremony, and it gave the scene a barbaric splendor. Banner and Tilfego began passing men laden
with silver, great bosses of it as big as saucers studding their
belts, silver bow guards and heavy bracelets jangling at their
wrists. Women crossed back and forth, draped with necklaces
of turquoise and clamshell and cannel coal worth thousands of
dollars. The crowd thickened as the two men neared the gate,
and it was slow going. Then Tilfego spurred his horse against
Banner and pointed at a copse of cottonwoods near the south
end of the great corral. A dozen horses were hitched beneath
the trees. Light from a nearby cookfire flickered high enough
for Banner to see the black, with the Broken Bit barely dis-
cernible on its dusty rump.

"Hackett," Tilfego said. "They must have drive our man
over here all right. He try to escape by going inside corral.
They would not leave their horse otherwise."

"Then we've got to get inside too. We can move faster on
foot. How about that hitch rack?"

Another line of horses stood at an improvised hitch rail
near the corral. They tied their animals to it, and began to
push their way past the Indians. The glow of the big fire inside the corral blossomed against the velvet backdrop of the
sky like a rosy nimbus, lighting the coppery faces all about
Banner. As they neared the gate, a young man on a pinto
shouted angrily at them.

"*Haish aniti, ha'at iisha?*"

"What he say?" Tilfego asked nervously.

"He asked who we were and what we wanted," Banner told
him. "A lot of them don't want white people at these ceremonies. You'll have to watch yourself." He turned to the Indian, speaking in Navajo. "I am Yellow Hair, the friend of
Adakhai. We look for him here."

The young man was unconvinced, and shouted to a pair of friends beyond Banner. They began to force their horses through the crowd, closing in on Banner and the Mexican, their faces ruddy with anger in the smoky firelight. But an old man called to them, telling them to cause no trouble on this holy night. Then an eddy of the crowd carried Banner and Tilfego through the gate.

The roar of the great fire in the center of the corral provided a constant undertone to the cacophony of other sounds. The crowd held back from its intense heat, leaving a large open space all around it, in which the dances were given. Many of the Navajos had brought their wagons, their horses, even their camping equipment into the corral, and when Banner found an empty Studebaker wagon, he climbed up on the seat, looking out across the veritable ocean of sweating faces and barbaric blankets and glimmering silver.

Many of the ceremonies had already been performed, and he saw that the Plumed Arrow Dance had now begun. The patient had been carried out close to the fire, where he sat on the ground, wrapped to the eyes in a buffalo robe. It was the same palsied old man Banner had seen at Red Lake. The two performers were doing a measured dance around him, holding up their plumed arrows, demonstrating how far they would swallow them, singing the First Song of the Mountain Sheep.

> *"Yiki Casizini*
> *Kac tsilke cigini*
> *Kac Katso yiscani . . ."*

Singing of the young man with his sacred implement, the holy young man with his plumed arrow. Giving three coyote yelps and thrusting the long arrows deep down their throats while the awed crowd watched.

"Can you see anything?" Tilfego asked.

Banner shook his head helplessly. "Not Adakhai."

"Maybe was not him?"

"Who else would have come over here?"

"I would, if they was chase me and I know this was here."

"Whoever it is, we've got to reach him before Hackett does. You go around toward the north. I'll keep going this way. We'll cover twice as much ground that way and meet on the other side. If you find him first, whether it's Adakhai or not, try to get hold of a chief and make him understand what's happening. If they know Jahzini's life depends on it, the Indians will help you."

Banner dropped off the wagon and shoved into the crowd, away from Tilfego. Through a break in the ranks, he saw that the dancers had pulled their plumed arrows out of their throats, giving three coyote yelps, and the first one had started blessing the patient. He was applying the sacred arrow to the soles of the patient's feet, his knees, his hands, his abdomen, giving three coyote yelps at each spot, until he reached the mouth, and had driven the bear's spirit from the patient.

Then, beyond the patient, beyond the dancers, clear across the compound, in the dense crowd on the other side of the corral, Banner saw Arles.

The man was not watching the dancers. He was lighting a cigarette and watching a point ahead of him in the crowd, and moving inexorably toward that point. In the treacherous firelight his face looked almost black. His mouth was held in that loose, meaningless grin.

It was a natural reaction, for Banner. He followed it without thought, pushed by a breathless sense of urgency. He pushed his way through the packed crowd to the first ranks and broke free and ran into the open, heading straight across the compound toward the other side. The heat of the fire struck at him in a searing wave, but he forced himself on. He was twenty feet out from the crowd when the earth seemed to spin from beneath him. He fell to his knees, blinded, every breath seeming to sear his lungs. A jeering cry rose from the crowd, and one of the young men shouted at him.

"Did you not think it was hot, *belinkana?* Did you not think our dancers were holy?"

Crouched there, shaking his head, Banner knew how foolish he had been. How the dancers ever stood the heat of that fire was one of the things no white man had ever been able to answer. Jahzini had taken Banner to a Mountain Chant when he was a boy, and he had seen a white man try to approach the fire. He had fainted before he had gotten within thirty feet of it.

Banner crawled back to the crowd, reached a wagon, pulled himself to his feet by a wheel. The Indians were still jeering and making jokes at his expense. He hardly heard them. His vision had returned, and he looked across the compound again.

He saw that the Plumed Arrow Dance was over, the two young men had retired to the Medicine Hogan. Other dancers were trooping into the compound. On the other side of the corral, in front of the first ranks of watchers, a little girl was swaying back and forth before a blanket on which a feather mysteriously followed every movement of her body. The Mountain Top Shooting Arrows entered from the west with their lightning sticks which were constructed like folding hat racks, that leaped in and out like painted tongues. They sang the ancient song to the Slayer and to the Son of Water, and the drums made the night throb.

The constant whirl of dancers made it hard for Banner to see beyond them into the crowd. But finally he realized that Arles had moved. No matter how Banner searched he could not see that sardonic face.

He began to stagger through the crowd, moving around the circle toward the other side. Time seemed to press against him. How many minutes left? How many seconds?

That Hackett and his men would think of doing it here was evidence of their desperation. It was their last chance to save themselves. It was Arles's last chance.

Yet desperate an attempt as it was, they might make it, with luck. All the Indians were gradually pressing in as close to the fire as possible, to watch the dances. It left open spaces between their rear ranks and the walls of the corral. A man could stand in those black shadows by the cedar-bough wall and break through to the outside immediately after shooting.

It was possible that he could get away without being identified.

Banner had almost reached the Medicine Hogan in the west end when he saw Big Red. The man stood beside an empty linchpin wagon near the hogan. For that moment the babble of sound seemed to fade. It was only the two of them, staring at each other across the dense mass of the crowd.

Then Big Red started toward Banner.

Anger ran rawly through Banner, filling him with the impulse to meet the man, to get his hands on something tangible. But he knew he did not have time for that. He turned to shove his way through the crowd in front of the Medicine Hogan, trying to get ahead of the Hackett rider. As he shouldered past a pair of young Navajos, one wheeled in anger, jabbing at him with an elbow.

"Juthla hago ni——"

Banner blocked the blow, pretending he did not understand the vile curse, and stumbled on. He saw that he had gotten past Red, that the press of the mob was holding the man up.

Then, fifty feet beyond, Joe Garry.

Desperately, Banner changed directions. But Garry wheeled to cut across and block him again. He tried to turn back, saw that would take him into Red again. He spun around a last time and tried to drive through the Navajos to the front ranks and open ground. It was too late. Joe Garry brutally shoved an old couple aside and stepped in front of Banner, one scarred hand on his gun.

"Don't be a fool," Banner said. "Pull that gun and they'll mob you."

"Nobody needs a gun, Lee," Big Red said.

He was right behind, and Banner started to wheel involuntarily. But Red grabbed his arm, checking his whirling motion, trying to twist his arm into a hammerlock. Banner fought to get free, but Garry lunged in and hit him in the face.

Blinded by the blow, held from behind by Red, Banner lashed out wildly with a boot. He felt it catch Garry in the stomach.

The man reeled back, doubled over, making a retching

sound. At the same time, Red twisted Banner's arm up into his back with a violent wrench. Banner could not help shouting with the stabbing pain. It bent him forward helplessly; his wild struggles were useless.

Then he heard Red grunt from behind, and he was released. He fell to his knees, sick with the pain of his twisted arm. It was a great effort to rise, to turn. He saw Adakhai standing above the fallen redhead, a shovel in his hands.

"*Ahalani, anaai.*"

Banner could not help his feeble grin. "Greetings, brother," he answered. "You came out of a cloud."

"I have been trying to catch up with you for some time," Adakhai said. "What are you doing here?"

"I came to help you," Banner said. He gestured at Joe Garry, still sitting on the ground, the pain of the kick turning his face to parchment. "That is one of the men who shot at you on the Yellow Gap cutoff this afternoon."

The Indian looked puzzled. "I was not shot at on the cutoff. I have been here since yesterday."

Banner stared at him blankly. "You mean you were not coming this afternoon to tell that you had seen the murder?"

The Indian placed his hand over his heart. "You saved my life, Yellow Hair. You showed me that a white man could understand our ways and our gods. You are my brother now, and if I had seen the killing at Yellow Gap, I would tell you. But I cannot say what is not true."

"Then they weren't after you——"

Banner broke off, wheeling around, staring into the crowd beyond. Then he began running again, knowing he had lost too much time already. He heard Adakhai call from behind, but did not answer. He passed the Medicine Hogan, plunging into the packed crowd again, pushing his way through.

All the dancers had left the compound now. Young horsebackers were dragging in new logs at the ends of their ropes to throw on the center fire. It was shooting up to the heavens once more in a great pyre. Sparks rained against the velvet backdrop of the sky like a host of miniature comets, and a diaphanous white ash was settling onto the spectators. The climax of the evening was about to begin. The Fire Dance.

From outside the corral where they had been spraying each other with the sacred medicine, the twelve young dancers began to run in, their naked bodies painted white, their cedar-bark torches blazing, their shrill cries of the sandhill crane filling the air.

"Prrr! Eh-yah! Prrr! Ehyah——"

Banner reached the spot where he had first seen Arles, and began looking frantically for the man, pushed this way and that by angry Indians as he forced his way through their tightly packed ranks. Even here the heat of the fire was so great that the Navajos could not stand still, and shifted constantly back and forth like a restless sea.

Out in the center the twelve dancers were cavorting about the pyre like fiendish marble statues come to life. Their chant was growing wilder as they circled. They had ignited their torches in the flames and were beating at each other with them, literally bathing themselves in flames.

> *"The time when they came out of the earth!*
> *Hostudi's fire is put upon us.*
> *But it does me no harm,*
> *I am holy with the fire . . ."*

And Banner saw Kitteridge.

The man was over by a line of wagons, a hundred yards away. The wagons were between him and the wall, but he was moving down toward the end of the line, his back to the wagons, his back to the shadows gathered blackly beneath the wall of cedar boughs. And it was in those shadows Arles would be. With all the attention of the crowd on the cavorting dancers. Waiting for Kitteridge to move out from behind the last wagon.

"Kitteridge," Banner shouted at the top of his voice. But the man did not seem to hear him over the chant of the dancers, the frenzied shouting of the mob, the frantic beat of the drums. "Kitteridge, watch out! Don't move from behind that wagon!" Banner screamed it. "Kitteridge, for God's sake——"

> *"The torch they put on me does not injure me,*
> *The torch they put on me does not injure me.*
> *I am holy with the fire . . ."*

Like flaming demons, dancing around the blaze, running into the bed of coals, scattering them and stamping them out, whipping each other with their blazing torches. And all the while Lee Banner, fighting to get free of the crowd, seeing that there was only a moment left, that Kitteridge would step from behind that wagon in another instant.

Banner did not shout again, knowing the man could not hear. As Kitteridge stepped away from the wagon, exposing his back to the wall, Banner finally broke free of the crowd, clawing at his gun.

In the same instant that he saw the first fluttering motion from the shadows by the wall, Banner heard the clank of spurs from behind him. His whole body stiffened with the impulse to wheel and meet it. But he knew that if he did, he would never save Kitteridge.

He threw himself full length onto the ground, firing at the movement in the shadows. Hackett's gun roared from behind. But the bullet passed over Banner's head and ate into the earth five feet from him.

Sprawled on his belly, Banner fired again into those shadows, wondering why Hackett's next shot did not hit him, and fired again and again, till the vague movement became a man, became Arles staggering out from the wall, doubled over, hugging his bloody belly, dropping his gun, pitching onto his face.

> *"I am holy with it.*
> *I am holy with it.*
> *I am holy with it . . ."*

23

There was a great silence. The dancers had stopped, the shouting of the crowd had stopped. Banner got to his feet, trembling in reaction now, turning to see why Hackett had not killed him.

The man lay on the ground ten feet behind Banner, ringed by a dense mass of Indians. His great cartwheel spurs held his heels six inches off the ground. He was dead.

Banner stared at him, a cottony taste growing in his mouth. It was as if his emotions had been numbed. He could feel no shock, no triumph.

He looked finally to see who had shot Hackett. Tilfego stood on top of one of the wagons, far down the line from Kitteridge. The grin made a Chinese mask of his face, and his gun was still in his hand. Banner raised his hand in a salute of gratitude, then turned to meet Kitteridge as the man reached him.

"You took a big chance for me," Kitteridge said, in a low voice. "I guess I owe you more thanks than I'll ever be able to give."

"Just tell me one thing."

Kitteridge's grin was feeble. "It's what I was coming down here to tell you. It took me a long time to think it out. A man gets twisted up inside when he's run like that for five years———"

"I think I understand, Kitteridge."

"I was the one Hackett's men jumped in the cutoff this afternoon," Kitteridge said. "They drove me in this direction. When I saw the corral, I thought I could shake them in the crowd———" He broke off, moistening his lips. "You were right, Lee. I saw Arles kill Wallace Wright. I was afraid my true identity would be discovered if I got hauled into court to testify. But at the last I knew that even if you'd rigged that telegram to suck me out, I couldn't let an innocent man die . . ."

Banner gazed at him a long time, wondering why he was so empty of reaction. Was this the way a man felt after so much? It was then that he became aware of the stirring of the crowd, and turned to see Adakhai, standing on the outer fringe, with Cristina. She was staring wide-eyed at Kitteridge, and Banner knew she had overheard his confession. She seemed to take her eyes off him with great effort, turning to Banner, starting toward him as she spoke.

"Ramirez told me Hackett had left town. I guessed what it meant. I knew that if they were after Adakhai he might seek refuge here. When I found nothing at Yellow Gap, I came on." She shook her head wonderingly, staring again at Kitteridge. "But it wasn't Adakhai——"

"You and I made the same mistake," Banner said. He knew there was one last thing he owed Kitteridge, and turned toward the man, forcing it out. "You'll want to know about Julia. She may have thought I was the one, Kitteridge. But you were always between us. Even when she didn't realize it herself, you were between us. She'll be waiting for you, in town."

Kitteridge met Banner's eyes a long time, as if letting it soak in. Then he grasped Banner's arm, voice husky with emotion. "You're really a man to ride the river with, Counselor."

Cristina was looking up at Banner, searching his face. "It seems to cause you no great pain, to tell him that."

He realized she was right. Somehow it did not hurt him as he had thought it would to cut the final bonds that held him to Julia. Maybe they had not been the bonds that he had thought they were. There had been passion, there had been intense emotion. But somehow it had not been as fulfilling as merely standing here looking down into Cristina's face.

"Perhaps, then," she said, "I can answer the question you asked this afternoon. No thousand years stand between us, Lee. I know that now." She lowered her voice till it was only for him. "Not even a foot, if you want it that way."

He would have taken her in his arms, but the crowd held

him from that. He put his hands in hers, and it was enough.

"Yes," he said simply. "I want it that way."

"*Qué barbaridad,*" Tilfego said, from behind them. "What are we waiting for? Let us all go in and get married."

Les Savage, Jr. was an extremely gifted writer who was born in Alhambra, California, but grew up in Los Angeles. His first published story was *Bullets and Bullwhips* accepted by the prestigious Street and Smith's *Western Story Magazine*. Almost ninety more magazine stories all set on the American frontier followed, many of them published in Fiction House magazines such as *Frontier Stories* and *Lariat Story Magazine* where Savage became a superstar with his name on many covers. His first novel, *Treasure of the Brasada*, appeared in 1947, the first of twenty-four published novels to appear in the next decade. Due to his preference for historical accuracy, Savage often ran into problems with book editors in the 1950s who were concerned about marriages between his protagonists and women of different races—a commonplace on the real frontier but not in much Western fiction in that decade. As a result of the censorship imposed on many of his works, only now have they been fully restored by returning to the author's original manuscripts. *Table Rock*, Savage's last book, was even suppressed by his agent in part because of its depiction of Chinese on the frontier. It has now been published as he wrote it by Walker and Company in the United States and Robert Hale, Ltd. in the United Kingdom.

Savage died young, at thirty-five, from complications arising out of hereditary diabetes and elevated cholesterol. However, his considerable legacy lives after him, there to reach a new generation of readers. His reputation as one of the finest authors of Western and frontier fiction continues and is winning new legions of admirers, both in the United States and abroad. Such noteworthy titles as *Silver Street Woman, Outlaw Thickets, Return to Warbow, The Trail*, and *Beyond Wind River* have become classics of Western fiction. His most recent books are *Copper Bluffs* (1995), *The Legend of Señorita Scorpion* (1997), *Fire Dance at Spider Rock* (1995), *Medicine Wheel* (1996), *Coffin Gap* (1997), *Phantoms in the Night* (1998), and *The Bloody Quarter* (1999).